THE INDULGEN̶C̶E̶S̶ ̶ LE

'I'd like to be spanked, please,' Katie said happily.

Tiffany gave her a dirty look, but Katie barely noticed, bouncing happily across to Duncan's chair and draping herself across his lap. He made something of an exhibition of it, applying a dozen firm swats to the bulging seat of her jeans before pulling them down and repeating the process on the pink polka-dot panties beneath.

By then Katie was warm, with the soft bottom-flesh sticking out around her leg holes glowing distinctly pink, but she was still blushing as Duncan pulled her panties down. She was given another two dozen on the bare, hard enough to set her kicking and break down her self-control – and to make sure we all got a glimpse of her pussy from behind . . .

Why not visit Penny's website at www.pennybirch.com

By the same author:

THE
INDULGENCES
OF ISABELLE

Penny Birch
writing as Cruella

This book is a work of fiction.
In real life, make sure you practise safe,
sane and consensual sex.

First published in Great Britain in 2008 by
Nexus
Virgin Books
Random House
Thames Wharf Studios,
Rainville Road
London, W6 9HA

www.rbooks.co.uk

Addresses for companies within
The Penguin Random House Group can be found at:
global.penguinrandomhouse.com
www.randomhouse.co.uk/offices.htm

The Random House Group Limited Reg. No. 954009

Distributed in the USA by Macmillan, 175 Fifth Avenue, New York,
NY 10010, USA

A CIP catalogue record for this book is available from the British Library

ISBN 978 0352 34198 3

Penguin Random House is committed to a sustainable future for
our business, our readers and our planet. This book is made from
Forest Stewardship Council® certified paper.

Printed and bound in Great Britain by Clays Ltd, Elcograf S.p.A.

Typeset by TW Typesetting, Plymouth, Devon

2 4 6 8 10 9 7 5 3 1

Symbols key

 Corporal Punishment

 Female Domination

 Institution

 Medical

 Period Setting

 Restraint/Bondage

 Rubber/Leather

 Spanking

 Transvestism

 Underwear

 Uniforms

One

'Oh, all right!' Portia snapped, and took down her knickers.

'You broke the rules, so you are to be punished,' I pointed out.

'Yes,' Sarah added, 'and do take that whining note out of your voice.'

Portia didn't answer but clearly she didn't agree. Her face was full of consternation as she got into position, kneeling in the old library chair with her bottom pushed out towards the rest of us. She'd pulled her knickers down as far as her knees, and the undergarment showed just beneath the hem of the loose white summer dress that she was wearing.

'Lift your dress,' Sarah ordered.

'I know what to do,' Portia snapped. Then she'd done it, exposing her bare bottom to the room.

I was always a joy to see her bare herself, partly because of her beautiful bottom but mainly because she was always so resentful about exposing it. Her bum cheeks were full and her tiny waist made them seem fuller still. They were also firm and as pale as cream. Every little movement made them quiver slightly and I could already see a hint of her pussy lips peeping out from between her thighs. She knew full well what she was showing and that knowledge was reflected in her angry, shame-filled expression. I've always found it particularly satisfying to see an upper-class English girl have her panties pulled down in readiness for spanking, and she knew that too, glaring at me as Sarah got up.

'You needn't look so smug, Isabelle. You might get it too.'

'I think not,' I told her.

Portia was about to answer, no doubt with some snotty comment. But whatever she'd intended to say gave way to a squeak of protest as her dress was tucked up higher still to leave her breasts dangling down in an expensive silk bra that matched her knickers.

'Sarah, you said a spanking!' she protested.

'That's what I intend to give you,' Sarah answered.

'Isn't it humiliating enough with my knickers down?' Portia demanded. 'And in front of everybody. I only—'

Again she broke off with a squeak, this time because the cups of her bra had been flipped up, leaving her plump little breasts swinging under her chest like a pair of small pink udders. Caroline giggled.

'You can laugh!' Portia retorted, her face now scarlet with embarrassment. 'Imagine how *you*'d look.'

Caroline merely stuck her tongue out, but she made a small, self-conscious adjustment to her far larger breasts. Portia turned her face to the window, struggling to hide her feelings as she gazed out across the rooftops of Oxford. We were too high up for anybody to see what was being done to her, although someone on the roof of the Radcliffe Camera would have had a fine view. But that was highly unlikely, so unlikely that not one of us was in a hurry to see Portia's punishment completed, except Portia.

'Spank me, then, if you have to!' she demanded, although it was barely a few seconds since her bra had been pulled up.

'All in good time,' Sarah said calmly. 'A dozen each, ladies?'

'That's not fair!' Portia retorted. 'The rules say a spanking!'

'The rules say six of the best with a cane,' Eliza pointed out. 'You should consider yourself fortunate.'

'Fortunate!' Portia gasped. 'I don't think a bare-bottom spanking in front of everybody is very fortunate. I'm not even ready for it!'

'Exactly,' I told her. 'Which is what makes this a punishment.'

'Well . . . maybe. But anyway, I'm not sure it's safe. What if somebody comes upstairs?'

'To go where?' I laughed. 'This is the only room and we've booked it.'

'What if one of the librarians came up?'

'Why should they?'

'Do try and take it like a lady, Portia,' Sarah ordered.

'But it's not fair!' Portia wailed. 'I only told Tiffany—'

'We've heard it already, Portia,' Jasmine interrupted. 'And Eliza is right. It should be the cane.'

'That doesn't make it any fairer,' Portia went on, now twisted back with her breasts and bottom flesh quivering with emotion as she began to defend herself again. 'I spent the night with Tiffany, and spanked her, and she enjoyed it, and—'

'We know,' Sarah pointed out. 'But telling outsiders about the society without the members' agreement is against the rules. Besides, there's still the issue of you taking other girls to bed behind my back, which we'll discuss in private.'

'You've already punished me for that!' Portia whined.

'I may have started, but I have not finished,' Sarah retorted.

Portia's lower lip pushed out into a sulky pout, but only for a moment before she began to complain again.

'Do be quiet,' Sarah ordered. But Portia took no notice, still protesting bitterly that her punishment was unfair.

She only stopped when her knickers were tugged down past her knees by Sarah.

'What are you doing?' she demanded.

'Taking your knickers right off,' Sarah replied.

'I'm already bare, aren't I?' Portia whined. But she lifted her legs one by one to allow the panties to be removed.

'I want you to be quiet too,' Sarah said.

'Sarah, no!' Portia protested as she realised where her discarded underwear was going. 'They're silk, Sarah, and—'

Her voice cut off as the panties were wadded firmly into her mouth, leaving her expression sulkier than ever.

'That's better,' Sarah said, and turned Portia's head to face the window once more. 'Stick that bottom out.'

As she spoke she had pressed down on the small of Portia's back. Portia let out a little sob through her mouthful of panty silk as her bottom cheeks spread to show off the tight wrinkle of her anus and her freshly shaved pussy lips. She held the position, though, the flesh of her bottom trembling and her face dark with blushes for what she was showing. She was already breathing deeply, while a bead of juice at the mouth of her vagina betrayed her arousal.

'Katie?' Sarah offered.

Katie got up, flushing with pleasure at being chosen first, which brought me a twinge of jealousy. I gave her a smack on the seat of her jeans as she stepped towards the library chair, and she gave me a brief apologetic look before addressing herself to Portia's bottom.

'I'll be gentle,' she promised, and began to pat at Portia's cheeks.

It can't have hurt, but that allowed Portia to concentrate on the humiliation of receiving a punishment spanking in front of the rest of us, as Sarah knew full well. For all her arousal there was nothing fake about Portia's shame. Over the previous year she had been growing gradually more dominant, increasing tensions between her and Sarah and making it ever harder for her when she had to have her bottom smacked. Now was no exception: her face was full of resentment even as the flesh of her bottom began to flush pink and her pussy grew slowly puffy in response to Katie's gentle slaps.

'That's at least three dozen, Katie,' Caroline pointed out.

'Oops, sorry,' Katie replied. She stopped spanking.

'You can go next, then, Caroline,' Sarah offered.

'Yes, please,' Caroline answered, jumping up.

Unlike Katie, Caroline was far from gentle, applying hard smacks to Portia's bottom and pausing after each to fondle the plump cheeks and tickle between them. Soon Portia was squirming and kicking her feet, which only encouraged Caroline. As a townie and part-time stripper, Caroline had always felt resentment at Portia's privileged background. To get Portia's knickers down for a spanking was a rare treat and not one that she intended to waste. She gloated over her victim's helpless excitement and nudity as she dished out her share of the punishment and rather more. That was all very well, but I knew that Portia craved attention and the best way to really humiliate her was to ignore her during her spanking.

'Even if she did break the rules,' I said, 'we do need to consider new members, especially now that Laura and Pippa have gone.'

'Seven seems enough to me,' Sarah replied. 'After all, we don't want to draw attention to ourselves. Do we, Portia?'

As she finished speaking she planted a firm smack on her girlfriend's bottom. Caroline moved aside, allowing Sarah to take over.

'So long as we are discreet I see no objection to new members,' Eliza put in. 'Besides, now that Isabelle is fully trained and both Portia and Jasmine seem to prefer to take dominant roles we are in danger of getting out of balance.'

'That's true,' Jasmine agreed. 'Especially when there are men around.'

'We can't really expect to use Dr Treadle's house unless we invite him,' Sarah pointed out, still spanking Portia but otherwise paying no attention to her at all.

They continued to discuss membership and premises, and I hid a smile at the ever-increasing resentment on Portia's face. Our discreet female-only society, the Rattaners, had now been in existence over a year. We had met once a month during term time, either at Laura's remote cottage – until she and her girlfriend had moved away – or at Dr Treadle's house, which was detached and also near the ring road. The noise of the traffic drowned out the cries and the sounds of smacked female bottoms, but of the seven of us only Jasmine and Caroline actually liked men. My own feelings were ambivalent, but I knew that private locations were always useful.

For the first meeting of the Michaelmas Term we had booked a private reading room in the Bodleian, ostensibly for a meeting of the James Malcolm Rymer Society. Rymer was a Victorian author so obscure that we could be confident that nobody else was likely to apply for membership, while the reading rooms on the top floor were sufficiently secluded for spankings to be dished out in them, especially the Latimer Room, which was up a little staircase of its own. I had run a series of tests with the aid of Katie and Caroline, spanking one while the other listened, and concluded that we were safe as long as the girl on the receiving end was quiet about it, a problem easily solved by stuffing her knickers in her mouth.

Portia's were about to fall out, and Jasmine stuffed them back in again as she took over. Like Caroline, she considered Portia somewhat stuck-up, adding to the pleasure of spanking her, while there had been ever-increasing rivalry between them during the Summer Term. She spanked hard, avoiding Portia's now-red bottom-cheeks in favour of the girl's still-pale thighs, which soon had her victim wriggling more violently than ever and sobbing with pain. Eliza followed Jasmine, applying twelve no-nonsense smacks to the tearful Portia's bum.

I rose as the last one landed, ignoring the pleading look from Portia's wide, moist eyes as I took her firmly around the waist. She was soaking wet, and her bottom-hole had begun to contract rhythmically in her excitement. I knew what she wanted, but she was supposed to be being punished and I intended to keep it that way. That didn't stop me stroking her to feel the heat from her hurt skin and the texture of her bottom, so full and fleshy and completely feminine that just to touch it made my own pussy tighten with desire. I could smell Portia too, the musky scent of her arousal and the perfume she used mingled together in an intoxicating fragrance, making the temptation to slip my hand between her thighs almost too much to resist. Suddenly she was pushing her bottom up, her dignity gone completely as she offered herself to me.

'Oh no you don't,' I said with a laugh, and gave her a hard spank.

Everybody had seen the movement, leaving Portia red-faced with embarrassment and trembling badly. I stepped back.

'Did you know that these rooms are sometimes used for tutorials?' I asked.

Portia gave me a wild look, the frustration burning in her stare.

'You wouldn't, I suppose, you being a scientist?' I went on as I walked across to where a tall blackboard was fixed between two bookcases. 'But they are, and have been for ever so long, which I suppose is why they have these.'

Portia's eyes went round as she saw what I'd picked up: a pointer, about two feet long, slender and made of some hard dark wood.

'I imagine that's Victorian,' Eliza remarked.

'Probably,' I agreed. 'But I dare say it can survive being applied to Portia's bottom, and the rules *do* say six of the best.'

The expression on Portia's face was close to panic, her eyes wide and her lower lip trembling. Streaks of eyeliner marked her cheeks where she'd been crying and her skin was flushed right down to her neck. Her nipples were stiff and her pussy had begun to open, but there was real fear in her eyes as she threw a pleading look to Sarah, who merely shrugged. I smiled, twitching the stick in my hand as I approached Portia once more.

She hung her head, powerful sobs now shaking her body and making her dangling breasts jiggle. I spent a moment fondling one of them, enjoying the soft, heavy feel, the stick resting across the flesh of her bottom. She was making it worse for herself, her anger and the power of her sexual reaction bringing out the sadist in me so strongly that it was hard to retain my poise.

'Six,' I told her. I stepped back a pace to measure my stroke.

I had every spectator's full attention, all five of them: Eliza calm as always, Sarah with one corner of her mouth twitching up into a smile, Jasmine openly delighted, Caroline grinning and half-consciously stroking herself through her top, Katie wide-eyed and frightened but perhaps the most excited of them all. As I lifted the pointer Portia flinched, her bottom cheeks tightening, her eyes closed tight. I made her wait, until her self-control began to break down and she started to sob. Then I brought the stick down hard across her bottom. She jerked and gasped at the impact, which left a long pale line across her flesh – a line that quickly turned to red.

'One,' I told her.

Portia could no longer control her shaking. Her breasts were shuddering, while the muscles of her tummy and sex had begun to make slow rhythmic contractions, as had her bottom-hole, which looked exquisitely rude. Again I lifted the stick and again I applied it to her flesh, a little lower, so that once she'd stopped wriggling about and clutching at her hurt cheeks she was left with two parallel weals marking her skin.

'Give her a five-bar gate, Isabelle,' Sarah instructed, 'and do it hard. I'd like her to be wearing her welts for a couple of weeks to remind her not to go behind my back.'

9

I nodded, ignoring an instinctive touch of pique at Sarah for giving me an order. Portia had hung her head lower still, her dark curls now tumbling down to hide her face, but I could imagine what she was thinking – about how it would feel to have to go about with her bottom decorated for the next few weeks. I was smiling as I lifted the stick once more, taking careful aim before bringing it down to lay a third stripe across her cheeks.

'Three,' I said. 'You're marking up rather nicely.'

Portia said something through her panties, maybe a rude word, maybe a thank-you – it was impossible to tell. I ignored her anyway, content that she already had her bare reddened bottom stuck up in the air. My third stroke had landed a little higher than I'd intended, so I gave her the fourth low down, across the meatiest part of her cheeks where they bulged out to either side of her anus.

'Four – and *do* try to keep still.'

I was trying hard not to laugh. Portia had begun to make little treading motions in the chair, making it hard to aim, and I waited until she'd managed to get herself under control again before giving her the fifth stroke. It was the highest, leaving her with five lines decorating her bottom. Once more I waited until she'd calmed down. Then I applied the last stroke, angled down across the others to create the five-bar-gate effect, making it absolutely obvious that she'd been caned – and by an expert.

'Six,' I told her. 'You may get up now.'

Portia stayed as she was, motionless for a moment before she broke. Her hand went back, clutching at her sex to masturbate herself even as the tears streamed down her face and her body shook with sobs. We watched in silence, allowing her to do what she had to, and to humiliate herself in front of us.

That was the best thing about Portia. She knew she was a stuck-up little brat, and what ought to be done about it.

It took just moments, her hand snatching at her pussy roughly at first, then to a rhythm, her fingers slapping at her flesh, faster and faster, until her vagina and anus went into spasm and she was coming. I could imagine the strength of her feelings as she did it, masturbating openly in front of the six women who'd punished her, a demonstration of absolute surrender and also an acceptance of the justice of her beating. That wasn't going to change her attitude, though, and the resentment was coming back into her expression even as her orgasm faded.

'Go and stand in the corner, Portia,' Sarah ordered as her girlfriend's shudders finally died down. 'Pull your dress up and put your hands on your head.'

Portia gave Sarah a sulky look but obeyed, scampering quickly into the angle of two bookcases and adjusting her dress so that both her smacked bottom and her breasts were bare. Her breathing was heavy and even, and she was still shaking, but we ignored her as Eliza spoke.

'We must at least consider new members. Does anybody have any suggestions?'

'We do,' Jasmine answered, with a quick glance at Caroline. 'Our friend Yazzie.'

'Only there's a bit of a problem,' Caroline put in. 'She's Mo's daughter. Mo from the Red Ox.'

I winced. The Red Ox was one of the pubs where they stripped. I had some extremely unsettling memories of it – and of Mo, a big half-Chinese man with a primitive attitude to women.

'She's really cute,' Jasmine was saying, 'and well into it, mainly bondage, but she doesn't mind having her bottom smacked. There's no need to look so worried, Isabelle. Mo doesn't know we're into her.'

'I should think not!' I answered. 'But what if he finds out?'

'Exactly,' Caroline agreed. 'He'd kill us!'

I nodded. Given his own behaviour it would be hypocritical of him to object to us playing with his daughter, but I knew he wouldn't see it that way. Men seldom do. Besides, it would give him a hold over me. I'd put a great deal of time and effort into breaking away from him and his friends, a group led by the truly filthy Stan Tierney who'd taken advantage of me during my first year.

'I'd rather not risk it,' I said.

Portia was making urgent gestures from the corner.

'Do take your knickers out of your mouth, Portia,' Sarah said.

'I didn't want to give you another excuse to punish me,' Portia explained, after taking the now-soggy scrap of silk out. 'What I want to say is that we should at least meet her, and Tiffany.'

I hesitated. I knew that if I put it to the vote I would probably lose. Sarah was likely to vote against me on principle, and Jasmine and Caroline were the only ones apart from me who had to worry about Mo. Katie would support me, maybe Caroline, but not Eliza, who was keen to find somebody for herself now that I was no longer under her discipline. I was quite keen to meet Tiffany as well, so the best bet was to arrange for Yazzie to be vetted by whoever was least likely to accept her. She'd be Jasmine's playmate, which would make Portia jealous, while Katie would be indifferent to another submissive woman.

'Katie and Portia can meet Yazzie,' I suggested. 'Jasmine and I can meet Tiffany.'

There was an immediate exchange of calculating glances, but nobody spoke up.

Tiffany Inglehurst was a first-year at Erasmus Darwin College, where Portia herself had been an undergraduate and where Sarah worked as the catering manager. She was also an out and proud lesbian, having joined the university society in freshers' week, which was apparently how Portia had met her. They seemed to have gone more or less directly from the UOLS stall to bed and had stayed there until Sarah's unexpected arrival, a scene that I was very sorry to have missed.

After her initial spanking for going behind Sarah's back a tear-stained Portia had admitted to telling Tiffany about the Rattaners. This confession had led to her group punishment. Given what Portia and Tiffany had got up to in bed together it all seemed fairly safe, and at least there was no difficulty with the introduction. Portia simply told Tiffany that two girls would be coming to interview her for membership, and that was that. It was really only a formality anyway, because as she knew about us already we could hardly turn her down.

It was going to be harder with Yazzie because she hadn't been told about the Rattaners. Katie and Portia were going to make out that they were customers for the corsets that Caroline made, which was true in a sense, and so pretend to meet Yazzie as if by accident. I was still half-hoping that they'd turn her down, but only half. Jasmine had shown me a photo that had seriously weakened my resolve. Because she was Mo's daughter I'd been imagining her as some sort of shapeless hulk with a huge round head and little piggy eyes, much like him. The truth was that while she was obviously Chinese, there the resemblance ended. She was tiny, and very compact, with great melting eyes and dark hair that hung down below her bottom, a bottom that Jasmine assured me was extremely spankable. Just looking at her photo was enough to make me want to put her across my knee.

All I knew about Tiffany was that she had red hair and was reading Politics, Philosophy and Economics. She'd also managed to get one of the first-floor rooms in the main quad at Erasmus, which suggested that she was pushy and not short of money. As we stood in the Victorian red-brick cloisters at the bottom of Tiffany's staircase Jasmine gave a little snort, conveying jealousy rather than the contempt she was hoping for.

'She's going to be another stuck-up little bitch, isn't she?' she suggested.

'Let's at least give her the benefit of the doubt,' I replied.

The rooms opposite Tiffany's belonged to a don, a Dr Welsh, while the one directly next to hers was an SCR guest room. I was in college myself, on the top floor of Old Quad, which was about the best that a third-year could hope for, and St George's was at least venerable and beautiful. Still, I couldn't help but feel a touch of jealousy at Tiffany's surroundings. As I knocked on the door I was telling myself not to be silly, but the pure English arrogance of the voice that answered made it hard to suppress my feelings.

'Come in.'

We entered to find Tiffany seated in a large leather upholstered armchair. There was an open fire in the grate, which I was sure was illegal, and she was toasting a crumpet on the end of a long brass fork. She was small and slim, with an oval face framed by copper-coloured curls held back with an Alice band.

14

Her expression suggestion absolute confidence, even a little disdain, making me wonder what Portia had told her.

'You must be Isabelle and Jasmine,' she said. 'Do sit down. I can give you ten minutes.'

'Ten minutes?' Jasmine responded. 'We really need to talk to you properly.'

'My PPE group are coming for tea,' she explained.

I'd assumed that she'd been making tea for us, but I realised now that there were too many cups, saucers and plates.

'Portia's told me all about it anyway,' she went on, 'so I know this is just a formality. But I do love to be spanked, especially by rough girls. Portia tells me that you two strip in pubs?'

I felt Jasmine stiffen beside me. I was still trying to find my voice to refute the accusation without actually telling a lie when Tiffany spoke up again.

'So I'm thoroughly looking forward to it and, hopefully, to dishing out a little as well. Be a sweetie and butter this crumpet for me, would you?'

She'd finished toasting the crumpet and put it down on a plate. I shut the door behind me and quietly slipped the latch into place, took three swift paces across the room and grabbed hold of her by the collar of her blouse. Tiffany hadn't even been looking and she dropped the toasting fork with a squeal of surprise and alarm, followed by a second yelp as I forced her down over the arm of her chair.

'Get her skirt up, Jasmine,' I ordered.

Jasmine hadn't needed to be told – she was already hauling the struggling girl's skirt high. It was tweed and quite tight, which made it difficult, and all the while she wouldn't stop kicking and protesting.

'No! Stop it, you idiots! My friends are coming . . . my friends!'

'Shut up,' Jasmine snapped, hauling hard on Tiffany's skirt to expose a pair of lacy black knickers.

'Unless you want Dr Welsh across the corridor to see you like this,' I advised, 'and your precious friends.'

I'd got Tiffany firmly by the scruff and Jasmine was holding her legs, allowing me to whip down the black panties and expose her small freckle-covered bottom to the air. The door was locked but she didn't know that, so I gave her a moment to imagine the humiliation of having her friends walk in to find her taking a spanking.

'Please, I'm begging you!' she pleaded. 'You can do anything you like to me, just not now. Not now, please . . . please . . .'

'Shut up,' I told her. Then I began to spank.

Tiffany's bottom was very soft, the flesh squashing out under my hand with every smack. She couldn't take it either, wriggling in our grip and begging us to stop, in a state of blind panic that only made it all the more fun. Jasmine was enjoying herself too, and after a moment she changed her grip, hauling Tiffany's legs wide to display the rear view of a sweetly turned little pussy covered with thick ginger fur. From between the lips hung the string of a tampon, and she was so slim that her anus showed too, a fleshy pink dimple in a nest of crinkly hair. My bottom-hole looks the same, which brought home to me just how unfair we were being, so I gave her a final hard smack and then let go.

'You . . . you horrible big bullies!' she sobbed. 'Portia said you were bitches, but . . . but that was so good! Do me again . . . please, just do it quickly.'

I glanced at Jasmine, who shrugged. Tiffany hadn't tried to get up, so we took hold of her by her panties and the waistband of her skirt and set to work, slapping a cheek each. She was wearing stockings, which made the sight even more alluring as her legs pumped in her lowered underwear, with her thighs and cheeks parting to treat us to glimpses of her pussy and anus as she wriggled under the spanking. We only stopped when the clock on her mantelpiece chimed five, which presumably meant that her fellow PPE students were due to arrive. She jumped up, grinning and rubbing at her bottom, her pretty face set in an expression of bliss.

'Ooh, that *was* nice!' Tiffany sighed. 'Now my bum will be lovely and hot while I'm serving tea. Come on, you'd better go.'

'OK,' I agreed, 'but a couple of things first. Everybody in the Rattaners is equal, whatever their background, and by the way I'm a Scot, and I've been through public school and finishing school, as I suspect you have yourself?'

She made to reply but thought better of it, pulling up her knickers instead.

'And I locked the door, by the way,' I continued. 'We do try to be discreet.'

Tiffany's response was a rather nervous nod. She smoothed her skirt down and began to sort out the tea things, not speaking but with her movements full of energy, like a mad imp. What I was saying didn't seem to be getting through to her at all but the warmth between my thighs provided the answer to what we'd come to find out. She could definitely be a Rattaner.

I didn't manage to see Katie until the weekend, when her blonde head and freckled face poked shyly around the side of my door just as I was putting the finishing touches to my essay. We'd spent part of the summer in Scotland, as well as two weeks backpacking in the Auvergne, and we slept together regularly, yet she still hesitated before kissing me, almost as shy as she'd been on the day we'd met. I pulled her close and made her open her mouth, allowing my hand to stray to the seat of the tight white trousers she was wearing so that I could cup one chubby bottom cheek as she melted to my kiss.

'How did it go with Yazzie?' I asked when I'd finally let her go.

'Great,' she answered, full of enthusiasm, only to start to look worried. 'Oh, I forgot. You're not that keen, are you?'

'I'm worried about her father, that's all. You know what that lot are like.'

Katie gave a sympathetic nod, then went on.

'Yazzie's really gentle and polite, and she takes the whole domination and submission thing really seriously. She even calls Jasmine *Kyou*, which is a suffix meaning "Lady" that Japanese submissives use.'

'I thought she was Chinese?'

'She is, or at least her mum is, and Mo's half and half. Apparently she was brought up by her mum, in London, but moved in with her dad a few months ago after he married this Jamaican woman.'

'Mo's divorced, then? That's no surprise. So what do you think?'

'I think she'd be all right. She loves to be tied up so that she's helpless and then to be spanked – or anything, really. It's being helpless that's important to her.'

'Eliza would appreciate that, and so would Sarah. What does Portia think?'

'She wasn't too keen at first but she changed her mind.'

I was instantly suspicious, wondering if Portia might have some ulterior motive, only to dismiss the idea. Yazzie was cute and no doubt she appealed to Portia's cruel streak, just as she did to mine. I was still doubtful, because the thought of Mo's reaction if he discovered that I'd been tying his daughter up and spanking her didn't bear thinking about. But everybody else seemed to want her, and it was important to keep Jasmine and Caroline firmly on my side.

'I suppose we'd better let her in, then,' I said. 'Now come and sit on my lap.'

Katie sat, and I was treated to the delightful sensation of her bottom settling on my leg. Just to have her with me made me relaxed, and also aroused because of the smell of her and the feel of her flesh – and the way her rounded breasts pushed out the front of her blouse, which I began to undo.

'Isabelle!' she squeaked. 'What if somebody comes?'

'They'll knock first,' I assured her, 'and the stairs creak. Now hush. I want to see you.'

Katie's top two buttons were already undone and she didn't try to stop me, although her mouth had come open a little and she'd begun to shiver with embarrassment and arousal. I undid a third button, allowing me to open her blouse and tuck it in at either side of her breasts, squeezing them together in her full-cupped white bra. She was quite a bit bigger than me, filling out her bra so that low, soft bulges of flesh showed above the cups. Her nipples, already hard, showed through the material. I stroked each of them with a crooked finger to make her sigh, giving her trembling a new urgency before gently easing each breast from its restraining bra cup to leave them jutting bare and beautiful in the cool autumn sunlight.

'Please, Isabelle, you're turning me on,' Katie said, half in protest, half in desire.

'Hush,' I repeated, and began to stroke her breasts.

She put her hands to her chest, cupping her breasts as if to protect herself but also holding them out for my attention.

'Put your hands on your head,' I ordered.

Katie obeyed instantly and closed her eyes, her shaking now so violent that her whole torso was quivering as I continued to tease her breasts. It felt wonderful just to control her and to feel her helpless reaction to my touch, even without the sight of her pretty, blissful face and bare chest, or the feel and the smell of her skin. I leant forward a little to take one stiff nipple, then the other, between my lips, sucking each one in and giving the gentlest of nips to her teats. She winced, and as I began to lick at her breasts she was making little sobbing noises in her throat.

'Trollop,' I told her, when I finally pulled back. 'You're as bad as Caroline.'

She shook her head.

'Yes, you are,' I insisted, again cupping one plump breast to stroke the nipple with my thumb. 'Maybe I should make you strip in pubs?'

Katie shook her head again, urgently this time. We both knew that I'd never make her do it, but it was nice to see her react.

'Perhaps even in the Red Ox?' I went on. 'In front of Stan Tierney and all his horrible friends, all leering at you as you peel your clothes off, touching their dirty cocks to the sight of your bare boobs, laughing as you peel your knickers down with your bottom stuck right out so they can see your rear view . . .'

She gave a sudden fierce shiver, as if she'd had a tiny orgasm, although she was still shaking her head. I laughed at her reaction and slipped a hand between her thighs to where her pussy made a soft bulge in her trousers. I began to rub her there.

'No, Isabelle, please,' she gasped. 'You'll make me all wet and the patch will show.'

'Good,' I told her. 'You can walk back to Foxson with a damp patch underneath and everyone will know what a little trollop you are. Either that or they'll think you've had an accident in your panties. I wonder which you'd hate more?'

Katie shook her head violently, just once, but made no effort to remove my hand. I continued to masturbate her, amused by the thought of her having to walk halfway across Oxford with a damp patch between her thighs and enjoying my power over her more than ever.

'I won't really make you strip at the Red Ox,' I promised her, 'but you will have to attend to some men this term. There's Dr Appledore for one. He can hardly expect to have me, but he's sure to want his little treats. I'll let him spank you – bare, of course – and touch you wherever he likes while you're over his knee. Then you can sit on his lap and pull on his cock for him while he feels you up, or maybe I'll make you suck him off. I do love to see that pretty face with a big, thick penis stuck deep in your mouth.'

Katie began to whimper and to shake her head again, with a desperate urgency this time, but she was coming, wriggling her bottom on my leg and pressing herself against my hand, with her breasts and hair bouncing to the motions. I watched as she came, utterly helpless in my hands and with her head full of the thoughts that I'd put there, of how I'd let my tutor spank her and make her gobble his penis.

It was hard to hold back until she'd finished properly, and the moment the shudders of pleasure had finished running through her body I was easing

21

Katie down to the floor. Both of us were far beyond the point of worrying about being caught, so I jerked up my dress and lifted my bottom to let her pull down my knickers without hesitation. A quick tug to lift my bra and I was naked for her – not very dignified, maybe, with my knickers around my ankles and my tits out, but I needed to come too badly to care.

Katie buried her face in my pussy, and as her tongue pushed in between my sex lips I closed my eyes in bliss. So many times she'd been on her knees for me, or licked me from behind, or had me sit on her face, but I never tired of the sensation, nor of having such a shy, pretty girl do something that I still felt was dirty. She seemed to get better every time, and now was no exception, with her tongue flicking and teasing in the folds of my sex. My breasts seemed to be straining in my hands, while every touch to my nipples was adding to the shivers already passing through me. Katie seemed to know, choosing exactly the right moment to suck my clitoris in between her lips. I screamed as I came, unable to hold it back, but with embarrassment at the thought of my neighbours hearing already flooding through me as I started to come down from my climax.

We were left red-faced and giggling as Katie finally rocked back from between my thighs. I kissed her quickly, tasting myself on her lips, before we adjusted our clothes. Since we were in the only part of the college not yet modernised all I had to wash in was a vast china sink, certainly pre-war and probably older. It was so big that I could have sat in it but I contented myself with a dab of water. As she had predicted, Katie had a damp patch – and it showed, outlining the swell of her pussy lips.

'You'd better borrow a skirt and a pair of knickers,' I advised her, trying to not to laugh.

She made a face and began to undo her trousers, only to stop as we heard the creak of the ancient wooden stairs.

'It's probably for one of my neighbours,' I said as Katie hastily fastened her trouser button. But the footsteps continued and came to a stop outside my door.

There was a pause. Then there came a knock, very faint, as if my visitor wasn't quite sure if she really wanted to come in.

'Hello?' I said as Katie hastened to open a window.

Again there was a pause, before the door opened to reveal a young woman, obviously a fellow student but nobody I knew. She was short, maybe not even five feet tall, with a round face framed in dark hair, big round glasses, and large round breasts pushing out the front of a purple jumper. Her waist was small and was completely hidden by the baggy jumper, but she had full hips and thighs that hinted at a bottom as big and round as the rest of her. She reminded me irresistibly of a slightly surprised owl.

'Isabelle Colraine?' she asked.

'Yes, hi,' I answered. 'How can I help?'

'I'd like to join the James Malcolm Rymer Society, please.'

Two

'Who is this owl girl, anyway?' Sarah demanded.

'She's called Amy Jane Moffat and she's reading maths at Newman,' I explained. 'She saw my room booking at the Bodleian and decided she'd like to join.'

'I said it was a stupid idea to call ourselves after a real author,' Portia said.

'She's a first-year,' I retorted. 'She's probably just trying to find her feet. Maybe if we arrange a reading group or something she'll get bored and move on.'

'*You* can,' Portia told me, 'but *I*'m not. And meanwhile, you ought to be punished.'

'Why?' I demanded.

'For introducing strange girls into the society!' Portia laughed. 'At least Tiffany's kinky!'

'I haven't introduced her to the Rattaners,' I pointed out, 'only to the supposed James Malcolm Rymer Society.'

'I still think you ought to be punished,' Portia insisted.

'Shut up,' I told her firmly. 'Never mind the Owl. How about Tiffany and Yazzie?'

'What do you think?' Eliza asked.

'Tiffany's a little . . . a little strange,' I told her, 'but she'd definitely fit in, and—'

'I told you so,' Portia interrupted, 'which makes it so unfair . . .'

'Do let Isabelle finish,' Sarah told her. 'And stop playing the brat. We all know what you're after but you're not going to get it, not in Katie's room.'

'I don't see why not,' Portia complained. 'Not me, of course, but Isabelle. We could gag her with her panties and—'

'Shut up,' Sarah said firmly.

Portia went quiet, but the sulky expression she'd been wearing since the beginning of the meeting only grew more intense. She was determined to get me punished after what had happened in the Bodleian, but it simply wasn't going to happen. I shook my head at her sadly before I went on.

'Yazzie is also acceptable to me, but with reservations. It's absolutely vital that her father doesn't find out, so I'd like to move for a temporary addendum to the rules to the effect that nobody is allowed to talk to Mo, Stan Tierney or any of those people.'

'We have to, occasionally,' Jasmine pointed out.

'Except for Jasmine and Caroline,' I agreed. 'Is that acceptable?'

'I certainly have no wish to talk to such people,' Sarah answered. Nobody else objected.

'And the punishment for any breach of this new regulation?' Eliza asked.

She had taken a book from her bag. Although the Rattaners was technically my society, everybody deferred to Eliza as the oldest and most experienced among us. I'd made her secretary and responsible for maintaining the rules, because I knew she was both honest and discreet. Even the notebook was written up so that the contents seemed to be no more than random columns of figures and symbols. But each entry had a meaning.

The punishment would have to be harsh, otherwise Portia was likely to break the rule just to make things awkward for me. That meant I had to make sure it was targeted squarely at her, which wasn't easy because for all her sulky attitude she was deeply into corporal punishment, at least when it was administered by women. Unlike Sarah she could even cope with men to some extent, but not with really dirty old men. The best choice would be Walter Jessop, who ran an antique shop in Whytleigh and liked nothing better than to fiddle with young women.

'The punishment is to be given to Walter for the night,' I said, 'for him to do anything to the offender that he wants.'

An expression of disgust crossed Sarah's face and Portia's eyes went wide.

'That is *disgusting*!' she said.

'Then make sure that you obey the new rule,' I told her, feeling well pleased with myself.

Eliza made a careful note in her book, then looked up again.

'We just need to agree on a venue, then,' she said. 'I've spoken to Isadore Treadle, and he's more than happy to act as host.'

'I bet he is,' Jasmine remarked.

'I suppose he'll want to tickle us?' Caroline added, half hopeful, half in disgust.

'That's only fair,' I pointed out.

'That's all very well for you to say,' Portia answered me. 'You won't be the one being tickled, or dressed up like some school tart, or getting spanked bare in front of him.'

'Do you have a better suggestion?' I asked.

'No,' she admitted.

'Then Dr Treadle's it is,' I concluded, 'and as he'll

obviously be there I suggest we invite Duncan Appledore as well.'

'If we must have men at all,' Sarah replied.

'At least Dr Appledore and Isadore are civilised people,' Eliza pointed out.

'It would be kind to invite Walter too,' Caroline said. 'He's letting me sell my corsets in his shop and share his stand at antique fairs and re-enactment events for nothing.'

'Hardly nothing,' Portia remarked with a meaningful glance at Caroline's ample chest.

'I do not!' Caroline protested. 'Well . . . only out of sympathy, and not often. Can he come?'

'I suppose so,' Sarah sighed. 'Is there any other business?'

'I still say Isabelle should be punished,' Portia said sulkily. 'At least a spanking . . .'

'You'll be the one getting a spanking if you're not careful,' I warned her.

'It's not fair,' she protested again, addressing Eliza. 'I get it, when it was perfectly obvious that Tiffany was suitable, but Isabelle gets us tangled up with this owl girl and she gets away with it! Who agrees that Isabelle ought to be spanked?'

I couldn't help but glance around the room as she spoke, because if they voted for me to get it I would have to submit. That would almost certainly mean being gagged with my knickers and getting six of the cane – or, if Portia had her way, being made to kneel bare for a spanking first, just as she had been. Fortunately she was the only one who thought I deserved it, while everybody else knew she was just being petty. Not a single hand went up except her own, so I'd escaped.

I couldn't help but feel sorry for Amy Jane, and tried my best not to think of her as the Owl. She was as shy as Katie, and like most mathematicians her brain seemed to work in a different way from everybody else's, so that she could seem to be thinking ahead of me all the time and yet miss nuances of tone and other social subtleties. Her first choice had been Merton, but she'd gone into the clearing system and ended up at Newman, which had been one of the last colleges to hold out against admitting female undergraduates and was still full of rowing hearties and rugger buggers. Even the girls tended to be sporty, extrovert types, so I could well understand that Amy Jane would want some different company.

I didn't mind that, and nor did Katie. The three of us got on well, and Amy Jane came to see me at St George's several times during the first two weeks of term. We'd arranged the Rattaners meeting for the Saturday of the second week, and as luck would have it Amy Jane asked if Katie and I would like to come and see a film with her that night. I had to turn her down, and she looked so hurt that I gave her a hug and promised we'd go out with her during the following week. At that moment Stan Tierney's leering face appeared in the window of the porter's lodge, next to where we were standing. He was still scouting for the same rooms he'd been responsible for when I was a first-year, including my old one, so it was impossible to avoid him completely. All I could do was ignore him, but I was terrified that he'd say something inappropriate in front of Amy Jane so I quickly made my excuses. She left, but as I turned back into college Tierney followed me, speaking as he caught up.

'She's nice. Nice tits. I like 'em fat.'

I walked a little faster, looking straight ahead, but he wouldn't shut up.

'Nice arse, too. Big and wobbly. Or is she firm? Some fat girls are firm.'

I walked faster still, until Tierney was struggling to keep up, but he wouldn't take the hint.

'What's it like to spank her? I bet she howls.'

'Shut up, Tierney – you're disgusting,' I snapped.

'Yeah? I'm not the one who likes to spank fat little first-years. What sort of knickers does she wear?'

'I don't know. She's just a friend.'

'Yeah, sure she is,' he laughed. 'Like your Katie's just a friend, and that stuck-up tart Portia. Don't forget that I know what you're like, Isabelle.'

'Will you just go away, please?'

'What, not good enough for you any more, ain't I? Nice, that is! I was good enough for you when you needed my help to get into Caroline Greenwood's knickers, wasn't I? And when you wanted to get your dirty little girls' society together.'

'How dare you!' I snapped back, finally losing my patience. 'You tricked me, you lied to me, you coerced me into ... into things I'd never do of my own accord!'

'You loved every minute of it!' Tierney sneered.

'You're vile,' I told him. 'Go away.'

He stopped, but he hadn't finished.

'You'll be back,' he said, 'begging for a suck of my cock like the little tart you are!'

I felt the blood rush to my cheeks as he spoke, not because of his words but because the Bursar was walking towards us in company with the College Secretary and some woman I didn't know. They might or might not have heard but they could hardly have missed my blushes, and they gave me distinctly peculiar looks as they passed. I hurried back to my room, my eyes full of tears – tears of anger, and also of frustration. There was absolutely nothing I could do, because Tierney knew far too much, all of which would come out if I made a complaint.

A cup of tea helped to calm me down, but I was left with a nagging suspicion that there was something wrong with what Tierney had said. Another cup and I'd realised what it was: how had he known Amy Jane was a first-year? Admittedly she *looked* like a first-year, with a satchel over her shoulder most of the time and the red and white Newman College scarf that made her look like an Aberdeen fan. That didn't actually guarantee she was a first-year, while it was also a little off that she had managed to pick up on the Rattaners so quickly. Not that Tierney knew anything about the supposed James Malcolm Rymer Society, and it was hard to see how he could have corrupted a first-year mathematics student from Derbyshire, especially when he couldn't have had more than a week to do it.

I tried to tell myself that the idea was ridiculous but it wouldn't go away. Tierney had tricked me before, and for all his sleazy manner and dirty habits he was no fool. Just possibly he'd come up with some Machiavellian plan to get me back under his influence, but if so it wasn't going to work, not this time. I'd been naive then, but not any more. This time I'd be careful and keep a careful eye on Amy Jane – on Tierney as well. If they seemed to be trying to draw me into anything I'd know what to do about it.

Getting ready for the Rattaners evening was less easy than it should have been, although the effort I had to put into secrecy always made it more exciting. There were altogether too many beady eyes around St George's for me to risk dressing there, or even for me to leave in company with Duncan. Not that there was anything wrong in going out with my tutor for the evening, but it would be sure to cause comment, which at the very least meant risking a breach of my own strict rules. Naturally I had to abide by them, but I was determined to get through the term, and the year, without having to suffer the indignity of a punishment.

I'd left quite a lot of my clothes with Jasmine and Caroline for the summer anyway, and their house was far safer than college. The beautiful black silk corset that Caroline had made for me in my first year was there as well, and I felt it deserved another outing. Just walking there from college felt deliciously naughty, knowing how I would be dressing and what was likely to happen, and the others were no less enthusiastic.

They were in the kitchen, Jasmine, Caroline and Yazzie, all three of them already dressed. Jasmine had chosen her image carefully, in order to reflect her desire to return to a dominant role but without giving Eliza, Sarah and me too obvious a challenge. She had put her pale blonde hair into a plait and coiled it at the back of her head, making her elfin face as strong as possible, while her purple satin corset would have been indecent had she had just an inch more chest. Black silk panties, seamed stockings attached to her corset by suspenders, and short black boots completed her look, which was more burlesque than either dominant or submissive.

Caroline had no such qualms. She was in one of her striptease outfits, a school uniform which would have had her sent home from even the most liberal of comprehensives. The skirt was in Royal Stuart tartan, but so ridiculously short that even as she leant across the table to retrieve a coffee mug for me it lifted to show off a pair of overtight white panties with as much bottom cheek spilling from either side as they managed to cover, leaving her yellow and black jasmine-flower tattoo on show. Her blouse was no better, with the buttons straining across her ample breasts and no bra beneath so that her nipples made dark circles under the fabric and pushed up two enticing bumps. She'd put her hair in bunches, tied with red ribbon, and had painted some freckles across her nose, while her choice of pink pumps and white ankle socks did nothing to soften her appearance. She looked like a slut, which she was proud to be.

Yazzie's outfit was less overtly sexual: a simple black dress so short that most of her thighs showed, along with black boots much like Jasmine's, while her hair was coiled up onto her head and decorated with a huge yellow silk flower. She was obviously the youngest among us, and unlike Caroline she actually looked quite innocent, but the three coils of coloured rope carefully laid out on the table in front of her suggested otherwise. She bobbed her head as I entered the room, greeting me.

'Isabelle *Kyou*. Thank you for accepting me.'

I smiled, pleased by the honorific, and held out my hand to be kissed. Yazzie responded well, bowing her head and pressing her lips gently to my skin, which sent a brief tremor of arousal through me. Mo or no Mo, I'd made the right choice.

'My clothes?' I asked, arching my eyebrows at Caroline.

'All laid out on the bed, sweetie,' she told me, jerking her thumb towards the stairs with a casual lack of respect that made my fingers twitch after the submissiveness of Yazzie.

Caroline had her back to me, and I took a moment to tuck her skirt up into its waistband before I pulled down her panties. It was a wasted effort as far as punishment went because she didn't even bother to cover herself but went on making the coffee. I gave her a couple of smacks anyway, hard enough to make her squeak, then went upstairs. Everything was laid out for me, just as she'd said: my corset, a pair of long black leather gloves, smart black shoes, stockings, black French knickers and a black leather pencil skirt, which was new. She'd obviously made it specially for me, which had me smiling in gratitude and promising myself that I'd do something special for her that evening.

I took my time over a shower and my make-up, then dressed, with my sense of dominance and control gradually rising with each article of clothing that I put on. The effect was certainly striking, although I felt that a hat would have added a nice touch and so I put my hair up and fastened it into a bun with one of Jasmine's combs and a piece of net. My new skirt was especially satisfying, although it came down almost to my ankles and was so tight that I could only walk with tiny, precise steps. I knew there would be a selection of implements in the workroom, and I selected an elegant bone-handled riding whip, the feel of which had me itching to apply it to somebody's bottom. It felt a shame to put my long coat back on over it all.

Dr Treadle's house was in Wytham Village, on the far side of Oxford, so Jasmine drove out to the ring road and around the city, which gave us plenty of time to talk. Yazzie continued to address me as *Kyou*, and evidently believed in maintaining formal roles, while Caroline was giggly and excited at the prospect of playing together. That made it very easy for me to slip into feeling both dominant and sexual, and by the time we arrived it seemed the most natural thing in the world for Yazzie to get out first and hold the car door for me. Indoors I let my coat slip from my shoulders and handed it to Yazzie, who was looking more than a little surprised at the sight of Esmond, Dr Treadle's stuffed ostrich.

'His tail feathers can be removed,' I told her, 'which is very convenient for tickling girls, especially girls who've been tied up.'

'Yes, Isabelle *Kyou*,' she answered, and her voice sounded as if she was about to come.

'I think you may have an interesting subject there, Dr Treadle,' I remarked as he closed the door behind us. 'You may enjoy her later, as a little thank-you for allowing us the use of your house.'

'I'd be delighted,' he answered.

He was looking as dapper as ever, in perfect black tie and with his neat white goatee beard newly trimmed, his cufflinks and the gold rims of his spectacles the only details of colour in his dress. Eliza was right to say that he was civilised, and he was exactly the sort of man I wanted to be associated with the Rattaners: mature, intelligent and calm, also tolerant and happy to put up with whatever we got up to while content with what he was offered in return.

Duncan Appledore was much the same, if slightly less pliable when it came to doing as he was told. He too was there, with his large and comfortable body relaxed into a large and comfortable armchair, a drink in one hand. Like Dr Treadle, he was in black tie but the otherwise sombre look of his clothing was relieved by a richly embroidered waistcoat. He had Katie on his lap, one hand gently cupping the curve of her bottom, at which I raised my eyebrows.

'I trust you're enjoying my girlfriend's bottom, Duncan?' I asked. 'No, don't stop, you are very welcome – but you, Katie, have earned yourself a spanking.'

She blushed and bit her lip, but her eyes were already shining with anticipation. I knew she'd come over with him, and she looked both sexy and

34

amusingly silly in her line-dancing outfit of skintight white trousers, a stars-and-stripes blouse, cowboy boots and a white Stetson hat. In my time I'd been made to dress the same way, which had been deeply humiliating, but it suited Katie. The only other person there was Walter Jessop, who looked distinctly out of place.

There had always been something seedy about Walter, but it seemed to have intensified over the summer. I was used to him being plump but he'd lost a little weight, which gave his body the impression of having sagged slightly, especially around the middle. His face was redder and his hair thinner, while his nose had begun to grow bulbous and was threaded with tiny purple veins. He hadn't bothered to dress for the occasion, unless a tweed jacket with leather patches at the elbows and a pair of baggy corduroy trousers was intended to represent some fetish I wasn't familiar with. One thing was certain: the threat of being given to him for a night would keep Portia well away from the Red Ox.

'Eliza should be here presently, with the others,' Dr Treadle announced, rubbing his hands together as he made for the sideboard. 'Drinks? And what entertainment do we have planned for the evening?'

'A Glenlivet for me, please,' I answered him. 'Sarah has a new game, so she says.'

It was actually something I was slightly worried about, because while Sarah and I had been allies most of the time, we had had our differences in the past and I didn't entirely trust her not to try and put me in some awkward position – such as bottom up over her lap with my smart black knickers stuffed in my mouth. Fortunately, unless I broke the rules she had no way of imposing anything on me without taking a risk herself – or so I hoped.

I'd no sooner sat down with my drink and retrieved Katie from Duncan's lap to sit her on my own when the doorbell rang. Dr Treadle went to answer it and Eliza, Sarah, Portia and Tiffany trooped in. Eliza wore a severe-looking tweed suit with a tight skirt, while the other three were in full riding gear of taut jodhpurs and white blouses, highly polished black boots and smart jackets. Sarah's jacket was black, while Portia's and Tiffany's were both red – or, technically, pink – and I couldn't resist a quip.

'I thought a red coat meant you were in charge, Sarah? So black implies . . .'

'Very amusing,' she replied. 'Especially as your entire outfit is black.'

The blood went to my cheeks in a blush that I was powerless to hold back, and which grew stronger as both Portia and Tiffany giggled. I buried my face in my glass in an attempt to hide my embarrassment and Sarah didn't press her advantage, instead making for the sideboard. The exchange had left me with an urgent need to exert my authority once more, and as soon as I'd swallowed my whisky I put the glass down.

'Right, you little flirt,' I said, and turned Katie over my knee.

She was taken completely by surprise, and barely managed a squeak of alarm before she'd been tipped up with the seat of her trousers, bulging with healthy young bottom, stuck out towards the room. I began to smack the taut globes. I had the full attention of the room on the instant. Even Sarah took the trouble to turn around to enjoy the view. All I wanted to do was make a show of Katie's submission to me, and perhaps warm her bottom a little to help her over her natural shyness, so I let her keep her clothes on and contented myself with three dozen smacks. Besides, just the feel of her cheeks through the tight white

36

material of her line-dancing trousers was enough to make me want to put her on her knees and make her lick me, and it was rather early for that.

Sarah had sat down, with a glass of white wine in her hand and both Portia and Tiffany curled at her feet, making me wonder what they'd been up to during the week. It seemed that Sarah had been quick to exert her control and make sure that both girls were hers rather than allow Portia to express her rising dominance. I immediately found myself thinking of how that was likely to affect the dynamics of power within the society, but Sarah had begun to explain her game and I quickly turned my attention to what she was saying.

'. . . Which is convenient as, of the twelve of us, six are dominant and six are submissive.'

Jasmine made to speak but thought better of it. Portia was clearly resigned to her role.

'The game is called joker, and this is how it works,' Sarah continued as she took a pack of playing cards from the pocket of her riding jacket. 'First, each submissive girl chooses a punishment, or something she'd like done to her or to somebody else. These are written down, in no particular order. We then cut cards, first the dominants and then the submissives. Whoever gets the highest card among the dominants gets first choice of partner, and whoever cuts the highest card among the submissives gets first choice of punishment, and so on. Is that clear?'

'Perfectly,' Duncan replied, 'and an excellent game if I may say so. Simple, yet effective, and very fair.'

It was also extremely cruel. Of the six girls, three would have to go to men, and it was the men who would do the choosing, while the chance for the girls of being able to play with their partner of choice was only one in six. Nobody was going to back out, but

37

Katie had started to tremble and she pulled herself closer to me.

'Choose me,' she whispered, 'if you can.'

'I will,' I promised her.

'I'll make a note of the punishments,' Eliza offered, taking her notebook and a pen from her bag. 'And we must veto anything that is too soft, or impractical. Who would like to start? Perhaps our new members?'

She was looking at Yazzie, who responded with a polite inclination of her head before replying.

'Thank you, Dr Abbot *Iemoto*. I would like to be tied, please, so that I am entirely at the mercy of my Mistress or Master.'

I couldn't help but feel a touch of pique as she spoke. They had explained the Japanese honorifics she used as we drove over, and the one she had given Eliza implied a respected teacher or an expert of great seniority. My own *Kyou* was respectful but less so than was *Iemoto*, while she had also used my Christian name as she did with Jasmine. Clearly she felt that my status was inferior to that of Eliza, and what made it worse was that I knew perfectly well that she was right.

'Good,' Eliza responded. 'And may I say that it is a pleasure to have somebody who understands that submission should mean *submission*, and not simply the gratification of her personal tastes. Tiffany?'

I wasn't sure who she was referring to, but I found myself colouring up anyway. After all, it was barely three months since she had given me my last punishment session, and she had never been shy about telling me I was a difficult pupil, especially when it came to taking enemas, which she loved to give, or having my mouth washed out with soap.

'I'd like to be spanked,' Tiffany said with relish. 'You can do it hard, and I don't mind if my bottom is bare, but I need you to be cruel about it, as if you've bullied me into it, the way Isabelle and Jasmine did me. I like to be teased too, and—'

'What was it you were saying just now, Eliza?' Duncan interrupted.

'Quite,' Eliza responded. 'Tiffany, you may rest assured that whoever chooses you will know how to deal with you properly. None of us are inexperienced. Katie?'

'Um ...' Katie replied. 'I'd like a spanking too, please.'

'Try and be original, Katie,' Portia mocked, 'at least a bit. Surely we all have to choose different punishments?'

'Maybe the strap, then?' Katie suggested. 'But not too hard.'

'Remember that you won't necessarily have to take your own punishment,' Sarah put in. 'It's the luck of the draw.'

'Of course – sorry,' Katie replied. 'OK, a strapping, given however the dominant pleases.'

'That's better,' Eliza replied. 'Caroline?'

'Being queened,' Caroline answered promptly.

'*Queened?*' Portia responded, with a horrified glance towards the three men.

Caroline shrugged. 'If you can't take the heat ...'

'Yes, but *queened*? Come on, Caroline!'

'Queened,' Caroline said firmly. 'And you have to lick.'

The look on Portia's face suggested that she was about to be sick, but she contented herself with a shake of her head.

'I just hope you get it yourself, that's all,' she said, 'from ...'

Portia stopped, perhaps realising that if she named a man he was almost certain to choose her. Then she knelt up to whisper urgently in Sarah's ear.

'Queened it is, then,' Eliza said. 'And for your own choice, Portia?'

'It's hard to compete, with sluts like Caroline around,' Portia replied. 'You can choose first, Jasmine.'

'Wetting your panties,' Jasmine said.

'How is the dominant supposed to participate?' Portia demanded.

'He can set the scene,' Jasmine explained. 'However he chooses. What's your choice, then?'

'A private striptease,' Portia said.

I could see her reasoning, because if she got it she wouldn't have to be touched.

'That's a little mild,' I pointed out. 'But I'm OK with it if it's done in front of the dominant and she has to bring herself to orgasm.'

Portia made to protest, but everybody else was in agreement and Eliza wrote it into her book.

'Let's cut, then,' Sarah said. 'Aces are high, and a joker means you have to swap places, whoever cuts it – hence the name. Isabelle?'

For once she'd given me proper precedence, not that it made any practical difference this time. But I thanked her as I picked up the deck of cards. Knowing full well what she and Portia were capable of, I gave them a good shuffle first, then placed them back on the table and cut the deck at the centre, praying it wouldn't be a joker. It was the five of clubs.

'Keep your card,' Sarah instructed. 'Eliza?'

Eliza cut a seven and Sarah a jack before passing the cards to the men. Duncan managed to get the ace of spades, assuring himself first choice of the girls, with Dr Treadle cutting a ten and Walter a queen. I was last, but it could have been worse. Duncan would, hopefully, choose Katie, and I managed to make eye contact with him as he went to the sideboard.

'It is by no means an easy choice with six such beautiful girls,' he stated as he filled his tumbler. 'But, as you all know, I have a particular penchant for Katie.'

I felt her relax against me and gave her an encouraging squeeze. Walter was eyeing the remaining girls and Portia's mouth had begun to twitch at one corner.

'Portia,' he said, and I saw her body sag in defeat.

It was better than getting her myself, while Katie was no longer available for Sarah. I began to smile.

'I shall have Tiffany,' Sarah announced, and gave me a knowing smile.

I ignored her, because although she had guessed correctly that Tiffany would have been my choice after Katie, I was last and the new girls were bound to be popular.

'Yazzie, if I may?' Dr Treadle said.

She bowed her head and crawled across from beside Jasmine to his feet.

'Jasmine,' Eliza stated.

That left me Caroline, which was rather nice as I'd only had a limited opportunity to play with her since Katie and I got together. I had always enjoyed her opulent figure as well, and she reacted beautifully to punishment.

'Time for the girls to cut,' Sarah said.

She was really enjoying herself, her voice full of sadistic relish as she tapped the cards into a neat pile on the table. None of the girls seemed particularly keen to cut first, but Yazzie finally leant out from where she was curled at Dr Treadle's feet. She got the three of clubs, about as low as it was possible to get, but only a serene submission showed on her face as she settled back. Tiffany cut a four, little better, and Portia a six, which had her biting her lip in consternation. Katie managed an ace, and she was smiling as she came back to me. Caroline followed, cutting a seven, with Jasmine last with another seven but of a higher suit.

'I'd like to be spanked, please,' Katie said happily.

Tiffany gave her a dirty look, but Katie barely noticed, bouncing happily across to Duncan's chair and draping herself across his lap. He made something of an exhibition of it, applying a dozen firm swats to the bulging seat of her line-dancing jeans before pulling them down and repeating the process on the pink polka-dot panties beneath.

By then she was warm, with her soft bottom-flesh sticking out around her leg holes distinctly pink, but she was still blushing as he pulled her panties down. She was given another two dozen smacks on the bare, hard enough to set her kicking and break down her self-control to make sure we all got a glimpse of her pussy from behind. She could come if she was spanked properly, and she even looked a little disappointed as she got up. But she didn't bother to cover herself, sitting her hot bare bottom down on my lap as she returned to me. I whispered into her ear.

'I'll make you suck his penis later.'

Katie gave a little shiver, but said nothing. Jasmine had stood up.

'I'll strip,' she said.

For her, it was the easy choice. She did it two or three nights a week, often for crowds of leering, drunken men. To perform for us was a simple pleasure, even when it involved bringing herself to orgasm in front of Eliza. It even allowed her to keep a degree of control.

'In the middle of the room, then,' Eliza stated. 'I don't wish to be greedy.'

Jasmine nodded, spent a somewhat puzzled moment trying to choose some suitable music from Dr Treadle's less than up-to-date collection, and began to dance. She was certainly good, strutting and teasing as she slowly removed her clothes, taking her time and making the best of her neatly rounded little bottom and pert breasts. Eliza took it in with a look of casual amusement, which stayed on her face even when Jasmine was down to her panties and crawling on the floor.

The panties came down slowly, with Jasmine's bottom turned towards Eliza in a gesture of unashamed sexual display if not necessarily submission. Eliza was smiling, and clearly enjoying the view, for all that I knew she'd rather have given Jasmine a firm spanking or inserted an enema hose up the tight little bottom-hole now being flaunted for her inspection. No disappointment showed in her expression, and there was a slight flush to her neck as Jasmine began to masturbate, alternately rubbing and showing off her sex until she'd brought herself to a shivering, heaving orgasm. We clapped as she finished: it had been a fine show. Two girls had now been put on display, and I was beginning to feel distinctly warm as Caroline bounced to her feet.

'I want to wet my panties,' she giggled. 'But . . . but I think it would be more fun if I took a dose of the strap.'

Portia shrugged, feigning indifference, but her expression betrayed her true emotions. It was the most painful of the remaining options but the least intimate, leaving her little choice but to thoroughly humiliate herself with Walter Jessop. I even felt a little sorry for her, mainly because I'd have hated to be in her position.

'Two dozen strokes, I think,' I told Caroline, 'as

you seem to be taking so much pleasure in being cruel to poor Portia.'

Caroline winced, but went to take her place on one of Dr Treadle's old upholstered leather chairs, kneeling on the seat with her arms resting on the back and her bottom thrust out for my attention. I took my time with her, first opening her blouse to leave her heavy breasts lolling naked beneath her chest and then twisting it up behind her back to make sure that everyone could see. Not that being stripped that way humiliated her at all, as it would have done most girls, but it was nice to have her on show. Her tiny school skirt only covered about half of her panty seat as it was, but I turned it up onto her back and spent a moment admiring the way the thin white cotton strained out across her ample bottom. The I pulled her knickers down.

'You have a fat bottom, Caroline,' I told her. 'A beautiful bottom, but a fat one.'

'I know,' she answered me, with a hint of a sob in her voice.

She was also firm, and her waist was tiny, making the way her bum cheeks flared more exaggerated still, and intensely feminine. So was the mingled scent of her perfume and aroused pussy, and the prospect of beating her was very appealing indeed. There was a selection of punishment implements arranged on a side table, laid out in much the same way as the drinks on the sideboard and the bowls of cashew nuts and olives, as if the devices were a perfectly normal part of the decor. I selected a heavy three-tailed tawse, which seemed about right for Caroline's resilience and the size of her bottom. Not that she was particularly tough, but she had been known to complain if she was not beaten thoroughly.

Caroline's stare followed me as I walked back to where she was bent waiting for punishment. She had pulled her back in without having to be told, ensuring that her pussy and bottom-hole were on show, as every girl's should be for a beating. I gave her a gentle smile for her obedience and stepped behind her, measuring the tawse across the cheeks of her bottom. Her muscles tightened in reaction, but went loose again as I lifted the thick leather strap, once more allowing her bottom to spread fully.

I brought the tawse down hard, creating a satisfying smack of leather on girlflesh, a noise that was repeated as I gave her the second stroke, and then the third. Caroline tried to keep still and to maintain at least some dignity, but I kept the strokes coming to a hard, even rhythm and she broke quickly. By the sixth she was kicking her feet and gasping. By the twelfth she was treading up and down on the chair and shaking her head because of the pain. By the eighteenth she was squealing like a pig and writhing under the blows, so that I twice caught her across the thighs before I was done, making her reaction more desperate still – and more enjoyable.

'If you don't want your legs smacked you must learn to keep still,' I told her casually. 'You may get up and give me a cuddle.'

Caroline didn't answer, but she came straight into my arms, trembling violently as I held her. Her eyes were a little moist, and her bottom hot and thick with welts, tempting me to stroke her hurt flesh as I soothed her, and to kiss her mouth to make her better and enjoy her reaction to the beating I'd given her. She responded, holding on tight to me with her naked breasts pressed to my own, completely surrendered to me.

'If you two have quite finished?' Sarah remarked.

'Sorry,' I answered, and broke away.

'No, no, carry on,' Portia put in. 'Have each other on the floor and we can all watch.'

'You're not going to escape that easily,' I told her.

Portia made a face at me but stood up, hesitating, although she didn't really have any options. Allowing herself to be tied up was out of the question, because it would have meant letting Walter do whatever he liked to her, which was sure to involve a cock up her pussy – and probably in her mouth, too – while being queened by him would be as bad if not worse.

'I'll wet my knickers for you,' she finally said in a voice so quiet as to be barely audible.

'I beg your pardon?' Walter asked, although he had obviously heard.

'I said I'll wet my knickers for you,' Portia repeated, a little louder and even sulkier than before.

'You'll wet your knickers for me,' Walter echoed with immense satisfaction. 'Splendid. First of all, I rather think we'd better have you in your knickers, just your knickers.'

Portia was pouting desperately, but she was the one who'd questioned Jasmine's initial choice and now she only had herself to blame. She began to undress, reluctantly and making no effort to show off her body, but removing her immaculate riding gear piece by piece until she was down to a pair of scarlet briefs, lacy where they curved tightly against her well-formed bottom while her pussy was cupped in smooth, heavy silk.

'Very pretty,' Walter remarked, 'and expensive too, I imagine?'

'Not particularly,' Portia answered. 'Twenty-four ninety-nine.'

'For a pair of panties?' Walter asked.

Portia merely shrugged.

'Spoiled rotten,' Walter said, with a shake of his head.

'Do you want me to wet in them or not?' Portia demanded.

'Yes,' Walter told her. 'But it's hardly polite to our host to have you piddle all over his floor, is it?'

'Make her sit on the loo in the bathroom,' Caroline suggested.

'I have a better idea,' Walter went on. 'Isadore, I noticed that by the front door you have an aspidistra in an old-fashioned china potty – late Victorian, I think. Might I borrow it? And perhaps I could also trouble you for a newspaper?'

'Certainly,' Dr Treadle responded, chuckling as he got to his feet.

The look on Portia's face as she waited for the preparations to be made was a sight to behold. She was fidgeting badly and obviously wanted to cover her breasts, but she realised that she'd just have looked silly. Everybody else was openly enjoying her plight as well, and she couldn't help but react, so that by the time Dr Treadle's fine red, blue and gold rug had been rolled back and the large china potty placed at the exact centre of an old *Daily Telegraph* she was shaking so badly that her erect nipples were visibly quivering.

'Your throne,' Walter offered, indicating the potty. 'Thighs well apart, please, and stick your bottom right out.'

Portia hesitated, but then she stepped towards the impromptu toilet, blushing furiously as she sank into a squat over the potty. She got into the position that Walter had ordered her to adopt, with her bottom stuck out and her thighs spread wide, so that he had an unobstructed view of the back of the seat of her knickers and also where the gusset was pulled tight to reveal the shape of her pussy lips.

'Don't feel you need to rush,' Walter said. 'I'm enjoying you just as you are.'

Portia threw him a last, absolutely furious look, then closed her eyes and hung her head a little, obviously trying to relax her bladder. It couldn't have been easy, and three times the muscles of her thighs and bottom cheeks went tense before she managed to let go. She gave a faint sob as her panty crotch bulged out under the weight of the pee, which quickly burst through, running from underneath her gusset and also out at one side to splash into the potty and trickle down her thigh.

There was plenty of it, very pale, and she'd obviously had a drink or two before coming to the party. Most of it went into the potty, but a little escaped down Portia's leg to drip onto the newspaper and the rest soaked into her expensive knickers, front and back, making them cling to her wet flesh to display the shape of her sex and her bottom cheeks. By the time she finished, the back of her knickers was soaked almost to the top of her bum crease and she was forced to take them off with her legs still set to either side of the potty, otherwise she'd have risked soiling the floor. As she did so she accidentally treated Walter to a show of the underside of her pussy which left him with a satisfied grin on his weather-beaten face as she walked quickly from the room with her sodden panties trailing from one hand.

Duncan began to clap, a response quickly taken up by the rest of us, and Dr Treadle got up to refresh our drinks while we waited for Portia to sort herself out in the bathroom. I was feeling highly aroused but also mellow, and was quite happy to enjoy the rest of the game before taking my pleasure with Katie and perhaps with Caroline as well. Tiffany was next: she had watched Portia's lewd little display with increasing astonishment, almost horror, which made the thought of watching her being put through her paces more exciting still.

'What do you want to do to me if I let you tie me up?' she asked Sarah as they took their glasses.

'Whatever I please,' Sarah responded.

'And queening is when you sit on somebody's face, isn't it?'

'That's right.'

Tiffany gave a single urgent nod. She was obviously embarrassed, giving a wry glance towards the men, but she laid herself down on the floor. Sarah was all smiles as she stood up to brace her feet either side of Tiffany's body.

'You know I'm going to do it bare, don't you?' she demanded.

Again Tiffany gave her nervous nod.

'But it's hardly appropriate that I should be bare when you're dressed, is it? Open your blouse and take down your jodhpurs.'

'How about her panties?' Walter demanded.

'She has no panties,' Sarah responded. 'She feels that they spoil the line of her jodhpurs.'

It was true. Tiffany had begun to expose herself, albeit somewhat reluctantly, and as she pushed her jodhpurs down we were treated to a display of her furry ginger pussy. She had no bra either, and her breasts, small, hard and high, were covered in freckles.

'That's better,' Sarah said, 'and rather pretty too. Now, I'm going to sit my bare bottom on your face and you're to lick me. Can you cope with that?'

'I asked for it,' Tiffany said, still nervous but with a touch of defiance in her voice.

I wondered just how experienced she was. For all my fantasies and a strong desire for sex with other women, I wasn't at all sure I could have coped with having a woman sit on my face at the beginning of my first year, let alone in front of an audience. Tiffany wasn't going to back out, though: she lay still and passive on the floor as Sarah bared herself and lifted her coat tails to make sure that the girl got a good view of what was about to descend on her face.

'You're to make me come,' Sarah ordered as she sank down into a squat, her bottom cheeks well spread.

Tiffany's mouth came open and her eyes grew wide as she stared up at Sarah's bum. Then they became invisible as her face was sat on.

'Now lick,' Sarah ordered, giving a little wiggle to make herself comfortable.

I was slightly disappointed to see that Sarah had sat down with her pussy rather than her bottom-hole over Tiffany's mouth but that at least meant that the little brat's nose was where it belonged. Not that she seemed to mind – she was licking busily and was plainly aroused. Her thighs had begun to come up and they opened as her excitement grew, showing off her pussy properly this time. I could see that she was wet and that her lips were puffy and the crease between them was glistening and pink.

Tiffany was a great deal more raunchy than I'd expected her to be, given her age and – presumably – her relative lack of experience, but I knew that Portia at least had been with her, and if she'd joined the lesbian society in Freshers' Week then she was obviously confident in her own sexuality. One thing she'd definitely done before was lick pussy, and she had Sarah moaning in no time at all. I wanted to join in, but it wasn't the right moment. When I had Tiffany I would be in charge, and I certainly wouldn't make an exhibition of myself the way Sarah was, clutching at her breasts and gasping in ecstasy as she experienced the attentions of her plaything's tongue.

Sarah had no sooner dismounted than Yazzie begun to strip off, which meant simply peeling her dress over her head. She was nude underneath and her pale, gently curvaceous body was hairless, as I saw when she dropped to her knees to pick up her bondage ropes between her teeth. I had the perfect view as she crawled back to Dr Treadle, with her milk-white bottom open to me and her neatly turned pussy and tiny pink anal star both on full show.

'Your boots too, please, Yazzie,' he instructed.

'Yes, Dr Treadle *Sensei*,' she answered, dropping the ropes.

'"Isadore" will do very nicely, thank you,' he replied as she quickly struggled out of her boots. 'That's better.'

'How would you like me, *Sensei*?' she asked.

Yazzie had got into a kneeling position, her knees planted wide to leave her sex vulnerable and her hands by her sides so that neither her breasts nor her bottom were obstructed from view. It was nice to see a girl make a toy of herself, although I really prefer a little fight or, better still, shyness.

'That will do nicely,' Dr Treadle told her. 'Now, let me see . . .'

His voice trailed off as he picked up the ropes. To the best of my knowledge he had no experience at all with bondage, but he clearly understood human anatomy. He quickly bound Yazzie's wrists to either side of her waist with one rope and tied her ankles together with another, leaving her helpless and pretty well immobile. He used the third rope to make a leash, fastening it loosely around her neck and tying the end off to the doorknob so that she was effectively captured. Then he left the room.

Yazzie didn't know what was coming. But I did, and I also knew why he'd insisted on her taking her boots off. Dr Treadle was soon back. In one hand he held a large ostrich feather, which has to be the most efficient instrument for tickling girls that there is. Yazzie saw, but her expression remained serene, at least until he touched the feather to the soles of her feet. I saw her muscles twitch as her mouth came open in surprise and she dissolved into giggles, completely unable to control herself.

It was funny, and I was laughing with the others as Yazzie's cool, submissive poise simply evaporated. When he applied the feather to the underside of her bottom she fell over, squirming on the carpet as her tickled her, making as much – or more – fuss as most girls do when they're spanked. Dr Treadle was grinning, evidently enjoying himself immensely while his cock grew to a hard bar within his trousers.

For any mixed swinging party to work, there has to be a point at which the men's cocks come out. If they don't then it's likely to fizzle out, as I had learnt during the previous year. Our three males were all older than any of the females, rather genteel and also reserved, which meant they'd probably need a helping hand – although, naturally, not mine. I gave Katie's bottom a smack.

'I think Duncan would appreciate your assistance.'

On her own Katie could never have done it, but on an order from me she could. Duncan had heard me and he adjusted himself in his chair to make a better lap for her. She settled herself and, with a little assistance, freed his cock from his fly. He was already half stiff and his penis grew quickly in her hand, a delightful sight because she managed to look innocent even with her bottom bare on his leg and her hand gripping his shaft, as if she were some naive young girl who'd been spanked for a punishment and then coaxed into masturbating the man who'd dealt with her.

As I'd hoped, with one man's cock out the inhibitions of the others dissolved. Walter beckoned to Caroline, who went to him after just a moment's hesitation, and soon there were two men with pretty girls on their laps and cocks growing stiff in eager hands. All the while Yazzie had been squirming on the floor, giggling helplessly as the ostrich feather teased her feet and between her thighs, her bottom crease and her breasts. Dr Treadle looked as if he was about to burst and got himself out only just in time, making a brief insertion of his erect prick into Yazzie's pussy before jerking himself to a frantic climax, his jetting sperm splashing all over her bare bottom and legs.

The new year was going to be a success for the Rattaners.

Three

We stayed at Dr Treadle's until the early hours of the morning. Once he had lost control of himself and spunked all over Yazzie's bottom there had been little or no reason to hold back. Even Portia had stopped sulking after a while, while I knew I'd definitely made the right choice in accepting the two new members. Yazzie was deeply submissive and receptive, which made her extremely useful, if less challenging than I might have liked. Tiffany was a brat, but that made her all the more desirable. She seemed to regard everybody except Portia as somehow different and inferior, but also sexual and rather frightening, as if she'd been dropped in with a gang of randy cavemen.

I was also pleased with the way the men had behaved, polite and obedient, and providing a useful masculine input. The Red Ox boys would have been another matter entirely, crude and demanding, which I knew would have given the party an entirely different flavour. Tierney in particular had a way of making everything focus on him and his particular preferences. I was very glad that he hadn't been there, and while it was tempting to let him know that there had been a party I managed to resist – only to discover that he knew anyway.

This happened on the following Thursday. I was walking around the quad, thinking vague thoughts about the influence of Metternich on nineteenth-century Europe, when Tierney appeared from one of the side passages. His grin was lewd even by his usual standards, and my first thought was that I'd accidentally tucked my skirt into the back of my knickers or that my nipples showed through my blouse. I hadn't and they didn't, so I feigned an interest in the architecture of the college roofs and hoped he'd realise that I didn't want to speak to him.

'Nice weekend was it, Isa?' he drawled. 'Smacked a few bums, I bet.'

There was a group of my fellow history students at the far side of the quad, and I was forced to make an abrupt change of course to avoid them overhearing.

'I don't know why you should think that,' I said. 'Leave me alone, please.'

'A bit hoity-toity this afternoon, aren't we?' Tierney said. 'I know what you get up to, Isa, and what I want to know is, why didn't you invite me and the boys?'

'That should be perfectly obvious,' I told him.

'Not to me it ain't,' he said. 'You love a bit of it. You posh tarts always do, once you learn to let go.'

I didn't answer, but he obviously wasn't going to go away and there were altogether too many people about for my liking. The lodge was close, and offered access to the relative anonymity of the street, but it also contained two boats' worth of rowers just back from the river. My own quiet corner of college was the only alternative, and I made for it.

'So what's the problem?' Tierney demanded as I changed course once again. 'Come on, you can tell old Stan.'

'Shut up and go away,' I told him, although I knew it was futile.

'No, really,' he insisted. 'You used to be well into us, so what's the problem?'

'You really are extraordinarily obtuse,' I told him. 'Just because you took advantage of me and pushed me into things does *not* mean I was "well into you", as you put it.'

'Didn't look that way to me,' Tierney said.

I answered with what was intended to be a contemptuous sniff but came out as something closer to a sob. We'd reached the bottom of my stair and I was steeling myself to keep him out of my room, by force if necessary, when I was rescued by the Chief Scout, who presumably wanted to tick Tierney off for slovenly work. I made a dash for my room, up three flights of stairs, slamming the door behind me and collapsing onto the bed. My head was full of memories of what Tierney had done to me and my heart overflowed with bitter shame because I knew full well that I'd been at least half willing. Yet there was no question that he'd used me, tricking me into tossing him off, sucking his cock, and worse.

My teeth were clamped over my bottom lip as I struggled to get the images out of my head, determined that I would not give in to my weakness and masturbate over the memories. There was only one other way my thoughts were willing to go, which was to ask myself how Tierney had known that there had been a Rattaners meeting. Everybody had been sworn to secrecy, and among the men I couldn't imagine even Walter Jessop telling him, not when it would mean losing any chance of future invitations. I couldn't imagine any of the girls telling him either, not even Portia, not when it meant being sent to Walter's for the night. That left Amy Jane, the Owl.

She and I had been to see a film the previous night, and while I obviously hadn't told her what I'd been up to at the weekend she knew that I'd been out with a group of friends. If Tierney had primed her it wouldn't have been hard to put two and two together, and now that I thought back I recalled that I'd seen Tierney on both the Monday and the Wednesday morning. Neither time had he done more than give me his usual familiar leer.

I could hardly ask Amy Jane. If it was true she'd simply deny everything, while if it wasn't I'd be putting myself into a highly embarrassing situation. Asking Tierney would be equally pointless, but if they were communicating then there had to be some link between them, and the Owl had to have a reason for feeding him information. Perhaps somehow he'd established a hold over her, which was just the sort of thing he liked to do. It was hard to imagine the Owl doing anything wrong, but it fitted the facts and also made her as much a victim as myself.

Perhaps I should have a heart-to-heart with her – but, again, that meant making some highly personal revelations. Amy Jane looked up to me, and I just couldn't bear the thought of admitting what I'd been up to. Even knowing that I'd performed striptease at the Red Ox was sure to horrify her. Only if I could catch the two of them red-handed would I be able to speak openly, and that wasn't likely to be easy. They could communicate by phone or email and I'd be none the wiser, although that wasn't really the way Tierney worked.

He liked his sex too much, and if he did have a hold over her he was sure to take advantage. Amy Jane was pretty, in a cuddly sort of way, while I was sure he would enjoy exploiting her shyness and personal insecurity. More importantly, her breasts were almost as big as Caroline's. There was no way on Earth he'd be able to resist trying to get his hands on them, and I bit my lip as I pictured the Owl with her top up and her big white boobs pressed together

57

so that Tierney could fuck her in her cleavage. If it was her, then he would meet her in person, at least occasionally.

On the other hand, he almost certainly hadn't done so in the last day. She and I had come back from the cinema at nearly midnight and I'd left her at the Newman lodge, while he had to be at St George's for work from eight o'clock. It was just about possible that she'd immediately cycled up to his house, but unlikely. Yet they'd communicated, and if I knew Tierney he'd have demanded a meeting at the earliest opportunity. Knowing that there had been a Rattaners meeting would have been sure to turn him on, and he'd have wanted to take it out on the most easily available female, and as soon as possible.

That meant, of course, that had I not been so brusque with him I would at that very instant have been impaled on his cock, one way or another, a thought that made my stomach lurch. As it was, it would be the Owl, perhaps sitting on his lap with her big breasts pulled out as she masturbated him, or on her knees with his fat white cock in her pretty mouth, even on all fours on his bed as he pumped into her from behind, enjoying the resilience of her ample bottom.

Tierney would be finishing work in just under half an hour, and as Amy Jane was hardly likely to entertain him in her room at Newman the meeting would be at his house if anywhere. I could follow him, although I'd have to be careful. He kept his bike in the service yard and my own was in the main shed, which made it easy to fetch it and position myself some way down the road where I could keep an eye on St George's.

Tierney emerged a few minutes before he should have finished work and cycled east, towards Magdalen Bridge and the Cowley Road. I followed at some distance, as I knew how to get to his house anyway, but he was so slow that I had to keep stopping. When we finally got to Cowley he didn't go to his house at all but to somewhere I knew only too well – the Red Ox. It was really a working men's club rather than a pub, and consisted of a low concrete shack with a car park and a storage yard at the rear. Every detail of the place was painfully familiar to me, and there was a lump in my throat as I stopped.

It seemed rather unlikely that Tierney would meet the Owl at the Red Ox, but if he did then she was sure to come the same way I had. I was going to turn away and try to find a café from where I could watch the road and the bus stop closest to the Red Ox, but just as I was wheeling my bike around a voice spoke from almost directly behind me, making me jump and spin around in surprise. It was Big Dave, the largest and most threatening of the Red Ox crew, at least in appearance. He was actually the least obnoxious of them and had even been known to stand up for me when Tierney was making a real pig of himself. I managed a shy smile while I struggled for something to say.

'You all right, love?' he asked.

'Fine . . . thank you,' I stammered. 'You just made me jump, that's all. I . . . I was just going to see if Caroline and Jasmine were here.'

'Stripping night is Saturday,' he told me. 'This is darts night. Could be they're around, maybe. Come on in and I'll buy you a half. This is Isabelle, lads. She's a student, but she's all right.'

I managed another smile for the group of eight or nine men coming towards us through the alleyway from which Big Dave had emerged. They were typical of the sort of men who used the Red Ox, mostly workers from the car plant, and while I didn't recognise any of them I found myself blushing at the thought that some of them might have seen me strip. None of them said anything, too engrossed in their own conversation to give me more than a rough but friendly acknowledgement, which gave me a twitch of pique, immediately followed by one of shame for my own reaction.

'You coming, then?' Big Dave demanded as the last of them passed me.

'Um ...' I began, and then realised that I could hardly refuse, because it would look very odd indeed if I didn't go into the Red Ox after claiming I'd been looking for Jasmine and Caroline.

'I'll just pop my head in,' I told him, and began to wheel my bike towards the Red Ox.

It was exactly as I remembered it, the outside seedy and disreputable, the inside a cloying fug of beer fumes and smoke. Quite a few people were there, and before I could pretend to complete my search for the girls and retreat Big Dave had brought me a half-pint of lager. All I could do was accept it, sipping thoughtfully and trying to look inconspicuous as I looked around.

Tierney was seated with his back to me, thankfully, and appeared to be engrossed in a heated conversation with a man who was either an Elvis impersonator or hadn't realised that it was no longer the 1950s. I also recognised Mike, the barman, who gave me a casual nod and a smile, just as if he'd never more or less forced me to strip naked in front of a couple of hundred leering men. Yet I found myself returning the gesture, and to one or two others as well, despite feeling distinctly insulted that none of them seemed to consider my presence at all out of the ordinary. Mo was also there, and Yazzie.

The last time I'd seen her she'd been on her knees, stark naked with her hands tied behind her back and her head buried between Jasmine's thighs while Caroline used a vibrator on her from behind. It was a shock to see her in ordinary clothes, a top and a denim skirt, but no more of a shock than the sound of her voice as she greeted me.

'Hi, Isabelle. All right?'

Gone were the meek tone, the sibilant accent, the respectfully downcast eyes, also the honorific. She sounded and acted exactly as she looked, an Oxford townie girl.

'You two met then?' Mo asked.

'Yes . . . at Jasmine's,' I said quickly, praying it was only the kinky sex that Mo didn't know about.

He merely nodded and took a swallow of his beer, leaving Yazzie to carry on.

'Do you play darts?'

'I have . . . once or twice,' I admitted, before taking the time to think my answer through. 'Just in the JCR, mostly.'

'Help us out, yeah?' she asked, jerking a thumb at the throng behind her. 'These gits have put up a hundred quid to a packet of nuts against us beating them.'

I made a face. A hundred quid against having their cocks sucked would have been more typical of the sort of bets the Red Ox crew liked to make, but even Mo wouldn't demand that sort of thing in front of his daughter – or I hoped not. It would also be immensely satisfying if we did win, to say nothing of my share of a hundred pounds. On the other hand just being in the Red Ox was making my stomach churn, and I knew that there were at least a dozen men there who thought of me as little more than some sort of animated sex toy.

61

'Thanks, but—' I began, only to be interrupted by the familiar voice of Jack, a greasy ex-Teddy boy who vied with Tierney for the title of the most squalid of the lot.

'If she's playing, let's make it two hundred.'

'Against the nuts?' Yazzie asked.

Jack began to speak and my skin went cold in dread of what he might say. But he thought better of it, presumably because of Yazzie's presence.

'Yeah,' he said instead. 'Two hundred against a bag of nuts. Five-oh-one and five on five.'

'You're on,' Yazzie answered on. 'Come on, Isabelle. So if we lose we have to buy them a bag of nuts – big deal.'

The last time anything similar had happened I'd ended up being the evening's amusement for a group of rowdy football fans, but I found myself smiling and nodding my head. Jack began to laugh, and that sealed it for me.

'Come and meet the girls,' Yazzie offered.

The only 'girls' I'd met at the Red Ox had been the men's wives, who looked on me as a complete slut, and the strippers. This made me hesitate but Yazzie had dragged me over before I could think of what to say. Sure enough, my teammates were three women I'd seen before: a mother and daughter, both dyed blonde and brassy, and a huge black woman who I was sure I recognised as a scout, but couldn't remember which college she worked for. They were introduced to me as Elsie, Sandy and Edna respectively.

'You strip, don't you?' Sandy asked immediately, and I felt myself blush scarlet.

'I used to,' I admitted, since it was pointless to deny it when I could vividly remember the expression of amused contempt on her face as I'd peeled out of a diminutive cowgirl outfit.

Sandy merely nodded and began to talk darts. The only man I knew in the group we were playing against was Jack, for which I was grateful, except that they seemed to think it would be best to put me up against him. He liked to think of himself as a professional gambler, but in practice he lived on benefits. His high opinion of himself meant that if he was against me he would probably try and show off, in which case I might beat him. That showed how little faith they had in me, even Yazzie, but I had never claimed to be any good.

Much the best player in the men's team was a tall thin man with an exaggeratedly large Adam's apple, rather alarmingly called Choker. He was up first, and beat Sandy so easily that I more or less gave up all hope of us winning. Evidently when the men had put the bet up they hadn't simply been bragging. Edna was better, if only by managing to annoy her opponent so much that he could barely aim straight, and she won, which left us level. Elsie put up a good fight but hit the wire with her last dart, costing her the game, and again I thought we'd lost and I probably wouldn't even have to play. Yazzie proved me wrong, winning really quite easily, and then I was up against Jack, who was sneering as he looked me up and down.

'Tell you what,' he said. 'To make a game of it I have to call out my shots, and if I miss what I said I was aiming for I don't get nothing.'

'You mean you don't get anything,' I pointed out, but he merely looked blank.

'Don't be stupid, Jack,' Choker advised. But Jack just laughed and leant close to my ear to whisper.

'Here's the deal, though. I win, and you can have the nuts, *my* nuts, right in your mouth while I toss off in that pretty face.'

The blood rushed to my cheeks, all the hotter because Jack's whisper hadn't been all that quiet and several people had heard. A ripple of laughter passed among the spectators, who I now saw included Tierney. He leered and raised his glass. They were obviously trying to annoy me, just as Edna had done with her own opponent, so I ignored them both, stepped up to the mark and managed to hit two twenties and a triple one, scoring a respectable forty-three. Jack responded with a confident nod and took my place.

'Twenty.'

His dart hit the double five.

'Shit. It's about time you got a new mat, Mike. It gets my balance all wrong. Triple twenty.'

He hit the one.

'Fuck! Jesus, Mike! Twenty.'

For once Jack's dart hit home, but a few minutes later I'd managed to finish with a double sixteen and he still needed over two hundred points. There was immediate angry recrimination from his teammates who felt he'd thrown the match away and were refusing to pay their share. Elsie and Edna joined in the argument, while I stayed well clear, but eventually the men were forced to pay up, with Jack contributing most of the money. By then I was feeling extremely pleased with myself – forty pounds in my pocket without having had to show off so much as an ankle. But I was also doing my best to ignore the nagging sense of disappointment beneath my triumph.

I was also having to tell myself that had the game gone the other way I would have refused to meet Jack's dirty demand. All I'd have had to do would've been to tell him to get lost, and there would've been nothing he could have done about it. But that didn't stop me thinking of what he'd threatened to do to me. He'd said he wanted me to suck his balls, and in such a way that his come would've splattered all over my face. It was disgusting, but as I cycled back towards the university I couldn't help thinking about how he might have gone about it – perhaps with me pinned on the floor so that he could dangle his scrotum into my mouth as he masturbated.

College was quiet, with only a few people about. I wanted to think about something else and so avoid what was beginning to look inevitable, but all my friends seemed either to be out or busy with their essays. In the end I went to bed, telling myself I would be strong and that I was a completely different person to the naive, susceptible girl who had allowed herself to enjoy being used so badly.

It was a lie. As I lay in the warm darkness of my room the voices of pride and temptation were warring in my head, one telling me that I should fight my feelings, the other that it didn't matter when nobody would ever know. I tried to escape into sleep, then to make excuses by telling myself I ought to do it specifically because that would let me sleep and I needed to get up quite early. The college clock chimed eleven, the quarter, and the half, before I told myself that if I was still awake at midnight I would give in.

I closed my eyes and tried to think soothing thoughts, of how good it felt to hold Katie in my arms and kiss her, how pure and fresh she felt, how to have her in my arms made me feel like a goddess, completely removed from the grovelling little slut who had stripped on stage at the Red Ox, who had been made to suck the cocks of men she didn't even know and had enjoyed every moment, who'd held her own bottom cheeks apart to let men into and up her, so dirty, so willing, so gloriously degraded . . .

My thighs came up and I was pushing down my panties under my nightie with a desperate urgency. A sob escaped my throat as they came off, but that didn't stop me pushing down my bed covers and kicking them away, nor did it prevent me from hauling my nightie up to show off my breasts. I closed my eyes, my head full of shame as I began to touch myself, stroking my chest and tummy and thighs with my back arched in rising excitement. Now it was too late, and I let my mind run as my hands sneaked down between my open thighs to find my sex.

I was sopping wet, puffy with arousal and extra-ordinarily sensitive, every touch of my fingers sending a fresh shiver of pleasure through me. For all my efforts to deny my feelings my body had betrayed me, and I was even regretting having won the game, because if I'd lost I would have been up at the Red Ox at that very instant, very likely with a large salty pair of balls in my mouth. It was a revolting thought, and utterly compelling, and as I began to rub myself with ever-increasing urgency I was once again imagining what would have happened.

I would probably have been done in the little storeroom at the back, where in the past I'd been made to do some truly disgusting things. Jack would have marched me in and told me to strip, gloating over my body as I removed my clothes, making me play peek-a-boo with my bra and stick out my bottom to peel my knickers down the way the men liked girls to strip. He'd have had his cock out long before I was completely naked, nursing his erection and showing off to me.

I'd have been made to take him in my hand, and to suck him, on my knees in the nude, before going down full length on the beer-stained floor. He'd have had to take off his trousers in order to straddle me, so that as he got down I could've felt his hairy muscular legs against my skin, with his cock rearing up above my face and his horrible scrotum dangling beneath. Horrible, yes, but I'd have taken it in my mouth, gradually losing control as the man-taste filled my senses, until my thighs came up and open in surrender, just as they had in reality.

Jack would've had Tierney in to watch too, and Big Dave, and Mike, all gloating down at me as I sucked and licked at the big leathery ball-sack, and all the time expecting a face full of muck. They'd have laughed as I got dirty, enjoying the sight of my spread pussy and the tuck of my bottom, probably rolling my legs up so that my bumhole showed too, perhaps touching me up, spanking me. That would have been best, to be thoroughly abused as Jack pinned me down, touched up and slapped about as my face was masturbated in.

They couldn't have resisted. They'd have fucked me, taking turns with me, cock after cock jammed deep up my all too willing pussy. They'd have spit-roasted me, made me taste my own juices on their cocks, maybe sodomised me too, and come up me, and over me, leaving my body slimy with their filth as I rubbed myself to orgasm after orgasm, exactly as I was now doing, with my bottom lifted free of the bed and my fingers clutching over and over at my dirty eager cunt, wishing that I really was in that grubby sordid club with my body sweaty and soiled on the filthy floor.

I was sobbing for my own deliberate degradation as I came down, and as I went slowly limp on the bed the clock outside struck midnight.

It was completely my fault. If I hadn't got a bee in my bonnet about Tierney and the Owl I would never have gone anywhere hear Cowley, still less the Red Ox. Once I was there I could still have backed out with at least moderate grace, but even then I had won my match and come away with my dignity intact. There was absolutely no excuse whatsoever for masturbating over the filthy fantasy that I'd managed to create, which had been stronger by far even than what Jack had suggested he'd do to me. It was all deeply humiliating, and it took all my willpower not to take it out on other people, especially Katie.

She and I had made an agreement when we'd first started going out that we'd sleep together at the weekends but stay apart during the week so that we had at least a fair chance of getting some work done. The arrangement had worked and had also helped to keep our relationship fresh, because my need for her would always grow stronger during the week so that when we did meet we would each be urgent for the other.

Technically, two women sleeping together was acceptable, although there were still social issues which we both preferred to avoid rather than confront. Spanking was another matter, especially at Foxson, where the walls were like paper and the 1960s design made the whole place a voyeur's delight. There was a quad of sorts, with one side only a single storey high to allow a view over the Cherwell and the fields beyond, with Shotover in the distance. Each room was a box, with a huge picture window, so that the interior of the quad was mainly glass and anyone with their curtains open was visible to at least two hundred others. I'd often threatened to spank her there, just because it made her so deliciously embarrassed, but in practice I'd always stuck to less noisy amusements, such as dripping hot wax on her bare bottom, and with the curtains firmly closed.

My own room was considerably more discreet, but on the Saturday we met in Summertown and so ended up at Foxson. The night was spent just cuddling, along with one session head to tail, more or less as equals. We had been that way for most of the summer, keeping our kinky activity special, and exclusive, perhaps in much the same way that Yazzie seemed to. The next day we'd agreed to meet the Owl, and we took a picnic down to the Parks to enjoy what was quite likely to be the last really nice day of the year – there was already a distinctly autumnal feel to the air.

I listened very carefully to the Owl's conversation, hoping for some hint of her association with Tierney, but she gave nothing away. Several times I almost said something myself but always stopped in time. If she *had* been talking to Tierney, then she was a very good actress because she seemed completely at ease, or as much so as her natural shyness would allow. A lot of the time she was talking about James Malcolm Rymer, and fortunately I had taken the time to read up on him. More awkwardly, she wanted to know when the next meeting was.

We had actually booked a reading room for the Wednesday afternoon, and because all the librarians recognised me I'd had no choice but to put it under my own name. All the Owl had to do was check the book and she would see. If she was linked to Tierney then she'd presumably checked already, and if she wasn't but saw the booking later it would hurt her feelings. The only thing I could think of was to say that the meeting was an hour later than the real time, so that she'd turn up after we'd finished all our Rattaners business and I could pretend I'd mis-remembered. It was a pretty clumsy excuse, but better than nothing.

'I'll see you there, then,' she said. 'For now, I've got to buzz.'

The Owl hadn't said anything about needing to be anywhere else, and as she receded across the meadow I wondered if she was going to see Tierney. I hadn't said anything yet to Katie but when I'd decided to she spoke first.

'Whatever are we going to do about her?'

'I don't know,' I admitted. 'I'm not entirely sure she's what she appears to be.'

'How do you mean?'

'I think she might something to do with Stan Tierney.'

'The Owl? Don't be silly!'

'I'm not being silly. I went to see a film with her in the week, and Tierney came up to me in college the next day. He knew we'd had a party.'

'Caroline or Jasmine probably told him, or maybe Portia's up to something. She's determined to put you down – you know that, don't you?'

'Yes, but I don't think she'd risk the punishment. And why would Caroline or Jasmine tell him?'

'Why would the Owl tell him, and how would she have known anyway?'

'She knew we were both out on Saturday night.'

'I suppose so, but still . . .'

'Maybe I'm wrong, but after what happened with the Line Ladies I don't trust him an inch. I followed him after work, but he just went to the Red Ox. I ran into Big Dave and ended up having to play a game of darts before I could get away.'

'Isabelle, you're not really supposed to speak to them.'

'I didn't have any choice. Anyway, I'm hardly likely to give the game away about Yazzie, am I?'

'That's true,' she admitted. 'But still . . .'

'If you tell anybody, Katie West, I swear you won't be able to sit down for a week.'

She stuck her tongue out at me. I made a grab for her, catching an ankle. She squeaked as I rolled her face down on the grass, and again as I hauled her towards me. The movement made her skirt come up and put her knickers on show to the entire Parks. The temptation to spank her was almost overwhelming, but we were in plain view of a good forty or fifty people so I held off.

'Later,' I promised her. 'Now, about the Owl. I suppose we'll have to arrange a reading from *Varney the Vampire* or something, just to keep her happy.'

'I suppose so.'

Katie had stood up to adjust her skirt, and we began to tidy up the picnic things. It was beginning to get cool, although not unpleasantly so. We were holding hands as we walked, indifferent to the occasional curious glance, and we crossed the river by Rainbow Bridge and began to walk north. To get back to the right side we were going to have to go right up to the Marston Ferry Road, but neither of us minded. That stretch of the river can be quite lonely, especially once the punting season is over, and we'd used the thick hedges of willow and hawthorn as concealment before.

I was in the mood for her from our brief tussle in the Parks and also because since giving in to my fantasies on the Thursday night I badly needed to reassert myself. Time and again after I've managed to get control of my life and my sexuality that little spark of submission and the desire to be degraded has sprung up again. But this time I was determined it wouldn't get the better of me.

'It's time you were spanked,' I told Katie as we reached the first of the hedges.

She responded with the faintest of smiles and I gave her hand a gentle tug, leading her away from the river. There was barely even a trace of a path on the bank, and I felt safe, yet sufficiently exposed to make what we were about to do feel delightfully naughty. Our hedge ended in a knot of trees, which proved to conceal a shallow bowl of dried mud, rough with hoof prints and smelling faintly of cow, although there were none in the field right then. Katie wrinkled her nose.

'Don't be prissy,' I told her, and sat down on a low willow branch. 'Over my knee.'

I'd cocked one leg up, and after a brief but nervous glance to either side Katie bent over. It wasn't an easy position for her, and she had to spread out her hands and her feet in order to balance herself properly, which left her in looking both vulnerable and awkward. I pulled up her skirt without ceremony, showing off her knickers which were white with a strawberry pattern and clung tightly around her ever so slightly chubby bottom.

'You can keep these up, at least for a little while,' I told her. Then I began to spank her.

Just to have her knicker-clad bottom to play with was wonderful. It was bliss to smack it and stroke the soft cotton of her panty seat, to admire the bulging roundness of her bum cheeks, and, best of all, to enjoy her absolute surrender. I could feel Katie trembling, and knew how much shame and embarrassment would be raging in her head, just as it had in mine while I'd thought of what Jack had threatened to make me do. Yet as always she was eager to please, allowing me to do whatever I wanted and taking as much pleasure in my control over her as in the smacks I planted on her bottom.

I began to play with her panties, tugging them up tight to let her cheeks spill out from either side and holding her by them with the material taut against her pussy as I continued to spank. Her bum globes were already quite pink, and she took it sighing and wriggling, abandoned to the pleasure of exposure and punishment. I pulled tighter still, lifting Katie by her hips so that she was forced to brace the toes of her sandals on the hard mud. Her thighs were well spread, her pussy a small plump bulge in her straining panty gusset, her cheeks parted so that I could see the tiny creases of flesh to either side of her anus where they led down beneath the material of her stretched panties.

'You make a fine sight from behind,' I told her. 'But maybe I can make it ruder still.'

Katie gave a faint acquiescent moan, then a squeak as I pinched the gusset of her knickers together, leaving her pussy lips bulging out to either side of the material much as her bottom cheeks were. Her panties were now tight against her clitoris, and I began to jerk on them and spank at the same time, making her gasp and shake her head in reaction.

'You're going to come, aren't you?' I said. 'You're going to come while your naughty little bottom is being smacked. How humiliating is that, to have an orgasm while you're being punished? You're a bad girl, Katie – a bad, bad girl. You need your bottom spanked long and often . . . and as for wanking off dirty old men, you bad, bad, *bad* girl!'

I was spanking hard, using the full force of my arm across the chubbiest part of Katie's bum cheeks and jerking continuously on her panties. She started to come, panting out her helpless ecstasy as her bottom bounced to the smacks, hopefully with her mind fully focused on the picture I'd just tried to put in her head of her sitting bare on Duncan's lap with his cock in her hand, a well-smacked little tart giving the man who'd punished her a hand with his inevitable erection.

Katie cried out at the peak of her orgasm, with shudder after shudder passing through her body, and I continued to spank her until she was lying limp and exhausted across my knee, her blazing red bottom stuck high. When I finally let go of her panties she nearly fell off my leg, but I kept hold of her torso, taking her around her waist as I began to stroke her hot cheeks.

'You came, and I didn't even have to pull your panties down!' I mocked. 'What a little disgrace you are, Katie West.'

Her response was a whimper. She'd come, and now it was my turn. But I wasn't comfortable, with the rough willow bark pressing into my bottom.

'You're going to lick me,' I told her, 'from behind. But first, let's have these off, shall we?'

I'd taken a fresh hold of her knickers as I spoke, and pulled them down and off. Katie would be bare while she licked me, with her red bottom showing to the air, and even if I wouldn't be able to see it I would still know. I wanted her yet more exposed, to keep her nervous and on edge, so I unfastened her skirt and took that off as well before letting her up. She was now naked but for her sandals and top, very obviously stripped for sex, which was just the way I wanted it, and all the better for having had her bottom smacked.

'Hang your skirt and panties on a branch,' I told her. 'Then come back.'

Katie scampered quickly across to the hawthorn bush I'd indicated, then back, throwing a single worried glance at her abandoned clothes.

'Good girl,' I told her. 'And how very undignified you look with your rosy little bottom on show – and your pussy, too.'

The position I was planning to get into wasn't exactly dignified either, but I was too turned on to care. And besides, Katie knew me too well to be impressed by any pretence of reserve. I quickly took off my jeans and knickers to leave me naked from the waist down before bracing myself against the willow branch, my bottom stuck out for her attention. She got straight to her knees, hesitated for just an instant, then buried her face between my bottom cheeks, licking eagerly at my pussy.

'That's my girl,' I sighed, and allowed my weight to settle onto the willow branch, only for a deliciously wicked thought to enter my head.

The bag in which we'd packed away the picnic things was resting against the trunk of the tree, within easy reach. I pulled it closer, rummaging in it, and Katie pulled back.

'Isabelle!' she protested. 'That's not very fair, sorting out the stuff when I'm trying to make you come!'

'Shut up and lick,' I told her. 'Remember, the longer you take the more likely you are to get caught with your knickers off.'

She gave a little tut, perhaps intended to remind me that I was in an equally embarrassing position, then went back to work. We'd had cherry tomatoes, and there were a few left, also some mayonnaise, which was messy but too good to resist.

'Take the rest of my things off,' I told her.

Katie didn't even stop licking, but pulled off my shoes and socks, to leave me entirely bare below the waist, just as she was. That made what we were doing riskier still, since I was now as likely to get caught bare as was Katie. But that just made it even more exciting.

Taking the tomatoes, I reached back under my belly. Katie pulled away, giggling as she watched me ease each of the small red fruits up in my pussy. They felt nice, and if they didn't fill me very much it was still a pleasantly unfamiliar sensation, because while I sometimes fucked Katie – with a variety of implements – she never fucked me. For a moment I was fighting back the memory of how good it felt to have a cock inserted into me, only for Katie to start nuzzling and kissing at my bottom.

'I'm glad you like doing that,' I told her, 'because you're going to have to lick this up.'

I'd picked up the bottle of mayonnaise, and Katie gave a little choking sob as she saw it and realised what I was going to do. She'd licked my bottom often enough, but it always got to her. I unscrewed the lid and reached back, poising the bottle over where my cheeks flared out to pour a thick stream of warm sticky mayonnaise between them. It trickled down over my bumhole and around where the last of the cherry tomatoes was stuck up my pussy, before it flowed on over my mound.

'Now lick it all up,' I ordered her.

Katie came close again, poking out her tongue to lap up the mayonnaise. Some of it had gone over my cheeks instead of between them, and she started with that. I relaxed, knowing that it would take her a little time to steel herself for the indignity of licking my bottom-hole clean but that she would eventually do it. Sure enough, the flicks of her tongue moved deeper, lapping the salad cream up from my crease, and lower still. She gave a tiny, broken sob, and then she was doing it, her tongue in my anus, lapping up the mayonnaise and burrowing deep into my bumhole.

Her face, no doubt smeared with mayonnaise, was buried between my cheeks, but she obviously didn't care, lost in her submission and thoroughly enjoying licking my bottom. I let her indulge herself for a while and move lower in her own time to suck the cherry tomatoes out of my hole one by one. Now that there were no inappropriate thoughts to spoil my feeling of dominance. I was completely in control, with my well-spanked girlfriend licking my pussy and bottom clean, kneeling near-nude in the dirt with her face filthy and her tongue exactly where it belonged.

We hadn't gone as far in a while, but Katie was as eager as ever, with her face pushed well in between my parted arse cheeks and her nose against my slippery bumhole as she tongued me. I thought she'd make me come like that, but she obviously wanted to make her humiliation as complete as possible so she returned her attention to my anus, rubbing my pussy with a knuckle as she licked.

For me, that was perfect. I was going to come and there was nothing I could do to stop it. I thought of her, my darling Katie in nothing but her sandals and top, her bare, smacked bottom on show and her face pushed in between my cheeks, licking at my open, slippery anus as she brought me to an exquisite orgasm. This was how it should be, not with some dirty bastard dangling his balls in my mouth but with my beautiful, obedient girlfriend applying her tongue to my bumhole. I cried out as I came, calling out her name and telling her again and again I loved her until my body finally gave way and I slumped down over the willow branch, blissfully satisfied.

Katie pulled back, giggling, and I managed to look around. Her face was a mess, smeared with mayonnaise and pussy cream. Quite a lot had gone down her top, while there was also some in her hair. I knew I wasn't much better, with my bottom and thighs all sticky, but fortunately there was a little water left among the picnic leftovers, along with some serviettes. We cleaned up as best we could, but Katie had to do her top in the river and walk back with the wet material plastered to her breasts almost as far as the bridge before it had dried. Even then we had to sneak into Foxson by the back gate.

Four

Katie and I spent the night together in her room, but I got up early to cycle back to St George's. Not many people were about and I used the pass key she'd given me to let myself out of the back gate, only to reach it at the same time as a group of scouts were coming in. Among them was Edna and I gave her a friendly greeting, which she returned. It was a little embarrassing, because I realised now that it was at Foxson I'd seen her but without ever really focusing on her as distinct from anybody else who was regularly about. I'd never really bothered to make a secret of my relationship with Katie, and scouts are notorious gossips, which meant that Edna might well know about us.

I put the thought out of my mind as I cycled back, concentrating on the forthcoming Rattaners meeting instead. The situation with the Owl was going to make it a little difficult, but after my weekend with Katie, especially her spanking and the aftermath, I was feeling both dominant and confident in my ability to keep everything under my control. If Portia was a brat about it I would know what to do, and I wasn't going to take any nonsense even from Eliza.

For the next three days I did my best to concentrate on work, something I've always tried to do no matter how interesting my social life may be. A lot of students find it difficult but it's really only a question of self-discipline. I even managed to finish my essay early, and Duncan rated it as on the border between an Upper Second and a First, which put the final touch to my confident mood.

The previous Rattaners party had been pretty well ideal, with a good venue, a good group of people and a good game to get things moving, so there wasn't going to be a great deal to discuss – although one good idea had occurred to me. Sarah and Portia were particularly skilful at arranging games with the right balance, and the one we'd played had been excellent. I'd even enjoyed the rule about having to switch if you drew a joker, because while I had very definitely not wanted to get one it had made me feel we were being fairer to the submissive girls and it had made the play deliciously tense, while there had always been the chance that Sarah herself would draw one. Only afterwards had she admitted to me and Eliza that the jokers hadn't even been in the pack, making us promise not to tell the other girls.

It had struck me that with a bit of thought I might be able to arrange an even better game, one that would seem entirely fair and yet would ensure that I would be able to dominate Sarah, perhaps even Eliza, although I was not at all sure if I'd dare in her case. In order to be sure of my success I would have to introduce some element of skill to give myself an advantage, and the darts game had provided me with the answer. I knew that Yazzie played, and that Jasmine and Caroline did occasionally, but to the best of my knowledge none of the others did at all. An idea, provisionally called 'Top Dog', had begun to evolve, and in my mind I was putting the finishing touches to it as I entered the Bodleian.

'I have the Latimer Room booked,' I told the librarian, who responded with a nod and didn't even ask to see my card.

I went up, to find that I was almost the last to arrive, despite being a few minutes early.

'You're all very keen,' I said.

'I wouldn't miss this for the world,' Sarah responded, putting down the book she'd been reading.

There was something in the tone of her voice that I didn't quite like, while Portia looked positively smug. Jasmine, Caroline and Yazzie were at the other end of the table, talking together, but they turned to greet me with wan smiles. Eliza was also there, standing at the window as she pointed out Oxford landmarks to Tiffany. Both had turned round as Sarah spoke.

'There you are, Isabelle,' Eliza said. 'Shall we begin?'

Her voice was stern, but that was normal for her. Tiffany's vindictive smirk might also have been normal, but I didn't like it at all.

'Is something wrong?' I asked.

Portia shook her head, as if my question was ridiculous.

'You know very well there is, Isabelle,' Sarah said, 'and I would have hoped you would be honest enough to admit what you've done.'

'What?' I asked, genuinely puzzled.

'Isabelle has been talking to that ghastly man Tierney,' Portia supplied, addressing Katie, who had just come in. 'What do you think we should do about it, Katie?'

Katie just looked blank, but I struggled to answer.

'No, I . . .' I began, and stopped.

'Don't try and lie your way out of it, Isabelle,' Portia said.

81

'It wasn't like that!' I insisted as my stomach began to tighten in very real fear. 'He . . . he came up to me in the quad and started saying all sorts of filthy things. I had to tell him to shut up.'

'You were at the Red Ox,' Portia pointed out.

'Sorry, Isabelle *Kyou*,' Yazzie added. 'I did not know, but I told only the truth.'

'That doesn't count!' I blurted out. 'I . . . I . . .'

'. . . Spoke to Tierney, and to the barman, and several others,' Portia finished for me, 'which is against the rule you yourself put forward last time. What was the punishment again, Sarah?'

'There's no need to be smug about it, Portia,' Eliza responded.

'Look, Eliza,' I appealed, 'this isn't fair at all!'

'It seems entirely fair to me, I'm afraid,' she answered. 'You yourself suggested the rule, and the same rules apply to everybody equally.'

'She suggested the punishment too,' Portia said with relish. 'To be given to dirty old Walter Jessop for the night.'

'I do wish we could watch,' Tiffany put in as she bent to lean on the back of Portia's chair, still grinning like a Cheshire cat.

'Ahem,' Eliza coughed. 'Isabelle has broken the rules, but there is no call to torment her unnecessarily.'

'Yes, Portia,' Katie put in. She slipped an arm around my shoulders.

I felt as if I was about to burst into tears, and all I could manage was a helpless shrug. To refuse point-blank would completely destroy my authority with the Rattaners and might even destroy the society, or get me expelled, which would be worse. I was going to have to go through with it.

'There it is, then,' Eliza concluded. 'Jasmine, perhaps if you would be kind enough to call Mr Jessop this evening?'

'OK,' Jasmine answered. 'Sorry, Isabelle, but it's only fair.'

I hung my head, feeling dazed, only for a sense of hope to spring up. They could send me to Walter, but he couldn't make me do anything, while I knew that Katie or Caroline would help me out by giving him some dirty little treat in return for his complicity.

'How are we going to know if she gives in to him?' Portia asked. 'You know what she's like when it comes to trying to worm her way out of things.'

'That's not true,' I lied.

Portia answered with a derisive snort.

'One of us could go with her,' Eliza suggested. 'Or perhaps Mr Jessop could take pictures?'

'No!' I said hastily. 'They'd probably end up all over the Internet!'

'Only we would see them,' Eliza assured me. 'And Mr Jessop, of course, but he has always been trustworthy so far. Afterwards I would delete them.'

I made a face, imagining Portia and Tiffany sniggering over photos of me bum-up over Walter Jessop's lap, doing a striptease, pulling on his wrinkly old cock, sucking it . . .

There had to be a way out.

'I propose that we abandon that rule,' I said. 'It was badly thought out.'

'Yes, it was!' Portia laughed. 'Let's vote. All those in favour of abandoning the rule about talking to Tierney and Co?'

To my surprise Portia had raised her own hand, and Tiffany followed suit, making the vote unanimous.

'So much for that,' Portia said. 'But you still have to be punished.'

'No, I . . .'

'Yes,' Eliza said firmly.

I slumped down in my chair, biting my lip. She was right, and I had nobody to blame but myself, which only made me feel worse.

'I think she ought to be spanked first,' Portia said, 'before we send her to him.'

'That's not part of the punishment,' I answered her, although I could barely get the words past my lips because of my growing feeling of chagrin.

'Not for speaking to Tierney,' Portia went on, 'but for lying, and for trying to wriggle out of your fair punishment. You'd do it to me, wouldn't you?'

'Yes,' I admitted, and threw my hands up in a gesture of despair. 'But still . . .'

'Good,' Portia said firmly. 'She gets spanked first. We can meet somewhere and—'

'Ahem,' Eliza interrupted. 'I see no reason for Isabelle to be spanked before she is sent to Mr Jessop. However, I am very disappointed in you, Isabelle. A dominant woman must earn the respect of others in order to deserve it – and that includes acknowledging her mistakes with a good grace. So I would have expected better of you when it comes to accepting a just punishment.'

'I know,' I admitted. 'I'm sorry.'

'Which is why I am going to spank you,' Eliza stated. 'Now come here.'

I went, too weak to resist the authority in her voice. She was right too, for all that she was going to thoroughly enjoy doing it, just as the others were going to thoroughly enjoy watching – with the possible exception of Katie, who looked genuinely sorry for me as I laid myself meekly across Eliza's lap. I had fondly imagined I would never again be put in spanking position, but despite the three months since what was supposed to have been my final punishment I found it embarrassingly easy to give in to Eliza's authority.

'Lift your hips,' she ordered, and I went up on my toes.

My long printed muslin dress was tugged up my legs and lifted onto my back, exposing my panties and making me wish I'd chosen something more ladylike. They were actually Katie's, but our underwear tended to get mixed up and it hadn't occurred to me that I'd end up showing them off, least of all to the giggling Portia. Not that they were indecent, just plain white cotton panties, except for the picture of a large yellow teddy bear stamped on the seat along with the legend 'A Bear Behind'.

'Oh dear, oh dear!' Sarah chuckled. 'I do wish I had a camera.'

'I'll use my mobile,' Tiffany offered.

'No!' I squeaked, but too late, the flash catching me just as Eliza put her hand to the waistband of my knickers.

'Stop it, or you'll be next,' Eliza warned. 'I freely admit that I have missed doing this, Isabelle.'

With that she took my knickers down, not just off my bum, but all the way down to my knees, leaving me showing behind. Again the phone camera flashed.

'Tiffany!' Eliza snapped.

'Sorry,' Tiffany answered quickly. 'I just couldn't resist it! I can see your cunt, Isabelle.'

'*You* are next,' Eliza informed her.

Tiffany went quiet, but knowing that she was next in line was very little consolation to me. It was her favourite thing, as she freely admitted, whereas I had openly stated that I would never get it again.

I was going to get it now, though, with my dress high and my ridiculous panties pulled down to leave me bare and vulnerable, with Eliza's hand resting gently on my bottom. It would be hard, too: a firm, no-nonsense punishment spanking. The thought set me trembling with apprehension.

The reason that Eliza hadn't started already was the suspicion that somebody was outside, coming up the staircase, their footsteps barely audible. Katie had already locked the door and was standing with her back to it, but it obviously made sense to wait. Unfortunately that meant me being held in place with my naked rear on show until Eliza was sure that we were safe, and even then I was left worrying what somebody would have been doing lurking outside the room when there was nowhere else for them to go.

'I had better be quick,' Eliza remarked, and laid in.

From the very first smack I was out of control, unable to cope with either the stinging pain or the awful humiliation. I did try not to howl, but my legs were kicking and the tears had started from my eyes before I'd had more than a dozen firm slaps applied to my wriggling bottom. Portia was laughing at me, and Tiffany was giggling uncontrollably for all that she had the same punishment coming to her, which made it far worse.

I just let go, blubbering my heart out and squirming over Eliza's lap, with my red-hot bottom jiggling and bouncing in my teddy-bear panties, my legs kicking or splayed wide to show off my pussy and bumhole to my eager audience. Even Katie was watching, her hand to her mouth in shock and sympathy, but her reaction wasn't important. What mattered was that I was being spanked in front of her.

'That will do, I think,' Eliza said, and then it had stopped as suddenly as it had begun. 'But I think a little corner time would do you good.'

She gave me a last gentle pat as I got up and I went to the corner, shuffling in my panties, which had fallen down to my ankles. I was still crying, with a big bubble in my throat that wouldn't go away and my nose damp with snot. Behind me, Tiffany was soon being given the same treatment, and making as big a fuss about it as I had. I didn't care because I was feeling too sorry for myself even to want to watch, and I only took a quick glance to make sure that she'd had her bottom bared. She had, with her expensive designer jeans in a tangle around her knees and a bright orange thong pulled well down. Eliza had even hooked one leg around Tiffany's calf, which hadn't been necessary with me and meant that Tiffany's bottom cheeks were fully spread with her pussy and bumhole blatantly on show. But even that failed to cheer me up. I'd been spanked, and that was all that mattered.

The same words kept going through my head as Tiffany was dealt with and I stood snivelling in the corner. I'd been spanked, spanked across an older woman's knee, spanked on my bare bottom and spanked in front of my friends, all things I loved to do to other women but hated having done to myself, and yet there was no denying the warm glow in my cheeks and the hot, moist feeling of my pussy. Maybe I hated it, but when it came to getting excited over it I was no better than anybody else. Then I was just another rude little tart. I burst into tears again at the thought, only to be told in no uncertain terms to shut up.

'Somebody's outside!' Jasmine hissed.

'Are you sure?' I demanded, snatching for my panties.

'They just tried the door!'

'Oh God! No, don't worry. Katie, get the book. I'll get rid of them.'

'You said we'd be safe, Isabelle!' Portia snapped.

'Stupid girl!' Sarah added, glaring at me.

Katie produced a copy of *Varney the Vampire* from her bag as Tiffany and I hastily adjusted our clothing. As Tiffany fastened the button of her jeans she gave me an encouraging grin, which I returned, the two of us now allies against the uncomprehending world despite the way we had treated each other. I made for the door, wondering what I would say. We had got badly carried away, even Eliza, but there was simply no reason why anybody should have come up to the top floor when the Latimer Room was booked, never mind try to get in.

I opened the door. It was the Owl, nearly three-quarters of an hour early.

'Isabelle?' she asked, sounding worried.

'Hi, Amy Jane,' I managed.

'I saw you earlier,' she said doubtfully. 'Did you get the time wrong?'

'Um . . . yes,' I told her. 'Sorry.'

'That's OK. I'm here now. Hi, everybody.'

The answering greetings sounded distinctly nervous to me, but Amy Jane didn't seem to notice. I was sure she'd heard what had been going on and I was frantically searching for a plausible cover story as she took a seat at the table. Unfortunately, a girl's bottom being spanked sounds like a girl's bottom being spanked, and really like nothing else – or at least nothing that was likely to have been happening in a reading room at the Bodleian Library. We had been relying on anybody approaching being heard on the stairs, but with me in the corner and Tiffany over Eliza's knee nobody had been paying proper attention and in any case the Owl's approach had been virtually inaudible.

'Have you been doing a reading?' Amy Jane asked brightly.

'Yes,' Katie told her.

'Don't let me get in the way, then.'

As Katie began to read, Sarah leant close to whisper in my ear.

'This is all your fault, Isabelle!'

It wasn't, but I was going to be punished for it anyway. I'd always teased Portia for the way she sulked about her punishments, but now I knew how she felt. It just wasn't fair, when everybody had agreed that the Latimer Room would be safe if we were careful. Admittedly I'd invented the James Malcolm Rymer Society and made the actual bookings, but the fact was that if they hadn't insisted on spanking me for talking to the Red Ox crew then there wouldn't have been a problem. But now there was, and only Katie and Caroline made any attempt to defend me while it was agreed that Eliza should punish me properly at the next Rattaners party.

In fact, the punishment probably was just, but for a different reason – one that I hadn't dared tell anybody. I was sure the Owl had heard, and pretty sure she knew what had been going on, but she hadn't said anything. That surely meant she was in league with Tierney and had kept quiet in order not to spook us during my chastisement. In consequence, he presumably knew that we'd met, from which he was sure to conclude that we'd be holding another party soon.

I had a pretty good idea what Eliza would do to me, but at least she was a woman and had been in charge of my discipline and training. Submitting to her would be deeply humiliating, and probably quite painful, but it was a lot easier to face than the prospect of going to Walter Jessop. I even thought about backing out, because considered outside the context of the Rattaners it was an unthinkable thing to do, sending a young woman to spend the night with a dirty old man as a punishment. Unfortunately, *within* the context of the Rattaners it was a perfectly *reasonable* thing to do, if perhaps a little harsh. Yet it was my own suggestion, and over the course of the previous year I'd voted for both Portia and Caroline to suffer similar fates. Both had gone through with it, and I'd thoroughly enjoyed the thought of their degradation.

Jasmine had arranged for me to go to him the following Friday, and she told me, which meant the intervening time seemed to pass minute by leaden minute and yet simultaneously to rush past. To make matters worse a message had come back, accepting my submission with pleasure and asking that I be dressed in a corset and Victorian split-seam drawers under a long coat. Caroline made the drawers specially, great lacy confections that no respectable woman would have been seen dead in, while Jasmine put her ha'p'orth in by insisting I put on one of her corsets, which was low-cut and scarlet. I added a chemise in the same style, stockings and boots, so that I wasn't actually indecent under my coat, although I was plainly dressed for sex, which made just cycling out to Whytleigh a hideously embarrassing experience.

It was bad enough knowing that under my coat I was dressed up as a Victorian prostitute, but as I rode the split of my drawers kept working apart, so that after a quarter-mile or so my pussy would be rubbing bare on the inside of my coat. I had to keep stopping to adjust myself, but at least by the time I got to Whytleigh I could tell myself I was wet because of the rubbing and not because I was aroused by what was about to happen to me.

Walter's house, and shop, was one of a row of old red-brick cottages facing the Cherwell across a strip of cobbles. It was already dusk when I got there, with the only noise a group of ducks paddling in the river and very little even to indicate which century I was in. I'd been trying to make it easier for myself by imagining I really was a Victorian call girl sent out to a client's house, but if anything the fantasy only made my feelings of humiliation stronger.

As I fastened my bicycle to the old-fashioned street light opposite Walter's shop I was thinking back to my first visit there. I'd been far less self-confident then, and had found it really quite easy to let my arousal at the thought of doing filthy things get the better of me. I had been defying the self-righteous minister who had done so much to turn me against religion and onto punishment. I was also defying my parents to some extent. All that was behind me now and my delight in having to play with a dirty old man's cock and balls was an embarrassing memory. I had sucked him off and let him come in my face and down my chest, something which was now once more a very immediate prospect.

It took all my willpower to cross the cobbles and ring the ancient bell. There was a light on in one of the upstairs windows, and I saw the curtain twitch aside and Walter's red, seamed face peer out, his loose mouth widening to a lewd grin as he saw that it was me. His face vanished, leaving me waiting, close to panic as I wondered what I could get away with, whether he'd want to spank me, to make me suck and lick on his ugly outsized scrotum, to slip his skinny little willy up my pussy to give me the first real fucking I'd had in nearly a year . . .

'Ah, Isabelle, good evening,' he greeted me as the door swung open.

'Good evening, Walter . . . sir,' I responded, re-membering how he liked to be addressed.

As I entered the shop I let my coat slip from my shoulders to show what was underneath, not really from any desire to display myself for him but because if I had to go through with it I preferred to maintain at least a little style. He looked me up and down appreciatively, then shot the bolts on the door and twisted the key in the lock. I was trapped, his plaything until the morning.

'Very pretty,' he remarked. 'Now, straight upstairs with you, I think.'

Walter was rubbing his hands together in eager anticipation, and he motioned for me to walk in front of him so that he could watch the sway of my hips and the wriggle of my bottom in my drawers as I made my way upstairs. Every step had either books or antiques piled to one side or the other, sometimes both, a clutter of objects that meant I had to place every foot carefully. His room was little better, with everything crowded together without the least sense of order, and even the bed seemed to have been hastily cleared, for me.

I stopped in the middle of the room and hung my head, wishing that my lower lip would stop trembling and trying desperately not to fidget. Walter stepped past me, avoiding a table piled with china knick-knacks, and picked up something that seemed very much at odds with the rest of our surroundings: a small, very modern digital camera.

'Stay just as you are,' he instructed. 'You do know that Eliza said I was to take photographs?'

'Yes,' I admitted.

My sense of chagrin was boiling inside me as he took careful aim and shot a picture of me standing forlorn in the centre of his room, my head hung and my hands folded in my lap.

'Excellent, excellent,' he said, checking the image in

his LCD screen. 'Now, if you would open your chemise?'

I complied, unbuttoning my chemise and opening it across my breasts. Walter took several pictures, all the while with the tip of his tongue poking out to one side. I found myself looking at the crotch of his trousers, where a little bulge had begun to appear, bringing blushes to my face and making my fingers shake as I held my chemise wide to show him my naked chest.

'Excellent, excellent,' he repeated. 'You have such elegant little breasts, Isabelle, artistic even. Now, turn around, and we'll have a few shots of you baring that delectable little bottom, shall we?'

I responded with a weak nod and did as I was told. With my back to Walter I pushed out my bottom, fumbled for the split in my drawers and slowly drew the 'curtains' wide. He was clicking away as fast as the flash would recharge, and took maybe ten or twelve pictures of me baring myself before he spoke again.

'Very sweet – you are an absolute darling. Now, stick it out a little more.'

What he meant was that I should show off my pussy and bumhole, but I deliberately turned my hips a little to one side in an effort to deny him the view.

'A little more,' he instructed, 'and turn your bottom to me.'

There was a firm edge to Walter's voice and I almost rebelled. But I found myself adopting the rude pose he was demanding, with my bottom stuck well out so that my pussy would show between my thighs and my bum cheeks would open to let him see between them. My bottom-hole is naturally brown, something I've always found embarrassing, and the burning sensation in my face reached a new intensity

93

as I heard the whirr of the zoom lens and realised that he was taking a close-up of my exposed genitals and anal region.

'Perfect,' he declared. 'That should keep Eliza and the girls happy.'

Walter put the camera down, and I allowed myself a touch of relief and gratitude. Evidently he felt that a few rude photos would be sufficient evidence of my surrender, but the girls had seen me naked a hundred times and so the pictures would be no more than mildly humiliating. Ones of me sucking cock or having my bottom spanked would have been far worse.

'I have you for the night, I believe?' he said. 'So perhaps a little amusement first, and then you can cook and serve my dinner.'

'Whatever you say . . . sir,' I responded.

Walter chuckled and sat down on the bed, his thighs splayed apart to show off the now prominent bulge in his old grey flannel trousers. Pulling two large pillows from beneath his coverlet, he made himself comfortable, with his back to the wall, very casually pulled down his fly and hooked his cock and balls free of his underpants. He looked obscene, there was no other word for it, fully dressed save for his weedy little cock and the bulbous mass of his huge scrotum, all of it protruding from his open trousers, his wrinkled face split into the most lecherous grin I had seen in quite a while.

'Suck my cock,' he told me, entirely unnecessarily.

I could have sat down on the bed and laid across his lap to take him in my mouth, but I got down on my knees before I could think about what I was doing. As I crawled between his open legs I was telling myself it was the sensible choice because it meant he couldn't grope me while I sucked, but I knew that was a lie. I'd gone on my knees by instinct, as a properly obedient girl should when she is to give oral sex to a man.

'What a good girl,' he remarked, chuckling.

He knew, because I'd made Caroline kneel at his feet to perform the same dirty task – Jasmine, too – while I'd looked on with haughty amusement as they attended to his cock and swallowed his come or took it in their faces if I ordered it. Now it was me on my knees, with his ugly genitals right in my face as I tried to find it in myself to do as I was told. I hesitated a bit too long.

'Come along,' Walter urged. 'This is no time to act the little madam, is it?'

I hadn't been acting the little madam, I'd been thinking of my dirty fantasy about being made to suck Jack's balls and trying to pluck up the courage to act it out. Walter made the decision for me, at least in part. As he'd spoken he had taken me by the hair, pulling me firmly forward until my lips were pressed to his bulging ball-sack. I caught the smell of him – and the taste – as I gave in, opening my mouth around his balls to suck in just as much as I could. To have my mouth full of scrotum felt as obscene and ridiculous as it no doubt looked and he chuckled once more as he began to move my head about.

'That's better,' he said. 'You have no idea how long it's been since I had my balls in a girl's mouth.'

It was not a question I was likely to be asking, at least not soon. My jaw was agape just about as far as it would go and I could hardly breathe, save to snuffle in the thick scent of cock and some cheap aftershave through my nostrils. Talking was out of the question, so I tried to suck, mouthing on the leathery skin and bumping the fat eggs of his testicles over my tongue. It felt every bit as rude and dirty as I'd imagined it would, helping to bring out the feelings of erotic humiliation that I knew I'd need to get me through the night.

When Walter finally decided I was being a good girl and relaxed his grip on my hair I began to lick instead, running the tip of my tongue over the skin of his scrotum and up and down his cock-shaft. He'd already been quite stiff, and now he quickly grew to full erection under my ministrations, while I was getting ever more randy and eager for my own humiliation. I wanted his balls back in my mouth, and gaped wide to push them in. At that he tightened his grip once more, keeping me firmly in place as I mouthed on the turgid bulk of his scrotum and rolled his balls over my tongue.

'Why don't your rub your little cunt while you're doing it?' Walter asked suddenly. 'I like you to have your fun too.'

It was about the most humiliating thing he could possibly have said, suggesting that I'd need to masturbate because he'd forced me to go down on him. Unfortunately it was true, but I shook my head, trying desperately to resist, although having been given permission made that harder by far. I closed my eyes and tried to think of the diplomatic relationship between the third Viscount Palmerston and Napoleon III, only to have both men appear in my mind with their genitals swinging from their open trousers. It was hopeless. My hand went back, to burrow into the slit of my fancy drawers and find my sex.

I was hot and wet and puffy, ready to be penetrated and ready to come. My finger found my clitoris and I was masturbating as I sucked on Walter Jessop's balls. It was a truly filthy thing to do, and for all my rising ecstasy I felt utterly humiliated. But the stronger that feeling grew, the higher my pleasure rose. I was going to come, my thighs already tight, my bumhole starting to wink, my pussy squeezing – only for a sudden burst of red across the insides of my eyelids to startle me. He'd taken my picture, with his balls in my mouth and my face set in utter bliss, and that was the final, appalling humiliation that I needed to trigger my climax.

My whole body went tight as my orgasm hit me, with the flash exploding in my face again and again, catching me with my cheeks bulging and as much of Walter's scrotum in my mouth as I could get, with my tongue stuck out to lap at his balls and shaft like some demented cock-hungry little slut, with my face pushed firmly against the slippery spit-wet mass of his genitals.

The shame of what I'd done and what I'd been photographed doing hit me long before the contractions had stopped running through my body, to leave me sobbing on my mouthful of scrotum with tears running from my eyes as he continued to take pictures. I still sucked, now broken to my task, and continued doing so until he spoke again.

'Now my cock,' Walter demanded. 'Suck me off – and you're to swallow properly, no tricks.'

He'd still been holding me down on his balls, and I pulled back gratefully, gulping in air only to have him stick his erection unceremoniously into my open mouth. I took him in hand, tugging on his little stiff shaft as I mouthed on the bulbous helmet between my lips.

'You've been taught well,' he sighed.

It wasn't exactly the first cock I'd had in my mouth, just the first for a very long time, but I couldn't help but feel resentful at the remark, as if how to suck men off had been an important part of my education. I hid my feelings, working on Walter's cock with every pretence of eagerness and wishing that I didn't feel like lifting my bottom to be penetrated from the rear despite having just come. My mouth was full of the taste of him, particularly his balls, making me want to gag and pushing up my arousal again at the same time. I closed my eyes, trying to think of anything but what I was doing and the overwhelming humiliation of my situation.

'That's perfect,' Walter gasped. 'Keep pulling, with just my knob between your lips. That's right . . . good girl.'

I obeyed, thinking it was the way he wanted to come and bracing myself for my mouthful of slime, only to catch the flash of the camera once more. He'd taken another close-up, just at the instant when I'd expected a mouthful of come, which no doubt meant that my expression had been one of utter disgust. Portia was going to love it.

'Hey, look . . .' I began, pulling my head up, only to have it eased firmly back onto his erection.

'Shut up,' he ordered. 'I'm going to spunk soon . . . yes, like that . . . just like that . . . oh, you are such a darling little tart!'

Walter finished with a grunt, pulling on my hair again and thrusting with his hips at the same time, jamming his cock down my throat even as he erupted. I started to choke, but he wouldn't let me up and a great mass of come mixed with snot exploded from my nose, all over his trousers. Even then he didn't seem to care, his eyes closed in bliss as he fucked my gullet with my eyes popping and my hands slapping futilely at his legs, spunk bubbling from my nose and the tears streaming down my face.

'Good, very good,' he said, and finally let go of my hair.

I came up, gasping for breath and trying desperately not to be sick all over Walter at the same time.

He'd reached for the camera, but he took one look at me and put it down again with a soft, dirty chuckle.

'Maybe not, on second thoughts. Would you like a tissue?'

I nodded earnestly, still unable to speak.

'Here we are,' Walter said, reaching out to his bedside table to retrieve a packet of tissues the normal purpose of which was all too obvious, and not so very different from their present use. 'Oh dear, I shall have to change my trousers. I do think you might have at least tried to swallow everything, Isabelle.'

'You stuck it right down my throat!' I protested. 'You're lucky I wasn't sick.'

'Now, now,' he chided. 'No hoity-toity behaviour, I said, or I may have to spank your bottom.'

I sat back on my heels, thinking bitter thoughts. He had the right to do with me as he pleased, by my own rule, and I knew he'd be making a report to Eliza. Refusing anything would only make my coming punishment worse, and she could be horribly inventive. I decided to behave.

'Sorry, sir,' I said, although my voice was thick with resentment.

'You probably will be, before the morning,' Walter assured me. 'Now, let me see how that last one came out. I was a little over-excited at the time.'

My curiosity was too strong not to want to look, and I bent forward. It was quite a good picture, at least in the sense that I was easily recognisable and it was quite obvious that I was masturbating him into my mouth with my lips around his helmet. I'd been right about my expression too, which gave the impression that while I was doing my sorry best I was hating every second of it. Portia was really going to love it, and I came to a quick decision.

'I'll make a deal,' I offered. 'If you promise only to send the first few photos to Eliza, the ones you took of me showing off, I'll be extra good.'

'Hmm, I'm not sure,' Walter responded. 'I know you, and I suspect that once you get going you'll be extra good anyway, but still . . . maybe, if I have no complaints by morning.'

It was a typical bit of manipulation, but it was the best I could hope for. The question was, how much was I prepared to suffer from him in order to reduce my humiliation in front of the girls?

Five

The answer was: a great deal less than I had expected. Having made me suck him off he told me to prepare and serve dinner, which consisted of grilled pork chops, well-boiled cabbage and mashed potato. Walter seemed to appreciate my cooking, because he ate so much that by the time he'd finished he could barely move, let alone make proper use of me. I let him fiddle with my bottom and boobs, even put a finger in me, but his cock remained obstinately flaccid. Even in bed he couldn't get properly hard, despite having me sit nude on his chest as I worked on him with both my hands and my mouth.

In the morning he had the opposite problem, waking up with a rock-hard erection, so that I was able to toss him off before he even realised what I was doing in order to escape the fucking he so badly wanted to give me. After that I left, which I had every right to do, and I was feeling distinctly pleased with myself as I cycled back towards the city. I had even managed to persuade Walter not to show the dirtier photos to Eliza, on the grounds that it wasn't my fault if his cock wouldn't behave the way he wanted it to. That meant the ones of me sucking, another he'd taken as I sat on his belly trying to bring him erect, and the close-up of my pussy and bumhole.

All in all, I felt I'd got away with it, or least with more than I'd expected to since I had been genuinely prepared to let him use me as he wanted. Nevertheless, I was going to have the photos of me in the nude shown round among the girls, and I still had my punishment from Eliza to come. She would not be so easy to manipulate, nor would she fail to do justice to the situation, that I could be sure of. Despite what I felt was a triumph with Walter, my entire carefully constructed wall of dominance was in danger of collapse.

I was determined that it wouldn't, and a very important part of maintaining it was my need not to be the only dominant woman brought low during the Rattaners evening. The game I had invented but never had a chance to put forward seemed an excellent way to make sure of that, and I worked on it during the week, along with two evenings spent practising at darts with Yazzie, Jasmine and Caroline. I seemed to have something of a knack for it, and managed to beat all three of them, both at darts and as my reward for victory. Yazzie was keen for me to come up and play at the Red Ox again, but I was feeling much too fragile to dare go near the place and so I turned her down.

The Owl had usually turned up at St George's at least twice a week, but she didn't put in an appearance at all, making me wonder if our little spanking escapade had scared her off, or if something had happened to break the agreement she had with Tierney. Either way, I knew that I would have to assume that Tierney and his friends knew about the forthcoming Rattaners meeting, and that they would be able to work out the date and the venue. Having them attempt to gatecrash the party didn't bear thinking about. Dr Treadle thoroughly enjoyed our company, but he was also a respectable academic in normal life and no doubt there were limits to what he was prepared to put up with. At the very least it would be highly embarrassing to have them hanging about in the road, and inevitably it would be me who got the blame. I would be severely punished and, worse, would probably be forced to resign as President, while we would surely lose the only good venue we had.

After all the trouble I'd been to in order to establish the society, that was unthinkable. I needed to be very sure that Tierney wouldn't turn up at Dr Treadle's, and the more I thought about it the more convinced I became that the only feasible course of action was to forestall him. Unfortunately I knew very well what that would mean. I had no money to bribe him, and I was in no position to threaten him, but I could offer him sex with Caroline. Even then he might not necessarily accept, when the choice was between a quickie with her and the chance of making a thorough pig of himself with all the submissive Rattaners girls.

I put it off all week, telling myself that it wasn't really necessary, that it was just too inappropriate to be considered, anything to delay the inevitable and because when it came down to it I knew that I could take a cock in my mouth or up my pussy if I really had to, whatever the circumstances and without hurting anything other than my pride. Really, there was only one major drawback, which was that it was clearly immoral of me to expect Caroline to do it when it was my responsibility. One of the many things that Eliza had taught me was that a dominant should never abuse her power, and even though I knew Caroline would go through with it I would be doing exactly that.

By Wednesday I had accepted that I'd have to do it myself, or at least promise to. I hate being dishonest, but Tierney had lied to me and tricked me so many times that in his case I decided to make an exception. Also, the thought of really doing it excited that part of my nature I'd been trying so hard to suppress. I was scared of how I might react, which made lying a great deal easier. Either way, I was absolutely determined that neither Katie nor the other Rattaners girls would find out.

That meant holding a private conversation with Tierney, which was easy. He always seemed to be lurking around, and I managed to catch him as he finished work on the Friday following my punishment from Walter. I didn't want to be seen with him, and I definitely didn't want him in my room where he could start making extra demands. So I did as before, waiting for him to leave and then cycling behind him at a discreet distance, only this time I waited until we were past the Picture Palace. Then I sped up, overtaking him and stopping my bike in his path.

'Isa?' he demanded, surprised. 'What are you doing?'

'We need to talk,' I told him.

'Oh yeah?' he answered suspiciously.

'Don't bother with any of your lies, Tierney,' I told him. 'I have a pretty good idea what's been going on.'

He shrugged.

'It's not going to work,' I continued. 'You won't be let in, and that's that, but I know what you're like, and that you'll try and spoil it for us if you can't get what you want, so I'm prepared to make an offer.'

'Oh yeah?' he said again, this time perking up.

'If you promise to leave us alone,' I said, 'I'm . . . I'm prepared to do the sort of thing you like – but not until after the meeting.'

Tierney applied one grubby fingernail to his nose and gave it a meditative scratch before replying.

'After *every* meeting, is that?'

'I suppose so,' I told him.

'Sounds good,' he answered, with what I felt was suspicious alacrity. 'How about that Katie?'

'Just me,' I insisted. 'I don't even want Katie to know about it, or any of my other friends.'

He nodded as I realised I'd just made a very foolish statement, placing myself more firmly in his clutches. Again he took a moment to consider before he spoke again.

'All right. Makes sense.'

I felt my stomach go tight.

'What will you want?' I sighed.

'Blow jobs,' Tierney answered without the slightest hint of embarrassment for his outrageous demand. 'Blow jobs, and we need you to play in the darts team next Saturday, against the Boar in Bicester. Little Yazzie says you're really good.'

It was the most bizarre combination of demands I'd ever heard, but coming from him it didn't really surprise me. Sex and the more sedentary sports both figured largely in his daily life, along with watching football and drinking lager. I couldn't help but feel grateful too, because I'd expected him to demand a lot more, and perhaps want to include other men if they'd been involved in his snooping. So it seemed that he'd been working alone, and now he had probably got what he'd been angling for all along. He was a fairly primitive creature, and for him having his cock sucked represented the peak of sexual pleasure. I was now going to be the one doing the sucking, or so he thought, and with luck that would be enough to keep him away from the Rattaners meeting.

* * *

I still wasn't sure that I could trust Tierney, and the prospect of my punishment wasn't the only thing that made me grow gradually more nervous during the course of Saturday. He was capable of just about anything, and I knew from bitter experience just how much pleasure he took in using me.

By Saturday evening I was such a state that I could think of nothing else, with every aspect of my predicament going round and round in my head: what Eliza would do to me, Sarah's cool amusement, the other girls' giggles or sympathy, which would be equally shaming for me, and the men's lust, which I was likely to have to satisfy. Then there was Tierney, overshadowing it all, so that although I knew Eliza would never permit it I was imagining him turning up in the middle of my punishment and demanding to have his cock sucked in front of everyone, or to take me upstairs for a fucking, or to sodomise me over Dr Treadle's tea table.

I cycled out to Jasmine and Caroline's house as before, but this time with Katie along to make sure I got her moral support right from the start. Yazzie was also there and greeted me respectfully, while Caroline gave me a hug and a kiss. Jasmine did the same, but there was something more than a little smug in her manner, and she insisted that I come upstairs with her immediately.

'Eliza says you're to dress in this,' she said, pushing open the door to their room.

I didn't even try to argue, but stared glumly as the costume laid out on her bed. It was embarrassingly familiar, my old Line Ladies outfit, which Eliza had frequently made me wear while I was in training, especially for spankings. Not only was it possibly the most ridiculous creation I'd ever put on – or, perhaps, 'been put in' would be more accurate – but it brought back some excruciatingly humiliating memories.

The least offensive item was the jeans, white flares with tassels down the outside of each leg and each back pocket done as the Stars and Stripes. The flag motif was repeated with the blouse, which was well tailored but actually appeared to have been made from a US flag. The boots were the same, vertical red and white stripes and the toes and the big square heels blue with added white stars. The hat was similar, the brim red and white stripes, the crown blue and with white stars. The little blue denim waistcoat was not the same, fortunately, just a flag on the single breast pocket, although it did have tassels and little metal horseshoes sewn on. The chaps were also plain, at least in their colour, but elaborately tooled and fringed, while the belt was a great heavy thing ideal for taking to girls' bottoms, buckled with a six-inch-wide boss showing yet another US flag. There were also nylon Stars and Stripes panties and a pair of short white socks with frilly tops. A similar outfit lay next to it, Katie's – although she really had brought hers for line dancing: it made her feel attractive, if also submissive.

'I might have known,' I managed to mutter.

'And I,' Jasmine said, 'am taking your place.'

She turned on her heel and strode from the room, well pleased with herself.

'Who's the one with a slave mark tattooed on her bottom?' I called after her.

'You'll pay for that,' Jasmine promised as she started down the stairs. 'Now hurry into your costume, or you'll come to Eliza with your bottom already pink.'

I didn't bother to answer but began to undress. There was a huge lump in my throat, and as I stripped I was thinking of how I'd have reacted if Jasmine had made the same threat just a week before.

I'd have caned her, or had her spanked by Portia, which would probably have been the best way to humiliate her. Now I simply felt sulky and resentful.

Naked, I went into the bathroom to wash, paying particular attention to my bottom as there was no chance whatsoever that I would get through the evening without my anus being given an airing. I even put a little dab of cream on one finger and slipped it up my rectum to make sure that I was properly clean inside – just in case. Inevitably that was the moment when Caroline chose to come in, giggling when she saw what I was doing.

'You know what Eliza's like,' I said, blushing.

Caroline just laughed and carried on with her business, watching as I took my finger out of my bottom-hole and washed my hands. I wondered if I ought to lubricate myself properly, but decided that it would be tempting fate. If they wanted to stick things up my bottom they could get me ready themselves, while I had no doubt at all that Eliza would bring everything she needed to take care of me properly.

Back in Jasmine and Caroline's bedroom I began to dress up in my Line Ladies outfit, feeling sillier and less self-confident with every single article of clothing I put on. I'd been told I looked pretty in it, sexy too, even dominant, but I'd never felt anything except ridiculous when I was wearing it. There was no bra either, so I left myself bare under my blouse, determined not to give Eliza any further excuses for punishing me. I also pulled my hair back in a ponytail the way she liked, even though I felt it added a peculiarly pathetic touch to my look. Katie had come up while I was changing, and must have seen the expression on my face as I considered my reflection in the wardrobe mirror.

'You actually look very nice, Isabelle, and I'll be dressed the same.'

'You're not going to be punished in front of everybody.'

'I'm sure to be punished.'

'That's hardly the same thing, is it? Sorry, Katie, I don't mean to be cross, but the situation with the Owl isn't really my fault, is it?'

She gave me a look with which I was all too familiar, when she knew I was wrong but didn't want to argue. I went downstairs, where the others were gathered in the kitchen. Jasmine had gone for black, and a slightly androgynous look, with leather trousers, boots and a black leather waistcoat. Caroline had chosen to go for an army look: minuscule khaki shorts and a khaki halter top that barely restrained her huge breasts. Yazzie was dressed as before, in a simple black sheath but carrying several hanks of coloured rope.

My feelings as we drove towards Wytham were very different from those I'd had before the first meeting, and stronger. In place of the sense of controlled excitement I'd had then I was near to panic, with my tummy fluttering and my pussy warm and open despite my best efforts at holding down my arousal. I knew how I should react, taking my punishment with a dignified acceptance, but they were going to see how wet I was. They'd know I was turned on, and that was the most shameful thing of all.

We were the last to arrive at Dr Treadle's. Everybody else was already in his living room, drinking and chatting casually about this and that as if it barely mattered that I was about to be put through my paces in front of them. The men were in black tie, Sarah, Portia and Tiffany in their riding gear, while Eliza was dressed in tweed. She alone bothered to do more than nod to me.

'Ah, Isabelle – and about time, too. We were beginning to wonder if you had decided that you couldn't face the evening.'

'No,' I answered.

'She's ready,' Jasmine said, and smacked the taut white seat of my jeans as she passed me. 'She's didn't even make all that much of a fuss.'

'Good,' Eliza responded. 'Do have a glass of wine, Isabelle.'

She was standing at the sideboard, and poured out a large glass from a bottle that was resting in an ice bucket. I took hold and drank it gratefully, my fingers trembling against the glass. Eliza went to sit down, watching me coolly. Walter Jessop was next to her, and gave me a cruel little smile. Only then did I realise that Dr Treadle had set up a computer to one side, and that the picture on the screen was of me holding my Victorian chemise open to display my bare breasts. A moment later it changed, to another from the same series, this one with my drawers held wide to show off my bottom and the rear view of my pussy.

I watched with horrified fascination as the slide show continued, waiting in dread for the ones that showed me sucking on Walter's balls and about to have my mouth spunked in. They never came, just my little display routine. Walter at least had kept his word.

'The pictures will continue to alternate for the evening,' Eliza remarked. 'Or at least for *most* of the evening, until you are suitably chastened. Now, drink up and come over here.'

My obedience was automatic. I swallowed the rest of my wine and stepped over to a clear area at the centre of the room. Eliza was smiling at me.

'First,' she said. 'Do you agree that you deserve this punishment?'

'Yes,' I said, although it took an effort to get the word out.

'Yes, you do,' she responded. 'It was your decision to book the Latimer Room, and to do so under the name of a non-existent society. Fortunately your friend Amy Jane either didn't realise what was going on, or is too well mannered to say anything – otherwise we might have been in serious difficulty.'

I hung my head, trying not to think of the consequences if the Owl had run screaming through the Bodleian denouncing us as a group of lesbian perverts. Eliza was right: I had made a serious error of judgement, and had dismissed alternative suggestions. I was also the one who'd allowed what was supposed to be a straightforward meeting to include punishment spankings.

'You also insisted on Portia being spanked in the Latimer Room instead of at our first party,' Eliza went on as if reading my mind.

'None of you seemed to mind,' I mumbled.

'I beg your pardon?' she demanded.

'I said, none of you seemed to mind,' I repeated, with my resentment at last rising above my feelings of shame and contrition.

'We had your assurance that it would be safe,' Eliza went on. 'We trusted you, Isabelle, and while I admit that we were perhaps a little too keen to have a punishment after the long summer break the responsibility must lie with you. This is, after all, your society.'

I returned a glum nod, although I couldn't shake the feeling that they were being unfair.

'Besides,' Eliza continued, no longer stern, 'I think we all know that, just as Portia thoroughly enjoyed her punishment, so you will enjoy yours. Won't you?'

111

'But I'm domin—' I began. Then I shut up.

Eliza's response was first a knowing smile, then a nod to Portia and Tiffany who were seated on chairs beside a bank of expensive-looking equipment that included a CD player and a camera.

'First,' Eliza stated, 'you will dance for us. Katie?'

As Katie stepped forward I realised that I hadn't been made to dress in my ridiculous outfit simply to humiliate me. They all knew how embarrassing I found the whole thing, and what had happened with the Line Ladies, so to make me dance was genuinely cruel. So was the awful music that Portia and Tiffany put on, some ghastly song sung in a Southern drawl with instructions for actions such as jumping up and down on my toes to make my boobs bounce, waggling my bottom and smacking each bum cheek in turn.

Katie had begun to dance, but I couldn't, at least not until I saw the look of amused contempt on Sarah's face. She was soaking up my discomfort, and the bigger a fuss I made the more she would enjoy it. I began to dance, trying to follow the sequence of utterly ludicrous and thoroughly lewd motions that Katie was going through. She didn't mind, but she liked to display her body, for all her shyness, and didn't even seem to object to the awful music. I was no good at this type of dancing either, and knew full well that I looked more silly than sexy, for all the lust in the men's eyes, so that by the time the music came to an end I was on the edge of tears.

'That was funny!' Portia giggled. 'But I think she should do it again.'

'Yes,' Tiffany agreed. 'She didn't start until halfway through.'

Eliza nodded, Portia gave a crow of sadistic delight and the awful music started again. This time I tried harder, determined not to give them the satisfaction of my embarrassment, wiggling my bottom and making my boobs bounce with almost as much enthusiasm as Katie, although the burning scarlet of my cheeks must have given away my true feelings.

'Again!' Tiffany demanded as the music stopped once more. 'That is the funniest thing I have ever seen – and where did you get those costumes?'

'No, that is enough,' Eliza said, to my immense relief.

'There's a shop in Coventry,' Katie began, skipping over to Portia and Tiffany. 'You can get all sorts—'

'No doubt,' Eliza remarked, throwing her a stern look. 'However, we need to consider the remainder of Isabelle's punishment. As we know, mentioning the society to somebody who has not yet been vetted means six of the cane, although I have now amended that to a spanking from everybody *and* six of the cane, as that was what Portia received. This case strikes me as similar, and so a similar punishment is required, if a rather sterner one. Isabelle's little dancing demonstration may be considered fair retribution for us having had to sit through an extended reading from *Varney the Vampire*, but for allowing Amy Jane Moffat to find out where and when we were meeting I suggest she be passed around for spanking—'

'To everybody?' I interrupted.

'*To* everybody, and *in front of* everybody,' Eliza answered, and her tone was enough to make me hang my head and mumble an apology as she went on. 'Unless any of you feel that it would be inappropriate for you to spank Isabelle?'

Only Yazzie so much as hesitated. Tiffany gave a scornful laugh.

'As I was saying,' Eliza continued, 'I suggest she be

passed around for spanking, caned, then sent upstairs in disgrace for the rest of the party.'

'That seems fair – generous, even,' Sarah said. 'Considering what might have happened if this Owl girl had realised what was going on.'

There was a murmur of agreement, and I found myself making faces at the floor. It was awful. After all the effort I'd made to exert my sexuality I was now to be spanked, and by the very girls I wanted to look up to me, and all the while with pictures of me showing off my breasts and bottom on the computer screen. Eliza had stood up to place one of Dr Treadle's straight-backed chairs in the space where Katie and I had been dancing, a position that would ensure everybody had a good view of me getting my bottom smacked.

'Most junior first?' Sarah suggested.

'Ooh, that means me!' Tiffany said happily, jumping up.

'It should really be Yazzie,' I said quickly, horrified by the thought of being put over Tiffany's knee.

'Yazzie then, and Tiffany next,' Portia said, smirking at my discomfort.

Yazzie had also stood up, although in a calm and dignified manner. Her voice was the same as she addressed me.

'May I apologise for any discomfort or shame I am about to cause you, please, Isabelle *Kyou*?' she asked.

I opened my mouth to point out that she obviously didn't care enough about my discomfort and shame to forgo the pleasure of spanking me, but I held back. At least she had the decency to realise that it wasn't really appropriate, while everybody else was happily awaiting their turn, even Katie.

'Thank you,' I managed instead as Yazzie settled herself onto the spanking chair.

She gave a polite nod. I stepped towards her, shaking badly. Being spanked by Eliza was one thing, but to be done by the junior girls, and in front of men, was infinitely worse.

'Please unfasten your jeans,' Yazzie said, 'and take them down. Leave your chaps as they are.'

I forced myself to obey, fumbling the button of my silly white trousers open. Only as I tried to push them down did I realise that for all her respectful manner Yazzie was in fact a sadistic little bitch. She'd told me to leave my chaps up, which meant that I couldn't get my jeans down properly, which left my panty-covered bottom sticking out through the gap in the chaps in a manner which I knew would look as rude as it did ridiculous.

'Oh look!' Tiffany giggled. 'She's even got Stars and Stripes knickers!'

'Which she will now take down,' Yazzie instructed. 'But first, she is to tuck her shirt up under her waistcoat.'

I made a face, although it was really no worse having to take my own knickers down than to have them pulled down by Yazzie and I knew that there was no chance whatsoever of being allowed to keep them on. She really was evil, though, making sure that everybody got a full view, back and front, by making me tuck up my shirt. I obeyed anyway, too used to spanking rituals to do otherwise, while I was fairly sure that if I argued about anything Eliza and Sarah would do it for me, or would ask the men to.

With my shirt tails tucked up, my ridiculous nylon panties were on full show, with every single person in the room watching as I stuck my thumbs into the waistband. Most of the observers seemed merely amused, and only Walter's face showed open lechery.

But Tiffany was biting her lip in sadistic glee. Portia just looked smug.

'Down they come,' she urged. 'Let's see pussy.'

I threw a glare at her but pushed my panties down at the same moment to leave them in a tangle with my jeans. My bare bottom and front view were now framed in leather and in red, white and blue material.

'Nice bum,' Tiffany remarked. 'You should show it off more often.'

'I've been trying to tell her that for years,' Sarah put in. 'She has a lovely bottom, and it's such a waste not to make proper use of it while she's young. The way I see it, the pretty young girls should stay submissive and only take on dominant roles gradually, as they learn and mature.'

'Oh, absolutely,' Tiffany agreed. 'I know that I'm a cutie and people will want to enjoy my body, so I'm going to make the best of it while I'm young. One has to be realistic about these things – although actually you too have a lovely body.'

'Thank you,' Sarah replied. 'I do my best to keep in shape. But the important thing is that authority only really comes with age.'

'Oh, absolutely,' Tiffany said again. 'Especially when it comes to spanking. I used to have an immense crush on the headmistress at Saint's, and my favourite fantasy was to be sent to her study for a good spanking. Although, come to think of it, imagining getting it from Matron was even better, because she was from Leeds, or somewhere like that, and she had a wonderfully rough manner—'

'Do you two mind?' I interrupted. 'If I have to be spanked, at least have the decency to pay attention!'

'Sorry,' Sarah said. 'Do carry on.'

'Go across my knee,' Yazzie ordered.

I was feeling thoroughly put out as I climbed into

spanking position across her lap. She was so small that I didn't feel at all comfortable, and was forced to brace my hands and feet well apart to stay in place, which meant making a much ruder show from behind than I would have done otherwise. Yazzie put an arm around my waist and her hand settled on my bottom. I winced, the shame of my position flaring up to colour my cheeks and put a huge bubble in my throat.

'How many smacks would be appropriate?' Yazzie asked.

'As many as you like,' Eliza told her. 'There's no hurry, after all. But do remember that there are eleven of us.'

'Of course, *Iemoto*,' Yazzie replied, and began to spank my bottom.

'That's a sight worth seeing!' Portia laughed. 'Just look at her face – what a priceless expression!'

I didn't answer, knowing that to rise to the bait would only make things worse for me, especially once Portia's own turn arrived. Instead, I tried not to react to the stinging slaps being applied to my bottom. Yazzie was small, and not too strong, but she knew how to spank so I obviously wasn't the first girl across her lap. But she wasn't trying to hurt me, either, content merely to impress on me what was being done, and for once I managed to maintain some dignity.

'That is enough from me,' she said, and it stopped.

'Goodie! My turn!' Tiffany squealed. 'Get up, Yazzie.'

I'd already half risen, which was all I needed to do, as they swapped places so fast that Tiffany caught my arm and pulled me down over her knee before I'd even had a chance to rub my now-warm cheeks.

'I am really going to enjoy this!' she declared as she took hold and began to spank me, only to stop after just a half-dozen smacks. 'Hang on, this needs to be done.'

As Tiffany spoke she had pulled up my knickers. Now she adjusted them carefully across my bottom, so that the nylon was evenly spread across my bumcheeks to show my shape.

'Knickers down, Isabelle!' she mocked, and suited her actions to her words, easing my panties slowly back down over my bottom to lay me bare once more. 'And . . . whoops a daisy!'

She'd pulled my cheeks wide, suddenly, catching me completely by surprise and deliberately showing my bottom-hole off to the entire room. All I could manage was a squeak of surprise and consternation, which was drowned by laughter from over half my audience.

'Do you know?' Tiffany asked, still holding my cheeks apart. 'You have ever such a rude bottom-hole – it's all brown.'

'I know,' I admitted sulkily. 'Now could you get on with it?'

'Temper, temper,' she chided. 'But fair enough, since you're so eager for your spanking here goes.'

Tiffany began once more to smack, with more enthusiasm than accuracy, catching my thighs and hips. It stung dreadfully. I had to bite my lip hard to stop myself losing control, and she was bringing the heat to my sex with embarrassing speed.

'I smell pussy,' she said suddenly, and the spanking stopped again. 'Oh, you *bad* girl!'

I gasped in shock as Tiffany inserted a finger deep up my vagina.

'You're all *wet*!' she chided, and began to spank me with her other hand as she eased her finger in and out of my cunt-hole. 'All wet and ready, and all because you're having your bottom smacked, you dirty, *dirty* girl!'

Her voice was full of laughter, adding to my nearly unbearable consternation as she spanked and fingered me, and yet there was no denying what her actions had done to me.

'Seeing as she's on heat,' Tiffany remarked as she slipped a hand between my thighs, cupping my pussy, 'shall I bring her off, girls? Shall I make her come while she's having her little bottom smacked? I bet it's easy.'

'You're being a bit greedy, actually, Tiffy,' Portia put in.

'You'll get your turn,' Tiffany answered, starting to masturbate me from behind as she slapped at my cheeks. 'Just let me get the little dirtbag off.'

'Later, perhaps, Tiffany,' Eliza instructed. 'We don't want to waste the entire evening on Isabelle's punishment. Remember, too, that she is supposed to spend time upstairs in disgrace.'

'OK, I suppose I can wait,' Tiffany agreed grudgingly. 'But I want to play with her later, because I know she won't let me once she gets back on her big domination trip.'

She'd let me up as she spoke, and now she stood herself, taking a quick glance at the finger she'd had inside me before speaking again.

'Open wide.'

I obeyed automatically, allowing Tiffany to push her finger into my mouth to have me clean up my own juices.

'Slut,' she said. 'Who's next, then?'

'I am,' Katie said. 'Come on, Isabelle.'

There was sympathy in her voice as she spoke, but her tone was still firm. In a way it was even more humiliating to be punished by her than by Yazzie and Tiffany. Katie was my girlfriend, my pet, the girl who had chosen me to give her the discipline she craved, and now I had to go bare-bottom over her knee.

She took me by the hand as she reached me, and kept hold as she settled herself onto the chair. I felt limp as I was laid back into position, and found I no longer cared about my legs being apart or what I was showing behind. Just two spankings and my will was already giving way, although what Tiffany had done had hardly been fair.

'I'm not going to do this hard,' Katie said as she began to spank me, 'because you know I don't think it was all your fault. But I am still going to do it, because that's what's been decided, and this club's only going to work if we all pull together.'

I nodded weakly, knowing that she was right, and that she was right to take her turn just as I was right to accept their verdict. That didn't stop me imagining how I'd take out my feelings on her once I'd got her alone, especially as her enthusiasm grew and she began to spank harder. Soon I was having to bite my lip again to keep control, and the last half-dozen spanks hurt more than anything I'd been given so far.

'There we are,' Katie said as she bent to kiss my bottom. 'That wasn't so bad, was it?'

It was hard to know how to reply when, for all my chagrin, the juice from my pussy had begun to trickle down the insides of my thighs. Just three of the eleven others had now spanked me, and already my head was full of thoughts of being made to masturbate in front of them, or to give oral sex to each of them in turn.

Caroline replaced Katie on the spanking chair and over I went once more. She was brisk and firm, but she took her time, bringing me to the very edge of losing my dignity completely before she stopped. Only when she'd finished did she really make me suffer, pushing me off her lap to rise before she turned to push out her bottom, with her big bum cheeks straining out the seat of her tiny khaki shorts.

'Kiss it,' she demanded.

I couldn't stop myself. It was no part of the punishment and I didn't have to, but I found myself rocking forward, my lips puckered up, to plant a single gentle kiss on the crest of one big khaki-clad bottom cheek. Caroline chuckled and walked away, resuming her seat on Walter's lap. I was left on the floor, kneeling, with my whole body shaking badly as Portia got to her feet.

'I have been waiting for this for months,' she stated, 'and I'm going to take my time with her. If you don't like that, then you can deal with me later, OK?'

Nobody contradicted her and she sat down, looking at me in cruel amusement as she patted the taut corduroy of her jodhpurs. I crawled over her lap, bracing myself as I had before, only for her to hook a leg around the back of one of my knees, spreading my pussy wider still and making my bum cheeks open to show off the rude brown hole between them. I began to sob as Portia's hand went to my bottom, but instead of starting to spank me she merely took a squeeze of my flesh, then turned her attention to my blouse.

'Not my breasts,' I pleaded as she tweaked open a button. 'You don't need my breasts showing to spank me.'

'You always do it to me,' Portia pointed out. 'Doesn't she, girls?'

'Being made to go bare-breasted is good for your humility, Isabelle,' Jasmine said, mimicking my accent and putting on a deliberately haughty voice.

I shut up as my shirt was opened, thinking of all the times I'd lifted their tops or unbuttoned their blouses to show their breasts off during spankings. Because of my waistcoat Portia had to pull each breast out, leaving them bulging from the neckline in a froth of blue nylon, which made me feel more foolish and exposed than ever.

'That's better,' Portia declared. 'And now, Isabelle, for your spanking.'

She gripped me hard around my waist and laid in, swinging her shoulders to get as much force as possible to my bottom as she spanked me. Three hard swats and my desperate efforts to maintain my dignity ended. It just hurt too much, while the way she was holding me meant there was no escape from the pain. I began to shake my head and kick about with my free leg, even though it did nothing to reduce my pain. In no time she had me thrashing in her grip and begging her to stop.

'Portia, please, I'm not used to it . . . it's been too long!'

'I couldn't agree more,' she answered me, gasping the words out because of the effort she was putting into dealing with my bottom. 'It's been *far* too long!'

'She used to get it from Eliza every week,' Sarah explained to Tiffany. 'But that was last summer, and it's been ages since Portia had her.'

'I think she needs it,' Tiffany answered.

At those words I burst into tears, because she was right. At least I felt I needed it now, with my bottom ablaze under Portia's hand and my entire body as ready for sex as at any time I could remember. I needed spanking, hard, and then to be put on my knees in front of the women who'd punished me to thank them in the best way I knew, with my tongue, and to suck the men off too. I'd lost control – the pain and arousal was just too much – and when Portia finally stopped and rolled me off her lap I collapsed to the floor, my knees up and open, my arms spread wide, my face a wet mess of tears and mucus, my pussy wetter still.

They could have had me there and then, making me service them one by one, but the rest of them were still firmly in control and the spanking continued. Jasmine went next, telling me that I wasn't worthy to be her Mistress as she slapped at my cheeks and pinched my nipples. Next came Sarah, genuinely angry for what I'd done, holding me firmly in place and spanking harder even than Portia to leave me snivelling brokenly on the floor, my eyes streaming tears. Eliza picked me up and gave me much the same treatment, only stern and silent, like a mother giving some badly needed but regrettable discipline to an errant daughter.

By the time she'd finished every last scrap of dignity and pride had been spanked out of me. It didn't even feel inappropriate to be put across Walter Jessop's knee and felt up while he spanked me, with his clammy fingers pawing my breasts and opening my bum cheeks to probe my bottom-hole. For Dr Treadle I was willing, wriggling my bottom and sticking it up for him as he spanked me with a caress to my cheeks between every slap of his palm. Duncan came last, and I well and truly disgraced myself by asking if he'd like his cock sucked when he'd finished with me. I was on my knees with his fly half undone before Eliza stopped me, turning from where she'd been pouring herself a glass of wine at the sideboard.

'Not with Isabelle, please, Duncan. She is to be caned and sent upstairs.'

'I do beg your pardon, Eliza,' Duncan answered. 'Isabelle, behave yourself.'

I'd forgotten all about the cane, and I was making faces as I stood up, frightened and excited at the same time, desperate to come but also eager to please. My whole body was wet with sweat, my bottom a blazing ball that seemed to swell from the tangled mess of my dishevelled clothing. Dr Treadle had gone to fetch the cane he kept for our parties, and as Duncan vacated the spanking chair I climbed up on it without having to be told, kneeling with my bare bottom stuck out and everything showing behind, waiting.

'Very good, Isabelle,' Eliza remarked. 'Now, six of the best, and then upstairs to bed with you.'

Dr Treadle returned and passed her the cane, an old-fashioned schoolmaster's whalebone that I myself had picked up in a junk shop in Edinburgh. I'd been so proud to have found it, and I'd used it that same evening to reduce Katie to tears. Later I'd administered it to Caroline and Portia at parties. All three of them were now looking at me, and while there was a little sympathy in Katie's eyes there was satisfaction too, while the others were gloating openly.

Eliza got into position, flexing the cane. I closed my eyes, trying not to think of how much it would hurt but rather of how it would add to my arousal, and how good it would feel to have a set of six neat welts across my bottom again, to stroke as I masturbated over what had been done to me. The cane touched my bottom, laid carefully across the crest of my cheeks for aim, lifted, and then came down again. I screamed as the thin shaft bit into my flesh, my body jerking so violently in reaction that I nearly upset the chair.

'One,' Eliza said calmly.

She waited until I could get a grip on myself, then gave me the second stroke, directly across the line of my anus. Again I screamed and kicked, my body shaking with sobs once more as I forced myself to get back into position. Eliza called the stroke and gave me my third an instant later, across the tuck of my bottom, which hurt even more than the others and set me bleating pitifully for a break, at which she waited patiently until I was finally able to push out my bottom into the proper position once again.

'Three,' she stated. 'And . . . four.'

Even as Eliza spoke the cane had hit me, lower still, where my bottom cheeks bulged to either side of my cunt, which left me gasping for air and clutching at the back of the chair, too hurt even to control my breathing. Any lower and she was going to get the crease between my cheeks and my thighs, which would be more painful still.

'Not my legs, please, Eliza,' I babbled. 'Don't cane my legs!'

'Cane her legs,' Portia advised.

'Be quiet, both of you,' Eliza said. 'Stick your bottom up a little more, Isabelle.'

I obeyed, shaking violently as I pulled my back in to make my cheeks rise and flare. Eliza tapped the cane against my bottom, higher than before, lifted the whalebone shaft, took careful aim and slashed it down exactly where she'd laid it, to create a fifth agonising line of fire across my flesh and thrust me forward so hard that the chair fell over, sending me sprawling on the floor.

'Sorry, sorry . . .' I stammered as I hurried to get up.

'Stay on the floor,' Eliza said, 'in a crawling position.'

I got onto all fours, looking up nervously as I opened my knees and lifted my bottom into the position Eliza had taught me. She gave a satisfied nod, laid the cane across my bottom diagonally and brought it down across my cheeks, setting me gasping and thumping the floor with my fists. She'd given me a five-bar gate, just as I had to Portia, and I knew that as with Portia the neat pattern of cane cuts would be decorating my bottom for at least two weeks.

'Not too bad, if I say so myself,' she remarked complacently. 'Now, Isabelle, off to bed with you, and then perhaps a game of joker, Sarah?'

'I need to come, please,' I begged, setting Portia and Tiffany sniggering with delight. 'Please, Eliza? Tiffy can do it . . .'

'Oh, yes please!' Tiffany called, immediately starting to crawl towards me.

'Oh no, you don't,' Eliza warned her. 'You go straight to bed, Isabelle . . . no, on second thoughts, I think we'd better have your trousers and pants off so you won't need to undress, and Yazzie ought to tie your hands behind your back. Otherwise I think I know what you'll be up to the moment you're alone.'

'At once, *Iemoto*,' Yazzie offered, and I had no choice but to peel off my lower garments and cross my wrists behind my back as she bound them firmly together.

'Now, up to bed with you,' Eliza ordered as Yazzie tied the cord off around my waist. 'A spare room has been made up for you. Sarah, would you be so kind as to give Isabelle a hand on the stairs?'

'Of course,' Sarah agreed. She rose to take hold of my bound wrists and steer me from the room.

The room next to the bathroom, the smallest in the house and furnished in a plain, masculine fashion, had been made up for me. A bed stood under the window, freshly made and with a green coverlet, which Sarah turned down along with the corner of the sheets and blankets beneath. I had to sit my hot bottom on the bed and swing my legs around to get in. By now I was almost out of my mind with frustration and self-pity at the thought of being sent to bed while the party continued downstairs.

'What just happened to you was well deserved,' Sarah remarked. 'And I think you ought to know that it won't be the last time.'

'What do you mean?' I demanded.

She merely gave a chuckle and turned away, only to stop, hesitant, glancing at the door and clicking her fingers in an irritable, indecisive manner that I'd seen her use before. Suddenly she nodded, as if she'd reached a conclusion, and pushed her jodhpurs and knickers down with one smooth motion, baring her full womanly bottom almost in my face.

'You are going to lick me, Isabelle,' she said, twisting sharply around. 'And not a word to Eliza.'

I didn't answer, because even as Sarah finished she took a firm grip on my ponytail and pulled my face against her sex. She was twisting my hair hard enough to hurt, and I was fully aware that she wanted me to lick her as much to exert her dominance as for the physical pleasure it would give her. That didn't stop me poking out my tongue and lapping earnestly at her pussy. I'd been spanked and caned, along with a dozen powerful accompanying humiliations, from having men watch me being chastised to being made to kiss Caroline's bottom, and I was in no state to resist an order to lick pussy from one of the women who'd beaten me. Sarah gave a quiet chuckle at my obedience, then a sigh as my tongue found her clitoris. She pushed her belly out, hard into my face, and twisted my ponytail tighter still.

'Lick, you slut,' she ordered. 'That's right, just there . . . harder . . . oh, you sweet little tart . . .'

She came, grinding herself against my face. It was no more than a minute since she'd put me to her sex, and now she pulled her clothing back up as swiftly as she'd stripped. My mouth was full of the taste of her cunt and my pride was long gone, leaving me babbling as she smoothed her jodhpurs around her bottom.

'Do me, Sarah, please . . . rub me off, please . . . please, Sarah?'

'What, and risk having Eliza catch us?' she laughed. 'I don't think so. Night night, Isabelle – sleep tight.'

'Sarah, please!' I begged again, but she was already at the door, which she left slightly open, no doubt so that I'd be able to hear the sounds of the party as I lay in my solitary bed.

Great sobs were racking my body as I let my head fall back onto the pillow. It was agony, worse than all the spanking, worse even than the cane, at least mentally. My bottom felt huge and hot, my pussy swollen and sensitive, both parts of my body in urgent need of my fingers. Eliza had known exactly what she was doing when she had made me strip from the waist down, leaving me acutely conscious of my bare bottom and legs and cunt, far more so than if I'd been completely in the nude. She'd known full well that left to my own devices I'd have rubbed myself sore over what they'd done to me, so she'd bound me to make sure I was well and truly punished, while being made to lick Sarah and left with the taste of her sex in my mouth added a last agonising touch to my frustration.

I could have screamed, and the tears were running freely down my cheeks. It just wasn't fair to treat me like this when they were going to play joker downstairs. I could already hear laughter, and Sarah's voice as she ran through the rules again. They'd have Katie, I knew they would, and at the thought of her with her white jeans and the polka-dot panties she was wearing pulled down and her pretty bottom stuck high for a playful spanking from one of the other girls I gave way completely, blubbering out my emotions in a full blown infantile tantrum of self-pity and resentment.

With that I wet myself, not because I couldn't

control my bladder but because I just didn't care. I felt it start to come and I just let go, pee spurting from my pussy with every wrenching sob to trickle down my thighs and backwards along my bottom crease and down my bum cheeks. The hot sharp piss made my welts sting furiously, but I didn't even try to stop it, letting spurt after spurt gush from my body to wet my skin and soil my sheets until I was lying in a soggy, sticky puddle of my own making.

Only when I'd finished did I slowly begin to return to my senses, and then my raw, unfocused emotion to gave way to a great wave of humiliation at what I'd done. To be spanked and left tied up was bad enough, a perfectly good reason to get in a bit of a tantrum, but for me, a grown woman, to wet my bed . . . it was just too much. They would find out, too, because whoever came up to release me could scarcely fail to notice and she would be sure to tell the others. In my imagination I could already hear Portia's laughter as she discovered that I'd wet the bed, and I began to panic, wriggling in my pee puddle, only to freeze at the sound of a footstep on the landing. I heard the bathroom door open and relaxed a little, only to stiffen once more as the door to my own room swung wide. My vision was hazy with tears, but the flame-red hair and riding gear of my visitor was unmistakable – it was Tiffany.

'Hello, Isabelle,' she said, her voice cruel but also conspiratorial.

'You . . . you can't come in here!' I blurted out, starting to panic once more. 'Eliza said—'

'What's she going to do, spank me?' Tiffany cut in. 'That would be lovely.'

'You made a real fuss last time!'

'I *like* to make a fuss. Now hush, I'm sure you want this as badly as I do.'

She had reached the bed, and now she put out a hand to stroke my hair. Just her touch was enough to make my pussy tighten and send a jolt of longing right through me, but it was not enough to overcome my shame for the state I was in.

'Look, Tiffany . . . Tiffy,' I gabbled. 'I want you, I really do, but . . . but this is not the best time, really . . .'

'Oh yes it is,' she said softly. 'I like you, Isabelle. I like the way you're rough with me, but I like my revenge too, and I don't suppose I'll often have you with your hands tied and your bottom spanked to get you in the mood.'

'The mood for what?' I asked. But she just giggled and continued to stroke my hair.

'Tiffany . . .' I began, but she put her finger to her lips and quickly turned around.

'I'm going to sit on your face,' she said. 'First, though, you know I never wear panties under my jodhpurs, don't you? And so . . .'

Tiffany had stuck her bottom out as she spoke, showing off the seat of her jodhpurs. They were truly tight, outlining not just the contours of her sweetly formed bottom but of her pussy too. She giggled and began to push her jodhpurs down at the back, gradually revealing her bare bottom, the neat freckled cheeks apart to show the tangle of ginger hair at her crotch, with her anus showing as a moist pink spot and her pussy lips pouting out from between her thighs.

'You like to spank it,' she said, 'so I hope you like to lick it too.'

'I . . . look, Tiffy . . .'

'Hush, just do as you're told for once,' she said, pushing her jodhpurs down and off, taking her boots with them.

She climbed onto the bed, cocking one leg across my body to spread her naked bottom over my face. My mouth came open by instinct, for all my unbearable shame.

'Do it well, and I'll return the favour,' she promised. Then she sat down on my face.

I'd tried to answer, to tell her that I'd do as I was told without expecting anything in return, but with her bottom in my face all I could manage was a muffled gulping noise.

'Come on, Isabelle, lick,' Tiffany demanded. 'I know you want to, and I know you like it, because Portia told me. She told me you lick girls' bums, Isabelle, so do it for me.'

As she spoke she wiggled her bottom, rubbing her pussy and her bumhole against my lips and nose. I couldn't stop myself. My tongue poked out, lapping between her sex lips to draw an ecstatic sigh from her above me. Again she wiggled her bottom, pressing herself firmly against my face, with her anus rubbing on the tip of my nose.

'Lick my bottom, Isabelle,' she begged. 'Please lick my bottom. I'd do it for you—'

She broke off with a moan as I gave in to her filthy demand – not that I'd had much choice. As she'd spoken she'd moved to bring her anus against my mouth, and I couldn't stop myself from doing it, sticking my tongue in up her rubbery little hole and filling my head with the taste of her.

'That's nice,' she sighed. 'I knew you were a dirty girl underneath, Isabelle. Oh, yes, like that. Isn't it nice to lick, just to be friendly . . . and why not do it to each other's bottoms when it feels so nice . . .'

Tiffany's voice trailed off to a sigh. I licked as best I could, eager to get my tongue as far up her bottom as it would go, but she'd lost control. She was squirming herself against me and purring like a cat, her bum full in my face so that all I could see was the twin curve of her little freckled cheeks rising above me. I could barely breathe, my mouth was full of the taste of her pussy and her bottom-hole, and she had me completely under her power. My thighs had come up and open, spreading my own sex for her, and I was wriggling my bottom against the soggy mess of the sheets where I'd wet myself.

Tiffany gave a little whimper, said something I didn't hear, and suddenly the bedclothes had been jerked down, exposing me completely. Shame and self-pity welled up through my ecstasy as she saw what I'd done and gave a squeal of shock and disgust, but she kept her bottom firmly in my face, and her words were broken and urgent as she began to talk again.

'Oh my God . . . you've wet yourself! You've wet yourself, Isabelle . . . Portia used to make me do that, and . . . and do it on me, but I'm not licking you like that, not like that . . . I don't want your pee in my mouth . . . I don't . . . oh God . . . fuck it, I have to.'

As she spoke she went down, burying her face between my thighs. Her tongue found my pussy and she was licking with frenzied urgency, lapping up the taste from my cunt. I rolled up, crossing my legs to trap her body, my cunt now spread in her face and hers in mine, both of us licking, pussies and bottoms too. She licked my cane welts and licked my anus, even rubbing her face in the pee-soaked sheets, while I did my best to return the favour, lapping her the length of her pussy crease and on up to her bumhole.

In no time I'd started to come, almost lost in ecstasy with Tiffany. But I was still conscious of the fact that had I not had my bottom smacked, not been caned and tied up, not been sent to bed in disgrace, and not got into such a tantrum over it all that I'd piddled in my bed, then I would never have known the moment of exquisitely filthy rapture that was now sweeping over me. Tiffany made it too, an instant later, and we came together with our mouths now pressed hard against each other's cunts for perfect mutual satisfaction. But as I came slowly down I was babbling my thanks not to her but to Eliza.

Six

Tiffany and I got away with it, but only just, and the aftermath was a nightmare. While the two of us were still head to tail Eliza called up to ask what was going on. Tiffany was forced to grab her clothes and make a run for the bathroom, from which she provided the highly undignified excuse that she'd got constipation. All I could do was wipe my face on the pillow and await my fate, which consisted of a brisk spanking with my face pushed into my wet sheets, being made to clean up my mess and remake the bed, then being sent down to Dr Treadle to apologise in front of everybody before going over his knee for yet another spanking.

All sorts of things had been going on while I'd been upstairs. Caroline was in the nude and she'd had her bottom caned, with what showed of her big pink cheeks as she nestled herself on Walter's lap stripy with stroke marks. Portia had been tied across the table and her blouse had been opened for hot wax to be dripped on her breasts by Jasmine, and she had apparently made an extraordinary fuss about submitting to her rival. Even Katie was bottomless, with two rosy cheeks showing behind as she served drinks, the result of a spanking from Duncan.

My ideas of making Sarah or even Eliza submit as well had seemed impossibly inappropriate, and I'd been too exhausted to try anyway. Even being naked from the waist down seemed completely natural, as did having my bottom patted and my breasts touched, although all the while it was as if it wasn't really me it was happening to.

It wasn't until the following morning that I was even roughly back to my normal self. But I could remember how I'd behaved, and how much pleasure I'd taken in what had happened to me. Katie was in bed with me, so I gave her a sound spanking and sat on her face in an effort to reassert myself, but that only went so far. I'd behaved like a brat about my punishment, and a complete slut too, letting everybody see how turned-on my spanking had made me, throwing a tantrum and then allowing Sarah and Tiffany to use me without so much as a whimper of complaint. That wasn't for me. That was for other girls: lovely girls, desirable girls, but still other girls.

I needed some time alone to think, because my feelings were so confused. That was impossible while I was with Katie, and also during the week ahead because I was determined not to let my emotional state get in the way of my studies. There was also the issue of what I had promised Tierney, which was distracting to say the least. All week he seemed to be everywhere at once, around every corner in college, and even in town, so that I'd quickly begun to suspect that he was following me. Twice he suggested going to my room to have his cock sucked, and both times I managed to make an excuse rather than refusing outright.

Eventually I was going to have to tell him he wouldn't be getting it, but that was not a happy prospect. He'd be furious, and I'd have broken his trust, which I'd never done before. That meant that in the future he wouldn't believe me, while there was still the issue of what the Owl might be telling him, all of which put me in an agony of indecision. At one extreme I could play him at his own game, plotting and scheming. Perhaps I could use the Owl to feed him false information, so that he'd turn up at the wrong place and time? Perhaps I could string him along with further promises until after the Christmas party? In both cases I'd only be storing up future difficulties for myself. But at the other extreme I could give in and suck his beastly cock for him, and my pride would not allow that.

The other issue was the darts match. I'd agreed to play and Yazzie knew that, which made it hard to back out. However, it would be in Bicester, at a strange pub, I'd be with four other women, and Tierney wasn't even in the team. I'd quickly decided to go, but to cycle to Bicester and meet them there rather than accept a place in the minibus they were hiring. My decision also allowed me to find more time to think, because I could start early, spend the day walking in the countryside, then join them later.

I chose a place near Quainton, in Buckinghamshire. During the summer Portia had told us about a stretch of old railway that still had its tracks in place. She'd wanted to be chained to it in order to fulfil a fantasy that was more a horrid thrill than anything sexual, but the rest of us had been happy to oblige. We'd stayed there all day and had seen not one single person, while on Eliza's insistence I myself had checked the line to make sure that it was cut at both ends and that there was no possibility whatsoever of the unexpected arrival of a train.

It was the perfect place to walk and to think, since if it had been deserted on a baking hot day in June it would presumably be deserted in November. I got up early and cycled out from Oxford. My head seemed to clear with every turn of the wheels, until by the time I'd reached the railway I felt calm and rational, really for the first time since my spanking across Eliza's knee. As I'd hoped, I was able to analyse my feelings, both about enjoying submission and about men.

For as long as I could remember, sex and discipline had been linked in my mind. As the ministers at home in Scotland had never tired of telling us, sex was a sin, and sin deserved punishment. To me, the essence of sex was to be entered from behind, and the focus of sex was therefore my bottom. Thus what better way to punish a woman for sexual sins than to spank her bottom?

Not that the ministers would have seen it that way, but it worked for me – except that it wasn't my bottom that should be spanked, but another woman's. That was the foundation of my sexuality, the one on which I'd built my relationships, first with Jasmine and Caroline, and then with Katie. Unfortunately, while I genuinely hated the idea of being on the receiving end there was no denying what it did to me and, for all my experience and training, that had not changed.

As I walked along the abandoned railway line, stepping from sleeper to sleeper at an exact pace controlled by their spacing, a nasty suspicion began to creep over me: that maybe there was nothing natural about my preference for being dominant at all. Perhaps it was simply a reflection of my pride. This made sense, and it also fitted in with my attitude to men. My preference has always been for women, but it would be a lie for me to claim to be anything other than bisexual. The difference in my attitude to men, though, is that, for me, sex with a man means having to submit myself to him and no amount of liberal or feminist theory has ever made me feel otherwise.

Having got that far, I discovered that I did not want to reach the obvious conclusion, and so turned my thoughts to Tierney and the Owl instead. I was convinced that she was spying on me, but I couldn't believe she would do it voluntarily. That meant Tierney had some kind of hold over her, which brought up some unpleasant possibilities. If only I could catch them together I would be able to talk to her and bring her over to my side, whatever she had done – short of murder, and it was impossible to imagine the Owl murdering anybody.

It was even difficult to imagine the Owl crossing an empty road when the little red man was showing, but it was very easy to imagine her getting upset over some indiscretion that I would have considered trivial. There were plenty of things it might have been, but whatever it was I needed to know, because that would put a stop to Tierney's tricks. Ideally, I wanted to know before we set a date for the Christmas party, so that would have to be my priority.

Having reached my conclusions I walked back to where I'd chained my bike to a fence and started out for Bicester. The air was distinctly cool, and I realised I'd almost certainly been right about my session with Katie in among the willows being the last opportunity of the year for outdoor sex. My knuckles were soon painfully cold, and by the time I got to the Boar I was chilled through. It was also dark, and foggy, a combination that made the warm smoke-filled atmosphere of the pub seem positively desirable, as was the company of my fellow human beings, even the rough working-class men and their slatternly companions who filled the place.

Nobody else from the Red Ox was there, so I treated myself to a double whisky and went to sit near the dartboard. A group of men and women were playing, very possibly our opponents, so I watched with interest. One of them in particular caught my eye, a massive man with a shock of greasy black hair and a moustache that made him look like a Mexican bandit, although he seemed more likely to be Turkish or Greek. He had the most colossal beer gut I'd ever seen, drank pints as if they were water and threw his darts with unerring accuracy. I could see at a glance that he was not only far better than me or anyone else from our team, but also far better than his friends.

I'd begun to consider our tactics when the door opened to admit a familiar figure, Stan Tierney. He was followed by Jack, Choker, and to my immense relief Edna, but that was all. They saw me immediately and Choker went to get the drinks while the others came to my table.

'All right, Isa?' Tierney greeted me. 'Budge up.'

He gave a friendly leer as he nudged my hip with his own and I hastily moved down the bench, only to find myself blocked by Edna, whose enormous hips and monstrous bottom occupied at least twice the space that I did.

'I didn't think you were in the team?' I asked as Tierney made himself comfortable next to me.

'The team's who wants to be in it,' he said, 'and I've come up to keep you company.'

He sounded genuine, even hurt, but the crafty glitter in his eyes sent a very different message.

'I thought Yazzie would be here,' I went on.

'Saturday, ain't it? She's stripping.'

'Yazzie strips? At the Red Ox!?'

'Yeah, sure. What's the big deal? *You* used to, before you got all hoity-toity on us.'

I merely shrugged, knowing that if I lived to be a hundred I would never understand the way working-class people think. Tierney, certainly, was oblivious to the impropriety of the situation, which would have given my parents apoplexy, never mind the ministers. Yet at least I wasn't at the Red Ox, and even if I was with two of the worst offenders from the crew and Choker, an unknown but suspect quantity, I was also with Edna, and immensely thankful for her presence.

'Whisky, straight up – yeah, love?' Choker asked as he put down what must have been at least a triple in front of me.

'That's right,' Tierney answered for me. 'She likes it straight up, does Isa.'

They all laughed, even Edna, setting my cheeks on fire with embarrassment. Choker set down the rest of the drinks and they began to talk about the darts match, except for Jack who had gone to speak with the captain of the opposing team. That turned out to be the huge man with the beer gut, who presently came over to find out who was playing against who. He was friendly to everybody, and had obviously met the others before.

We were playing to the same rules as when I'd joined in at the Red Ox, and I found myself up against a middle-aged woman who appeared to be going bald. She was also a good darts player and beat me, although not by a large margin. Their captain, Osman, also managed to dispose of Jack, but Edna and Choker both won, leaving Tierney playing against a tiny man so old that he appeared to be almost fossilised. I was still surprised when Tierney won, and was also rather surprised that no suggestions of sexual forfeits had been made, which I'd been half expecting despite the presence of Edna.

It was good to have won, although after getting so nervous about what Tierney might do I felt more relief than anything now it was over, and also experienced a strong sense of anticlimax. The others were thoroughly pleased with themselves, having lost the same match three years running. Jack in particular was full of himself, despite having lost against Osman, and happily accepted Osman's demand for a rematch at the Red Ox, this time with stakes instead of simply for the honour of the thing.

I paid little attention, drinking the whiskies they insisted on buying for me until I realised that if I didn't stop it would be dangerous for me to cycle home. Tierney himself had just pressed a glass into my hand, and I decided to make it my last.

'Fancy coming back to the Ox?' he suggested, with a wink so lewd he might as well have got his cock out. 'Or maybe my place? Nice and quiet at my place, it is.'

'No, thank you,' I told him. 'My bike is outside.'

'Twenty miles,' he said, 'and it's a nasty, foggy night.'

'It's ten,' I corrected him, 'perhaps twelve back to St George's, and I have lights.'

I produced one from my coat pocket, just in case he got any ideas about pinching them so that I'd have to go in the minibus.

'Suit yourself,' he said. 'But don't forget you owe me that blow job.'

He turned away, leaving me blushing crimson because he'd made no attempt at all to keep his voice down and there were people all around us, including Osman and the little wizened man Tierney had beaten. I took a swallow of my whisky, wishing that Tierney didn't get to me so badly and so easily, also that my fingers would stop shaking. Osman had heard, because he was grinning as he turned to me. But he didn't make an issue of it, simply asking where I'd learnt to play darts and if I'd be there for the rematch.

Twenty minutes later I'd finished my whisky and decided it was time to leave. The rest of the Red Ox team were scattered around the pub, talking to different people, and I quickly made my goodbyes. Tierney had been right about the fog, which had come down with a vengeance, giving the street lights yellow halos and making the car park an illuminated island in a sea of dirty white. My bike was chained to a lamp-post – or rather, it wasn't.

It took me all of one second to go from the initial horror of thinking I'd had my bike stolen to the realisation of who had stolen it, and I was back in the pub inside ten. Tierney was by the bar, making no doubt sexist remarks to a young and buxom barmaid. I went straight over to him.

'Where's my bike, Tierney?' I demanded.

'Fuck me, Isa!' he answered, jumping back in surprise. 'What's up with you?'

'Where is my bicycle?' I repeated, louder.

'How should *I* know?' he retorted. 'Where you chained it up, I suppose.'

'No, it is not,' I told him, 'as I suspect you know perfectly well. Now come on, this is beyond a joke. I want my bike.'

People were looking at us, and I was on the edge of tears. As Tierney answered me his voice was soft and considerate.

'Hey, hey, don't be like that, love. I haven't nicked your bike. Why would I?'

'The place is full of fucking tea leaves,' Jack put in. 'But don't worry about it. You can come back with us.'

'Oh, and then I suppose you want . . .' I began, my voice heavy with sarcasm, only to stop.

The Red Ox men had been perfectly well behaved all evening, at least by their standards, Edna was with us and there were about twenty men and women within hearing range. I was tired and drunk, it was a foul night out and a long way home.

'OK, I'll come with you,' I said, and quickly wiped a tear away. 'Thank you.'

'That's the way,' Tierney answered, then turned back to his barmaid. 'Here, love, get us a whisky, one of those fancy ones, and better make it a double.'

'On the house,' the girl answered, and lifted a tumbler to the optic of a bottle of Laphroaig.

I accepted it gratefully, feeling silly now for accusing Tierney and so grateful to the rest of them that I couldn't stop the tears. Osman and another man even went out to search for my bike, and it was nearly closing time before they returned, empty-handed. By then I had no choice anyway. I was feeling drunk and emotional, in no condition to ride. As we went outside and the cold air hit me I found myself having to hold on to Edna for support, and she guided me into the minibus where I slumped down in one of the rear seats.

My emotions were a mess, and I closed my eyes, the drink singing in my head as I made myself as comfortable as I could. I felt the minibus start, and then somebody sat down next to me: Tierney. I knew he was going to take advantage of me, but I didn't care any more. After all, I'd promised . . . and at least Tierney wasn't as decrepit as that old pervert Walter Jessop.

When he began to feel me up I barely reacted. I had my coat done up, and he'd put a hand under a lapel to fondle my breasts through my jumper and blouse. I wasn't even sure if he knew I was awake, but the outrage I should have felt at his behaviour just wouldn't come. Soon he'd got my nipples erect, and before I really knew it he'd pulled my clothes up, including my bra, and had opened my coat. My breasts were naked and his fingers were pawing at my flesh to explore my shape and tease my nipples even more as I felt his lips press to my ear.

'How about now, Isa? Nobody can see.'

Tierney was right. Edna was driving, with Choker beside her on the broad front seat and Jack immediately behind. I could suck Tierney off, nobody would be any the wiser and I'd have kept my word.

'Here, look,' he said. 'Look how horny you get me.'

I opened my eyes to find that he had his cock out, a fat pale rod sticking up from his scruffy jeans, visible each time we passed under a light. He was fully erect, and not for the first time I had to admit to myself that for all his other faults he did have a nice cock, big and meaty and perfectly suckable. I'd thought so the first time I'd taken him in my hand, two years ago, and I felt the same way now as I allowed myself to be guided gently but firmly down into his lap.

Something inside me was screaming at me to stop, yelling that I was betraying myself, that I had been tricked and that what Tierney was doing to me was abuse. It was a lie. I'd promised to suck his cock and I was going to. My mouth widened to take it in, then it was full. As I set to work, Tierney gave a low moan, perhaps from pleasure, perhaps from relief that I'd finally given in to him, and to myself. I knew I was drunk, but sometimes drink lets you do things you want to but otherwise wouldn't dare, and what I wanted right then was his cock.

'Hang on,' he grunted as he adjusted himself to pull out his balls.

I went straight down on them, as I had on Walter's, mouthing on the plump leathery sack to fill my mouth with the taste of him while I tossed off his cock. It felt deliciously dirty, and better still as his hand slid under my chest to grope at my breasts, so wonderfully rude, to suck off a much older man in the back of a moving van. My top was up, my bare little boobs in his hand, his cock hard in my mouth as we drove through the night with his friends just feet away. That made me a slut, and I knew it, but that was what I wanted, and more.

My hands went to my jeans, fumbling the button open and pushing them down over my hips. Tierney saw what I was up to and pulled up my coat, showing off the seat of my plain white panties to the window. I didn't care, far from it. If the world saw what a dirty pig I was, all the better, but Stan had more sense and eased me down to the floor beside him, with my legs cocked wide. I took his cock in again, stuck a hand down my knickers and began to rub myself.

'That's my girl, good and dirty,' he drawled.

I just purred. It felt wonderful, in the warm darkness, with a cock in my mouth and my hand down my panties, drunk and randy, my tits out and pussy warm and wet and willing . . .

'Fuck me, Isa's giving Stan a blow!' Jack swore.

'The dirty little cow!' Edna exclaimed. Her outburst was followed by a wordless grunt of astonishment from Choker.

'Uh, uh,' Tierney said firmly as I tried to rise. 'You stay right where you are, missy.'

He'd twisted his hand in my hair, keeping me firmly down on his erection, and I wriggled, but not so very hard. I'd been getting to close to orgasm, and the thought of being watched while I sucked Stan off was good because it was dirty and humiliating too, and the thing that turned me on most of all was the disapproval in Edna's voice. I nodded, and then as Stan eased his grip I pulled my head up.

'You don't have to hold me down. I don't mind doing it in front of them. If you like you can take turns.'

'Jesus shit!' Choker gasped.

'Why, you little tart!' Edna snapped. 'What you need is a good smacking!'

'Yes, please,' I sighed. 'Why don't you spank me while I suck the boys off?'

'Jesus, Joseph and Mary!' she said.

'Pull over for a minute, Edna love,' Jack asked.

'I will do no such thing!' Edna retorted. 'If you want the dirty little tart you can have her, but not when I'm around.'

'We won't be long, and you don't have to watch,' Jack pointed out. 'Come on, love.'

Edna merely speeded up, the force of the acceleration, pushing my face onto Stan's cock and pressing his helmet down my throat.

'Nice – do that again, Isa,' he rasped as I began to gag. But I pulled back, showing off now by easing my lips up and down his shaft with long, smooth motions.

'Jesus, I'd like a piece of that!' Jack sighed. 'For fuck's sake, Edna, will you pull over? Anybody would think you'd never watched us make a bitch give head!'

Edna responded with an angry grunt, but a moment later the minibus had begun to slow down. We were well out of town, and had pulled off into a darkened lay-by, where Jack and Choker came round to the back of the vehicle. They wasted no time but simply took me, Choker sitting down and jerking my hand from my pussy onto his cock, while Jack pulled my body out into the central aisle. I managed a feeble protest as I realised that I was going to be fucked, but he simply pulled my panties down and began to rub his half-stiff cock in the wetness between my legs.

I let him, and took Choker in my mouth to help him get hard, sucking eagerly while I tossed off Stan's cock and Jack's prick stiffened against my sex and between my bum cheeks. A moment later I felt my cunt fill, a glorious sensation after so long. They'd made me into a spit roast, rocking back and forth with one cock in my mouth and another up my pussy-hole. At that moment the interior light went on.

'Filthy little bitch!' Edna spat. 'And you a college girl and all – not that you're any better than the rest of us, sleeping with that Katie West. Little tarts, the pair of you!'

Every word she spoke sent a stab of humiliation through me – perfect sexual humiliation. She was right. Katie and I *were* a pair of little tarts, playing spanking games and licking each other's cunts every weekend, and with other women several times a term. I was a filthy little bitch too, a complete slut, only too pleased to indulge men, women, one at a time or all together, as long as I was thoroughly used.

'Can it, Edna, I'm going to spunk!' Jack grated. He'd begun to fuck me at a furious pace, jamming his cock in and out of my cunt-hole so fast and so hard that I lost my breath and Choker's cock slipped out of my mouth.

An instant later and Jack was there, first up my hole and then all over my bottom, jerking himself and swearing viciously as hot come splashed out onto my bare skin. Edna hadn't taken kindly to being told to shut up and she gave him a barrage of abuse, which he ignored as he finished himself off over my cheeks and wiped his helmet on my anus. Choker, now erect, caught me by the hair, pulling my head back into his lap and I took him in again.

'I've got to fuck her,' Stan grunted, and then he was clambering over my body as I began to move my head up and down on Choker's cock.

Jack moved back, Stan eased himself in up my hole and I was on a spit roast again, only now I was basted with spunk as well. I put my hand back, determined to come while they used me, to find my panties sticky with Jack's mess and more jism gushing out of my gaping pussy as Stan Tierney pumped himself in and out. His balls were slapping at my fingers as I started to rub my cunt and I snatched them, squashing them against my pussy to masturbate with.

'What are you doing, you mad bitch!?' Tierney yelped. 'Ow! Isabelle!'

'The dirty fucking tart!' Edna grunted.

I didn't even slow down, crushing Stan's scrotum against my slippery cunt and bumping his balls onto my clitoris, my orgasm rising in my head even as Choker jammed his erection deep into my gullet. My stomach lurched as he began to fuck my throat, Tierney cried out again in pain and I was there, riding my orgasm on their cocks, one in at either end as deep as they would go, for one long perfect moment before everything seemed to explode. Spunk squirted from my nose as Choker came down my throat. Tierney snatched my hand away from his balls and began to drive himself into me once more, calling me a bitch over and over again until he too reached his orgasm.

He did it right up me, while Choker was still holding me down on his cock, so that gushes of spunk exploded from my nose, my mouth and my cunt at the same instant, filling my panties and soiling my jumper, and all the while I was still snatching at myself, greedy for more as peak after peak of orgasm ran through me until I collapsed as the men finally let go of my body. I was coughing up spunk, with more oozing from my open cunt hole behind, all in full view of the disgusted Edna as Tierney moved to one side. As I felt a clot of Jack and Stan's mingled mess fall into my lowered panties she delivered her verdict.

'A common whore, that's what she is, for all her airs and graces.'

There was nobody to blame but myself. I'd got drunk and I'd given in, allowing Stan Tierney of all people to touch me up, to make me hold his cock, to suck him. He'd shared me with his dirty friends, spit-roasting me on the floor of a minibus, using me back and front as a receptacle for their spunk. No, I'd done all of that, but I hadn't been *made* to do anything. I'd been willing from start to finish, and in front of a woman who had been utterly disgusted by my behaviour. They hadn't even manipulated me.

The next morning I lay staring at the ceiling of my room, aghast at my own behaviour. My head was throbbing from the whisky and my mouth and pussy were sore from the fuckings, but none of that physical discomfort seemed to matter next to what I'd done, with each awful detail running through my head over and over again.

Letting the men have me hadn't been the end of it, not by a long way. Afterwards I'd thought I was going to be sick and Edna had helped me out of the van and into the bushes. I'd managed to keep my dinner down, but she'd still been telling me off and I'd propositioned her, suggesting that if I was such a naughty girl she ought to spank me. She'd told me she had a good mind to do it, at which I'd suggested it ought to be over her knee and with my panties down in front of the men. That had earned me a slap in the face, which had at least sobered me up enough not to proposition her for actual sex. She'd also had to hold me up while I peed in the bushes, and had had to help me wipe the men's mess off my bottom and my pussy. I'd never be able to look her in the face again.

Once back in the minibus I'd passed out, which had probably been for the best. Instead of taking me home for more, Tierney had adjusted my clothes and dropped me off at St George's. I could vaguely remember the porters laughing over the state I was in, but as Tierney was a scout he'd simply claimed that he'd found me staggering drunkenly around the town and no questions had been asked. That meant no trouble from my college, for which I was duly grateful, as indeed I had been to Tierney, allowing him to feel me up as he stripped me and put me to bed and even giving his cock a last quick suck before he left.

I washed at my sink, but my efforts to tell myself that I was somehow washing the men's dirt from my body came to nothing. They'd taken what I'd offered, no more, and if they'd been rough with me that was simply their nature. To pretend that they had tricked me, let alone forced me, would have been dishonest, both to them and to myself.

For the rest of the morning I stayed in my room with the curtains drawn, feeling sorry for myself and trying to resist the gradually rising urge to masturbate over what I'd done. Finally I realised that the only way to save myself was to get up and go into hall for something to eat. As I picked at a cheese salad I was thinking through the likely consequences of what had happened. On the good side Tierney was sure to be impressed by my behaviour, and if he thought he was going to get more of the same he would, hopefully, leave the Rattaners alone. Unfortunately he was sure to expect another session before the end of term, a thought that set me biting my lip with chagrin. I still needed to make sure there was a connection between him and the Owl, and then break it.

Choker and Jack didn't matter, because they were Tierney's creatures and would follow his lead, so as long as I stayed clear of the Red Ox they wouldn't be a problem. Edna was another matter, and it was even possible that she would report my behaviour to the authorities. Sleeping with Katie was one thing, and acceptable as long as we were discreet, but group sex with three men from Cowley was sure to cause comment, maybe even get me sent down. I was going to have to speak to Edna. I was also going to have to speak to Katie, because it was only fair to warn her, but I would have to pretend Tierney had taken advantage of me or she'd be upset.

Then there was my bike. If I reported it stolen, the police and therefore the college authorities were going to want to know what I'd been doing in Bicester. While there was no rule against playing darts in seedy pubs, questions might be asked and that again might land me in trouble. They would want to speak to Tierney, and maybe to Edna as well, which could only be a bad thing, while the chances of recovering the bike were pretty slim anyway. It wasn't even insured, and I had no spare money to buy another one.

I had meant to walk up to Foxson after lunch, but I simply couldn't face it. My head hurt, my legs ached, and my jaw muscles were sore from too much cocksucking, making it painful to speak. It made more sense to get an early night and go first thing in the morning. That way I could catch not only Katie but also Edna, which would spare me an embarrassing and possibly disastrous trip to the Red Ox to find out where she lived. Mike would probably tell me, while the others, especially Tierney, were sure to expect something in return, something rude. As always, the thought disgusted me, and yet I was thinking of the possibilities as I stripped off and collapsed back into bed.

Sleep caught up with me before I could disgrace myself, but my dreams were full of rough lecherous men who were eager to abuse me, and when I woke up again I immediately knew there was no hope of avoiding it. My nipples were stiff, my pussy was wet, and a thousand dirty thoughts were crowding into my head all at once. It was warm, and dark, making it all too easy to give in as my hand snaked down under my belly to find my sex.

I was face down, and I'd woken clutching my pillow, which I pushed down to raise my hips as I remembered how dirty and how eager I'd been, and how wonderful it had felt. The men had well and truly used me, but I knew it could have been worse, and in my imagination it was. I thought of how Edna might have taken me up on my offer and spanked my bare bottom in front of the men. They'd have thought it was hilarious, and the sight of me naked and wriggling in my pain would have got them going again.

Once she'd finished they'd have fucked me as they had before, one cock in my mouth and one up my pussy, laughing and jeering as I was made into a spit-roast for their amusement. All the while Edna would have been calling me a slut and a whore, and telling me that I needed to be spanked more often. She'd do it again, and would keep me held down across her knee while the men had me from either end, first Tierney with his lovely big cock in my mouth while I was still being spanked, then Jack entering me from behind.

That was a particularly satisfying fantasy, so I got up onto my knees and pushed the bedclothes down, imagining myself held down firmly across Edna's lap while the men used me. Perhaps, when she realised just what a little slut I really was, she would decide to take advantage herself, not by making me lick her but by whoring me out to passing motorists. She'd put up a sign by the road, offering me for sale, with the words 'Cheap Tart' in large red letters to describe me.

I'd be kneeling in the damp grass by the roadside, with one man up me and another in my mouth, again and again as I struggled to satisfy a queue that would grow faster than I could satisfy them. Already I was on the edge of orgasm, teasing my clitoris with a single finger as I imagined myself being sold, a cheap tart, available to anyone for anything at ten pounds a time – no, five pounds, or even one. I wouldn't even get the money. Edna would take most of it and give Tierney, Jack and Choker the rest as a treat for reducing me to a state in which I could be casually whored out.

Maybe Edna would need to hold me in place across her knee, applying occasional spankings to keep me in mind of who I was, what I was, and to amuse the men. No, I'd be too willing, eager for every indignity, swallowing spunk and guiding the men's cocks in up my slippery hole. Soon I'd be too slippery. Some bastard would complain that he couldn't get enough friction up my cunt and demand his money back. Edna would tell him to bugger me instead and up his huge erect cock would go, up my bottom-hole, jammed in so deep that his balls would be pressing against my empty cunt as he used me.

At the thought of being sodomised for a pound it all got too much. I came, screaming into my pillow, clutching at my cunt, and at the last moment I put my other hand back to stick one finger in up my sweaty, slippery bottom-hole.

Seven

The reality of Edna was very different from the fantasy, and I was feeling pretty glum as I set off on foot towards Foxson the next morning. Katie at least could be counted on to be understanding, even if my confession wasn't going to do much for my role as her dominant, self-controlled partner. Facing Edna was an appalling prospect, though, and worse because I would almost certainly have to ask to speak to her in front of her fellow scouts, who would probably have been told all about me.

It took a lot of courage simply to keep walking, but as I entered the main gate of Foxson I stopped in my tracks. There, resting against a post at one end of the college bike shed, was my bicycle. At first I thought I had to be mistaken, and that it was just another one of the same make and colour, but closer inspection proved that it really was mine. Even the chain was with it, complete with padlock but sawn through.

The only feasible explanation seemed to be that it had been found and that Edna had brought it back to Foxson because she didn't know which college I was at. Nothing else fitted, but there was no sign of her, nor of any of the other scouts. There was a single porter on duty who made me wait for ages before he would condescend to speak to me and seemed to resent answering a simple question and taking a note for Edna to say I would be in Katie's room. This left me angry as well as puzzled as I made my way up.

It was still a few minutes before eight, so I knocked gently and let myself in, meaning to wake Katie with a kiss if she was still asleep. She was, but she was not alone. Beside her a round head stuck up above the covers and beneath the duvet was the outline of a rounded hip, features immediately recognisable as those of the Owl. As I stood there staring the facts slipped slowly into place. The Owl was in league with Tierney, intimately. She had been in Bicester, and had pinched my bike to order so that I'd have to go back in the minibus. Then she'd ridden it back herself, come to Foxson and seduced my girlfriend while I was being fucked silly by Tierney and his friends.

My temper snapped. One hard wrench and the covers were off the bed, revealing Katie in her nightie and the Owl in panties and top. Another hard wrench and the Owl's panties were down, exposing her fat white bottom to the light streaming in through Katie's curtains. She gave a squeak of surprise and tried to turn around, but I was ready for that and grabbed her arm, twisting it up behind her back even as I laid into her bottom, spanking her with every ounce of my strength. Katie jerked upright, her mouth wide in astonishment as she saw me.

'Isabelle! What—'

'Believe me, she has this coming to her!' I snapped back, still spanking the struggling, wailing Owl.

'We only shared a bed!' Katie exclaimed. 'Isabelle, stop it!'

The Owl was howling her head off, while her big round bottom cheeks were already flushed a rich pink, but it was the alarm in Katie's voice that brought me to my senses. I stopped, but I kept my grip on Amy Jane's wrist.

'It's nothing to do with you sleeping together,' I said. 'Go on, Amy Jane, tell Katie what you've done.'

The Owl's answer was incoherent, but just to hear her squeaky, piping voice brought my anger back to the boil. I laid in again, spanking her as hard as I could across both fat bum cheeks, only to stop again at the sound of another – horribly familiar – voice.

'Why, you dirty little bitches!'

I twisted around to find Edna standing in the doorway, her great brown hands on her gigantic hips, her dark moon face set in an expression of astonishment and outrage. Before I could react she had slammed the door and I had been thrust hard down on the bed, falling across Katie and the Owl so that I was bottom up as Edna's massive fist closed on the scruff of my neck.

'So you like a bit of spanking, do you, you filthy stuck-up little whores!' she screamed. 'I'll show you, I will. I'll show you what a real spanking is like, you dirty, filthy—'

She broke off, too furious even to speak properly, and now it was my turn to squeal in shock and helpless outrage as my skirt was hauled high to show off the seat of my tights and the panties beneath, only for it all to be jerked down in one brutal wrench. Now my bottom was bare. Edna hit me, her hand landing across my bum cheeks to jam me down on top of the Owl who was struggling frantically underneath me, her own hot bare cheeks rubbing against my tummy as she squirmed. Katie was screaming and batting at Edna's arms, which only served to enrage the big woman even more and ensure that my spanking was delivered with a force far beyond anything I had ever suffered before. When it suddenly

157

stopped my first sensation was relief, then a sick feeling as I caught a new voice, male and full of authority.

'What in *God's* name is going on here? Catherine? Mrs Jellaby?'

Edna had let go of my neck, and I jerked up my panties and tights as she began to babble an explanation that was half apology and half righteous indignation.

'. . . Right here, all three of them in the same bed, it's not right,' she finished as I finally managed to find my feet.

The man standing in the doorway was of medium height, lean, grey-haired and very, very angry. He was also familiar to me as Dr Smith, a member of the history faculty and Dean of Foxson College.

The four of us stood in a line in front of Dr Smith's desk, myself, Katie, the Owl and Edna. I felt sick to my stomach, I couldn't control my blushes or my shaking, and I was on the verge of tears. Katie and the Owl were both crying, but Edna's homely features were set in an obstinate scowl. Dr Smith's anger had faded to exasperation, but there was little or no sympathy in his voice as he spoke.

'I wish to know *precisely* what happened,' he demanded, 'from each of you. Mrs Jellaby?'

'I'm a union member, you need to know that,' Edna answered him without the least hesitation, 'and if I lost my temper, sir, then I say it ain't surprising. It's a disgrace, it is, the way students carry on nowadays, sharing their rooms, and girls too. I try not to say anything, but three girls together in bed, and playing their dirty games, that's too much, and I know what that Isabelle is like, because just on Saturday night she did something you would not like to hear about, and—'

'Mrs Jellaby, please.' Dr Smith interrupted the flow of words, during which I'd been growing ever more embarrassed, although I wouldn't have thought it possible. 'Now, you say you caught Miss West in bed with Miss Colraine and Miss Moffat?'

'I did,' Edna confirmed.

'Very well,' he said. 'I appreciate you might feel that this was improper, but—'

'Improper!?' Edna snapped. 'They were playing their dirty little games, they were, right there on the bed, spanking games. Isabelle, she was spanking Miss Moffat's bottom, she was, and if there's one thing I can't abide it's people who think that kind of thing is good for kicks, and I'm sorry if maybe I lost my temper, but that Isabelle—'

'Excuse me,' I put in before she could make some even worse revelation about my behaviour. 'I think there's been a bit of a misunderstanding here.'

Edna would have carried on, but Dr Smith raised a hand and she went quiet, glaring at me. I swallowed the lump in my throat and began to speak.

'I didn't spend the night at Foxson, although I admit I sometimes do. Katie ... Catherine West and I are lovers, and so when I came to visit her this morning and found Amy Jane ... Miss Moffat in her bed I ... I rather lost my temper. Then Mrs Jellaby came in and seems to have got the wrong idea, but I don't want to make an issue of what happened. In fact, I'd like to apologise to her for my behaviour, and to the rest of you.'

I stopped, unable to go on for the lump in my throat. My tears had started to come, and before I could stop myself I'd broken down, sobbing. Dr Smith drew a long sigh.

'Miss Moffat?' he asked.

'I ... I came to see Katie yesterday,' Amy Jane

stammered, 'and we went to the bar, and I didn't think I was safe to bicycle back to college, so I stayed. We didn't . . . we didn't, you know what, Isabelle, I promise, I really promise!'

She'd turned to me as she spoke, her voice breaking with emotion. Dr Smith shook his head and rested his face in one hand.

'That's true,' Katie confirmed. 'It was just a misunderstanding.'

There was a long silence before Dr Smith spoke again, and when he did it was brisk and stern.

'Very well. So long as neither Miss Moffat nor Miss Colraine wish to take this matter further I feel that it should be dealt with internally, at least insofar as that may be possible. However, I feel that I should make certain points clear. Foxson is a modern forward-looking college and we pride ourselves on our tolerant, liberal attitude. We realise that a proportion of our students will be homosexual, and we feel that it would be wrong to discriminate against those students. I am fully aware that you, Catherine, have been in a lesbian relationship with Miss Colraine for a . . .'

He carried on for some time, with both Katie and I growing gradually pinker and the Owl looking as if she was about to burst. But the final humiliation was reserved for the end.

'. . . Your choice of action in what you imagined was revenge for Miss Moffat's behaviour suggests an unhealthy obsession with corporal punishment as it pertains to the erotic, which is something I am not prepared to tolerate here at Foxson. In short, if the three of you wish to spank each other kindly do it elsewhere.'

My face was on fire by now and Katie's was the colour of beetroot, while Edna had begun to look

160

smug. The Owl appeared to have passed beyond the ability to react.

'My decision is as follows,' Dr Smith continued. 'Mrs Jellaby, however moral you may feel your actions to have been I think you should be thankful that Miss Colraine does not intend to press charges for assault. You will therefore receive a written warning. Catherine, Miss Moffat, while I feel that you may have been foolish you clearly had only passive involvement with events and so I do not propose to take further action. Miss Colraine, on the other hand, has acted abominably and I find myself obliged to pass the matter on to the authorities at your own college. You are at St George's, I believe?'

'Yes,' I confirmed.

'And the Dean of Arts there is Dr Duncan Appledore, is it not?'

'Yes,' I repeated, and for all my overwhelming chagrin I was struggling to stop the corners of my mouth twitching up into a smile.

'I shall telephone him immediately,' Dr Smith finished. 'You may go.'

We went, hurrying from his study and downstairs in a state of embarrassed silence. Edna turned away without even bothering to thank me for not trying to make life more difficult for her, which I could very well have done, but I was in no mood to make an issue of it. Everybody seemed to be looking at us, and we couldn't get out of the building fast enough.

We'd reached the bicycle shed before the Owl finally spoke up, her voice thick with self-pity and recrimination.

'That hurt, Isabelle. And I didn't do anything with Katie.'

'I'm sorry,' I told her grudgingly. 'But . . . but what do you expect?'

'Well, not *that*!' she replied.

'And why not?' I demanded, my temper flaring up again. 'I'm sure you've got your reasons, but I am your friend and you could have come to me.'

'But I didn't do anything!'

'I'm not talking about spending the night here, Amy Jane, as you perfectly well know. I don't mind what you did or didn't do with Katie. In fact, I hope you had a really good time together. But I *do* care about you spying on me and telling Stan Tierney about everything I do, and—'

'Who's Stan Tierney?'

'Oh come on, Amy Jane, there's no point in lying now. If you don't know Tierney, how did my bike get there?'

I pointed at the bike, expecting at least a flicker of guilt. The Owl shrugged, looking completely blank. I was on the edge of losing my temper again, but Katie had put a consoling hand on my shoulder and I managed to bite back my anger before I could say too much. If the Owl wasn't prepared to admit to what she'd done there was nothing I could do about it, bike or no bike. But I was determined to have one last try.

'My bike was stolen on Saturday night, in Bicester,' I explained. 'Because my bike was stolen I had to come back to Oxford in a minibus, which is why . . .'

I trailed off, realising that I could hardly admit to what had happened in the minibus.

'I've never even been to Bicester,' the Owl told me. 'And I couldn't have brought your bike here anyway, because I came on my own.'

She sounded as if she was about to start crying, and as she walked over to place a hand on the saddle of the old yellow bicycle she rode a terrible weight of guilt began to grow inside me.

'Oh,' I said. 'But then . . .'

At that moment a porter emerged from the lodge, not the man I'd spoken to before but the one who was usually on duty when I came to visit Katie.

'You got your bike, then?' he asked, gesturing to it.

'Yes, thank you,' I answered. 'But who brought it?'

'Mr Jellaby, Edna's hubby,' he told me. 'Some bloke called Osman found it, he said, chained up where you'd left it.'

'No, it wasn't,' I retorted. But a seed of doubt had already begun to grow in my mind. 'Um . . . thank you, anyway.'

The porter gave me a friendly nod and went back into the lodge, leaving me wondering if I had really been so drunk, and so silly, that I'd gone to the wrong lamp-post. It didn't seem likely, especially as Osman and his friends had gone out to look for it, but perhaps a car had been in the way? In any event I now had it, and I'd just falsely accused the Owl.

'I'm sorry, Amy Jane,' I said.

'I have to go,' Katie put in. 'Let's talk again when we're not so upset.'

I nodded, kissed her and went to get my bike. My emotions were more confused than ever, and I was astonished at myself for losing my temper so badly. I knew why, though: what Amy Jane had done, or what I thought she'd done, had forced me to come face to face with something inside myself that I'd been trying very hard to bury, and in the minibus I had let it out with a vengeance. Now it looked as if she might be innocent after all, which made me feel awful.She fell into step with me as we left Foxson, both of us wheeling our bikes. I didn't know what to say, and just riding off seemed impossibly rude. In the end she spoke first.

'Your club isn't really anything to do with James Malcolm Rymer, is it?'

We were well clear of the gates of Foxson, walking between rows of red-brick houses with nobody in hearing range, but her question wasn't at all what I'd been expecting. I had no idea what to say, because if she was in league with Tierney she presumably knew anyway, and if she wasn't and I admitted it I'd be lining myself up for another punishment from the Rattaners. As a car passed us I found myself glancing guiltily at the driver, half expecting it to be Eliza or Sarah. The Owl spoke again.

'It's some sort of private lesbian society, isn't it?'

'What makes you think that?' I asked, trying to sound surprised and failing miserably.

'For a start you hardly know anything about him,' she responded, 'and all the members are women, and I know you and Katie are a couple in an open relationship, and Portia Anson-Jones was on the UOLS stall at the Freshers' Fair. You can tell me, Isabelle.'

The Owl sounded hurt, as no doubt she felt she had every right to be. I bit my lip, not wanting to lie but very sure that I shouldn't admit to the sort of things we got up to at Rattaners parties. I decided to compromise.

'You're right, in a way,' I admitted. 'We keep it secret because we don't feel we fit in at UOLS, and you know what student politics are like.'

'But isn't Portia the treasurer of UOLS?'

'Exactly.'

'I don't understand.'

'We're ... we're just rather old-fashioned. Yes, old-fashioned.'

'That sounds fun. Do you dress up?'

'Yes, sometimes.'

The Owl didn't answer, and we continued to walk. Slowly I began to feel that I might have got away

164

with it, or at least not dug myself any deeper into the ground, until she spoke again.

'Would you mind if I came along? I wouldn't be any trouble, I promise.'

'It . . . it's not really suitable,' I said hastily. 'Why would you want to come, anyway? Wouldn't you feel uncomfortable?'

'OK,' she said, 'I understand. You don't want me there.'

Her voice had begun to break towards tears, making me feel even worse.

'It's not that!' I promised her. 'It's just that the society wouldn't suit you. We . . . we play games and things, sexual games, and everybody has to join in, because spectators make us feel awkward . . .'

I'd said far too much, and my voice trailed off. I was desperately searching my mind for some way to put her off without hurting her. She had stopped, and so did I.

'Wouldn't it be better to find somebody to go out with?' I suggested. 'A man, I mean. There are lots of very attractive men in your college.'

'Do you think anybody would want me?' Amy Jane demanded as a tear began to form in one huge brown eye. 'I look like a bloody owl!'

'I wouldn't say that,' I lied, having done so several hundred times. 'Actually, I think you're pretty.'

'No, you don't,' she sniffed. 'You think I'm short and fat and frumpy. You wouldn't want me, would you? Katie spent all night with me and we didn't do a thing!'

'Come on, Amy Jane,' I protested. 'It's just that it would have been wrong for her to do that. You're not a lesbian.'

'I'm not anything!' she protested. 'I've never had sex, never! You smacking my bottom was the only vaguely sexual thing that anybody's ever done to me! I wouldn't mind what you did, I wouldn't even mind joining in. I just want somebody to like me.'

'I like you.'

'Not like that – properly!'

Amy Jane burst into tears, bawling her eyes out as her body shook with powerful sobs. There was a huge lump in my own throat, and I was horribly ashamed of my own behaviour. I put my arms around her as best I could with her bicycle between us, leaving my own to clatter to the pavement.

'Don't cry, please,' I urged. 'Look, um . . . it's not even that simple. I'd have to propose you to the society, and two of the others would have to . . . to interview you. But, Amy Jane, you do need to actually enjoy sex with other women!'

'I might,' she snivelled.

I held on to her, genuinely wanting to give her some comfort, although my head was full of visions of Portia or Jasmine giving her a playful spanking and Amy Jane running straight to the university authorities with tales of perversion and sexual abuse. Eventually I would have to tell her that if she wanted to join the Rattaners she have to accept being spanked, but with her crying her eyes out against my chest it didn't seem a good time to bring up the subject. Besides, I was the one who needed spanking, both for my appalling behaviour and for my stupidity.

Nor was that all. Having finally managed to drop Amy Jane off at Newman I started back towards St George's with my head full of conflicting emotions and the most inappropriate thought imaginable trying to force itself to the front of my mind. Edna Jellaby had spanked me, panties down and bare bottom, the way it ought to be done, and she had spanked me to teach me a lesson, as a genuine punishment. It was immensely arousing.

I knew full well what I'd end up doing if I went back to my room, but to avoid St George's meant avoiding Duncan, who would undoubtedly want to speak to me. He was going to be genuinely angry as well, although at least I didn't have to worry about being hauled up in front of the disciplinary committee and rusticated or even sent down. With luck he'd simply lecture me and then use the situation as an excuse to put me across his knee, to which he'd be very welcome.

When I got to college there was a note in my pigeonhole asking me to come and see him at two o'clock, more than four hours away. The wait was agony, with my feelings swinging wildly between genuine worry for what he might say and arousal at the thought of the predicament I'd put myself in, along with a jumble of other worries about Katie, the Owl, Tierney, Edna and a dozen more. By the time the college bells struck half past one I could wait no longer.

I went to Duncan's room, only to find that he wasn't there at all. I was forced to stand outside like a naughty schoolgirl waiting for admission to the headmistress's study, an image both terrifying and appealing. When he finally rolled up he took one look at me and laughed, which had me pushing my lower lip out in sulky resentment.

'You look quite the picture, Isabelle,' he chuckled, opening the door. 'Come in. Now, what's all this that old Peter Smith has been telling me?'

'It's all rather complicated,' I told him. 'But, basically, I lost my temper with Amy Jane, the girl we call the Owl. I spanked her.'

'Ah ha. And she is a candidate for the Rattaners, this Amy Jane?'

'No! Yes . . . in a sense. That's half the problem . . . well, part of it, anyway. As far as I know she's completely innocent, but she says she wants to join. You know who I mean, don't you? The small, rather round girl you've seen me around college with occasionally.'

'Absolutely, and your description of her as an owl is certainly apt, if rather unkind. Peter tells me you caught her in bed with Katie, which sounds less than entirely innocent, but I don't see why you were angry. I've always understood that you and Katie have an open relationship?'

'Yes. That wasn't why I spanked the Owl . . . Amy Jane . . . and I don't think she did anything with Katie.'

'So she's not even a lesbian? Not that it excuses your conduct. Good God, Isabelle, do you have any idea what the consequences would be if what we do became public knowledge? First you indulge yourselves in spanking games in the Bodleian Library, and now this!'

'I know . . . sorry. Anyway, this woman, Edna Jellaby, who's a scout at Foxson, came in and thought we were . . . were having spanking sex, so she did me – to teach me a lesson, she said.'

'A college scout spanked you? And is *she* a candidate for the Rattaners?'

'No, far from it, but you see . . . actually I'd rather not explain, if you don't mind, but I realise I shouldn't have done it . . .'

'I'm sorry, Isabelle, but I'm afraid you're going to have to explain. So, first you chose to spank some entirely innocent first-year, and while you were doing this a college scout entered the room and began to spank you in reprisal, as a genuine punishment rather than for pleasure? She must have had some reason to

168

do so, surely? College scouts are not normally in the habit of spanking students, after all.'

'Yes, in a sense,' I admitted miserably, and realised that I was going to have to tell him everything. 'The thing is ... is that last Saturday I was playing for a pub darts team in Bicester ...'

'A pub darts team in Bicester? This has something to do with Mr Tierney and the Red Ox, doesn't it?'

'Yes. Sorry.'

'Do go on.'

'He was there, and so was Edna Jellaby, who's in the team as well. They got me drunk ... no, I got myself drunk, mainly because my bike had been stolen so I had to go back in the minibus, and ... and Tierney took advantage of me ... sort of ... not at all really, but I ended up being very silly, and doing things ... and Edna didn't like it at all so I suggested she spank me, several times. Then she caught me with Katie and the Owl, and I think she wanted to teach me what a real spanking is like. That's all.'

Duncan was staring at me, apparently struck dumb by the enormity of my behaviour, which seemed a little unfair after all the Rattaners parties he'd attended.

'You know how it is,' I said weakly.

'I'm not at all sure that I do,' he replied, shaking his head. 'It is one thing to enjoy one's sexuality, Isabelle, and I trust that nobody could justifiably call me a prude, but there is such a thing as discretion. Oh dear, oh dear, what *is* to be done with you?'

Again he shook his head, as if in despair, but this time he turned to look out of the window, contemplating my fate. I waited a full minute before speaking.

'Couldn't you just spank me?'

'I *could*,' Duncan replied, 'and I am certainly tempted, if only to assuage my feelings. However, I cannot help but think that to do so would be somewhat akin to punishing a car thief by giving him the latest model from Mercedes-Benz. No, when it comes to your personal discipline I shall leave the matter to Eliza, who understands these things so much better than I.'

'Eliza? Surely it would be better not to tell Eliza?'

'On the contrary. This is not a matter that can simply be swept under the carpet, Isabelle. The incident occurred in Katie's room at Foxson, did it not?'

'The curtains were shut. Are you *sure* you don't want to spank me?'

'How many people do you suppose know about it?' Duncan demanded, ignoring my question.

'Nobody actually saw – at least, not when I was spanking the Owl, or when Edna did me, because she shut the door, but I suppose it was rather noisy, and there were a few people behind Dr Smith when he came in, and . . . look, Duncan, I really do think that a bare-bottom spanking would do me the world of good . . . oh, and speaking of bare-bottom, I was bare for Edna, and so was the Owl for me. A lot of people saw us go to Dr Smith's study.'

'Exactly. People who have since dispersed to laboratories, libraries, lecture theatres, tutorial groups and so on right across Oxford, each and every one of them with an excellent titbit of gossip to pass on. By this evening everybody from the Chancellor to the local dustmen will know, and doubtless the story will have been suitably embellished along the way. We can only pray that the tabloid press doesn't find out, although as they have no lurid pictures to go with the story I don't suppose they'd be all that interested. No, it is a serious matter, which must be discussed promptly, and discreetly, which would certainly make a change. Honestly, Isabelle, I really am appalled by your foolishness, and—'

Duncan broke off, shaking his head in exasperation. Then he spoke again.

'Actually, I *am* going to spank you. Come here.'

My stomach lurched at his words, delivered in such a commanding tone that it never even occurred to me to disobey – besides which I'd never needed it so badly. Duncan went to his settee and sat down, allowing me to drape myself across his lap. My skirt was pulled up and my tights and panties taken down for the second time that day, and for the second time not for the enjoyment of seeing my bare bottom – but for purely practical purposes, to humiliate me and ensure that my spanking really hurt. I was already sobbing, with the tears starting in my eyes even before he'd laid the first hard smack across my cheeks. But he'd only given me six when he stopped.

'It's just too noisy,' he said, 'and so are you. But there must be something . . .'

His voice trailed off. Then he suddenly hauled me up, keeping a firm hold of my hand. Without the least idea of what was going on, I allowed myself to be frogmarched into his bathroom.

'Bend over the bath,' he instructed. 'Or, if you prefer, the toilet.'

I chose the bath, bending into it with my bottom stuck out over the edge. My cheeks stung a little from the earlier slaps, and I felt off-balance emotionally. On the far side of the bath was a large wooden-handled bath brush, ideal for application to naughty girls' bottoms. I winced.

'I . . . I'll try not to be noisy,' I promised. 'But it might be best to make me take my knickers in my mouth.'

'I am not planning to spank you,' Duncan stated, opening his medicine cupboard.

'No?' I queried, surprised, and thought of what else could be done to bare-bottom girls. 'You're not going to fuck me, are you? Because . . .'

I trailed off, feeling distinctly aggrieved at the idea of being casually fucked. It was a bit much of him to simply assume that because I didn't mind a spanking he had access to my pussy.

'Hang on a minute,' I said. 'Duncan, I don't—'

'Do you agree that you deserve to be punished?' he demanded.

'Well . . . yes,' I admitted. 'I feel I ought to be spanked, but . . .'

'Spanking is noisy,' he reminded me. 'Impractically so. Now, hold your bottom cheeks apart. I am going to sodomise you.'

'What!? Duncan! I . . . but I don't *want* to be sodomised! OK, you can fuck me, but not up my bottom, please? That's hardly fair!'

Despite my words, which I believed I meant, I had reached back to spread my bum cheeks, just as I'd been told to do. Duncan had selected a tube of cream from the cupboard, some product intended for the relief of haemorrhoids.

'Are you sure that's the right thing to use?' I asked in alarm as he squeezed out a long white worm of the substance onto one finger. 'And really, I'm not at all sure you should be sodomising your students, and—'

'It is designed for application to the anus,' he pointed out, interrupting me, 'and no doubt will serve very well to lubricate yours.'

'Yes, but—'

I broke off with a gasp as Duncan wiped the cold haemorrhoid cream onto my bottom-hole. Then I gulped as a finger was pushed up my rectum. He had put his other hand to his crotch, massaging his cock through his trousers, but I still couldn't believe he was simply going to bugger me while I was bent over the bath, and without so much as a may-I? Yet I kept my bum cheeks spread as he lubricated my bottom. I was panting slightly as my anus slowly grew loose, not particularly happy about what he was about to do but unable to think of any good reason why he shouldn't. After all, I wasn't supposed to like it.

'If you wouldn't mind?' he asked. 'Take me in your mouth.'

Duncan had flopped his cock out, and I obeyed his instruction, turning a little to open wide and let him feed it in, all the while with his finger working my bumhole gradually more open. His cock was thick, heavy in my mouth even when flaccid, and as I began to suck I was telling myself that it was best to relax and let him get my anus properly open, and that there was no point in protesting when I was going to be buggered anyway.

'More cream, perhaps,' he remarked, and squeezed out a second worm, this time directly between my cheeks so that he could work it into my already slippery anus with the finger he'd already got dirty.

Duncan's cock had began to grow in my mouth, stiffening gradually to the motion of my lips and tongue, a strange sensation that I'm sure I'll never get fully used to. I gasped as a second finger was eased into my bottom, but I already felt juicy and slack, if not sufficiently to accommodate the fat penis swelling in my mouth.

'I do not intend to hurt you, Isabelle,' he said, now slightly breathless. 'But am I right to expect that sodomising a girl can make an effective punishment?'

'Yes, it can, believe me!' I told him as he pulled his now-rigid cock from my mouth.

Duncan was right. Even if it didn't hurt, the idea of being made to take a man's cock up my bottom was unspeakably humiliating, especially after being bent over a bath and having my anus lubricated with haemorrhoid cream. It was hard to imagine a more disrespectful way to treat a dominant woman – the only trouble being that after being passed around for spanking and then surrendering myself to Tierney and his cronies it wasn't at all easy to think of myself as a dominant woman. I was more like an eager little slut. Even so, being bent over the bath and fucked up my bottom was a pretty humiliating prospect.

'Keep your cheeks open,' Duncan ordered as he finally eased his fingers from my bumhole. 'Well open.'

I gave a single dumb nod and pulled my bottom cheeks apart wider still, stretching my now gaping anus wide to his view. He reached into the medicine cupboard once more, this time to pull out an old-fashioned gentleman's shaving brush with a rounded ivory handle that looked uncomfortably suitable for ramming up a girl's bottom-hole to keep it open. Obviously it was going up mine.

'You'll need to have this in you for a while,' he told me, and pushed the cold hard end against my anus.

My ring spread, accommodating the brush handle quite easily and leaving me with a tuft of badger hair sticking out from my gaping bottom hole. Duncan sat down on the toilet, puffing as he masturbated, with his eyes fixed on my penetrated anus and distinctly juicy pussy, then flicking to my face. I knew that my expression would be full of consternation at the prospect of being buggered, because I felt thoroughly put upon, but that didn't seem to bother him. What he was going to do to me might be intended as a punishment but it was obviously one he was going to enjoy dishing out.

Duncan's cock-shaft was finally hard, and he was pulling vigorously at it. His prick was still glossy with my spit, while his heavy balls were bouncing and squashing against his trousers with every tug. I forced a smile, realising that I really was going to be buggered as he stood up with his erection in his hand. He was still masturbating as he pulled the shaving brush from my bottom-hole and placed it carefully in the sink. I stayed open as it came out, my anus squashy and wet as his helmet touched between my cheeks, plugging my rectal ring.

'Do you have to do this?' I asked apprehensively as my bottom-hole began to spread out around his helmet. 'Really?'

'Your question,' he grunted, 'rather presupposes my answer.'

Duncan pushed. I gasped as my anal sphincter gave way and then his cock was up my bum, or at least its head was. I could feel it in my bottom-hole, bigger than the handle of the shaving brush and also warm, stretching me wide. I was now officially being sodomised. Not that Duncan had finished, not by a long way. I was still holding my cheeks open, allowing him to see what he was doing as he fed himself in up my anal hole. The sensation had me panting in no time, unable to control my breathing as the bloated, urgent sensation in my rectum grew. But that feeling was merely physical, and was as nothing compared with my emotions.

I had a man's cock up my bottom. My anus had been penetrated and my rectum filled with six inches or more of fat, hard penis. It was unbearably humiliating, and I was soon sobbing with reaction. It was a punishment, there was no doubt about it, to have my panties pulled down and my bottom stuffed with cock by my own tutor, about the only male authority figure I had. He was the man to do it, to sodomise me in fair retribution for my behaviour, to make me show my bumhole and put his cock inside it, to bugger me hard and make me thoroughly sorry for what I'd done.

'There,' he said. 'Now I am fully in you.'

He was: his balls were pressed to the mouth of my empty cunt, my bum cheeks spread against the front of his thighs and the mass of his belly. I braced myself, holding on to the bath so that he could push up me properly, my feet set wide and my hands clutching the far side. Slow, heavy tears were trickling down my face as he began to move his thick, stiff shaft in my rectum, long, easy thrusts that felt so deep that it seemed his cock would soon be poking out of my mouth. I hung my head, not to hide my weeping, but in abject surrender, and as the spittle began to run from my open mouth I didn't even bother to suck it back up.

I knew that Duncan never hurried, and as my rectal ring pulled gently in and out against his erection I let my mind drift to what I'd done, and what was being done to me in order to make up for my behaviour. It was completely appropriate, a punishment to fit the crime, and I was soon wishing that Amy Jane had been there to watch Duncan work his penis in my hole and see the tears trickling down my cheeks, Edna too, and Eliza, so that they could have taken turns spanking my naughty bottom before I was sodomised in front of them.

That thought stayed in my head, and in a few short moments my awful shame and consternation had begun to give way to pleasure. I bit my lip, knowing that it would be the final surrender if I masturbated while I was being buggered to punish me. But I couldn't stop myself. My hand went back and I found my cunt, touching my empty pussy-hole, then the taut ring of my anus to feel it pull and push against Duncan's shaft, an overwhelmingly dirty sensation.

I started to rub, sobbing with emotion as I masturbated and thinking of how I should really have been dealt with, smacked hard by Amy Jane and Edna, Katie too, and then Eliza. They'd have taken my panties down, and would have made me pull them up again between spankings, except after Eliza had done me when they'd be left down so that Duncan could grease my bottom-hole and sodomise me in front of all four of them. After that I'd be sent up to bed with my hands tied behind my back as I had been before, to cry my eyes out into my pillow while the spunk leaked from my buggered bottom-hole.

My anus began to tighten around Duncan's cock-shaft, contracting hard as my orgasm rose up. My pussy constricted too, blowing out air in a long rasping fanny fart that sent a last shudder of embarrassment through me – and then I was coming. I bit my lip, desperate to stop myself screaming. This seemed to bottle up the power of my climax inside me, bringing my orgasm up to a painful intensity until at last it burst. Duncan clapped a hand over my mouth as the scream broke from my lips, muffling the noise, but only partially.

He grunted and I assumed he'd come through the contractions of my anus, bringing my pleasure up to a second peak at the thought of having a man ejaculate up my bottom as part of a punishment. His hand locked tighter on my mouth as a second scream rose up in my throat, but this time he managed to keep me quiet and his hand stayed firmly in place as I came down slowly from my orgasm. Only when I was completely finished did I realise that his grunt had not been ecstasy but annoyance, and that he was panting for breath.

'I have to sit down,' he gasped, and I felt his cock start to pull away from my bottom hole.

I turned around in concern as Duncan pulled out. His hands were shaking and he was red in the face, but his cock was still hard, rearing up above his balls in the opening of his flies, sticky and glistening. I shrugged and smiled, more concerned for him than for myself even though my legs felt weak and my bumhole wouldn't close.

'Must you always be so noisy?' he managed to mutter, shaking his head as he sat down on the toilet seat.

'Sorry,' I replied, 'but I expect I'll be walking around like a pregnant duck for the next few days – if that's any consolation.'

Duncan managed a grin and leant back against the cistern. Then he spoke again.

'I did actually intend that to be a punishment.'

'It was,' I assured him, 'and I feel much better for it. But if you don't think that was enough, how about this?'

As I spoke I got down on my knees in front of the toilet, so that his cock was rearing up in front of my face. I hesitated, but then nodded to myself. It was best to get it over and done with, I thought, and before common sense could get the better of me I'd taken his slippery cock in my mouth, determined to suck until he came. Then I would swallow.

Eight

'I would like to propose Amy Jane Moffat for membership.'

Every single person in the room turned to look at me. Portia finally broke the silence.

'Very funny, Isabelle. Ha, ha.'

'I'm serious,' I insisted. 'She guessed more or less what goes on, and she wants to be considered for membership.'

'You mean you told her about us?' Portia demanded.

'No,' I said firmly. 'Well, not exactly . . . anyway, I've been punished for that already.'

'Oh no, you haven't,' Portia assured me gleefully. 'That's a spanking from each of us and six of the cane – again!'

'Not here,' Eliza said firmly.

We'd decided to meet in her room at the biology labs, where it was safe to talk. On a Saturday afternoon, with no students about, it would probably also have been a safe place to spank. But Eliza had ruled against it, a decision for which I was now immensely grateful.

'At the party, then,' Portia said.

I shrugged. Given what was likely to happen to me at the party a quick session across their knees and six cane strokes would be a useful warm-up.

'Isabelle,' Eliza went on, 'do you really think Amy Jane is suitable Rattaners material?'

'The Owl!' Tiffany laughed. 'Hardly.'

'Not really, no,' I admitted. 'And she doesn't know what we get up to, unlike Tiffy before she was accepted, Portia. She thinks we're a lesbian society whose members like to dress up, that's all. I think she should be vetted, but tactfully, maybe just hinting at mild corporal punishment – an initiation ceremony perhaps. That way she herself can make the decision not to join. Obviously I can't be involved in vetting her, and nor can Katie.'

'I'll spank her fat arse for her,' Portia offered. 'I bet she'd run a mile!'

'I don't think you're really the person for the job,' Sarah responded. 'I'll do it.'

'She has a thing about her weight,' I pointed out, 'so I suggest Caroline goes too.'

'Thank you very much, Isabelle!' Caroline retorted. 'You wait.'

'I didn't mean to be nasty,' I said quickly, 'and you know I don't think you're overweight, or the Owl . . . Amy Jane either for that matter. It's just that—'

'I understand,' Caroline interrupted, 'and I intend to take it out on you at the party. Isabelle is being punished, isn't she?'

'That depends on whether we have a party,' Eliza responded. 'After what happened at Foxson, I'm not at all sure that it would be advisable.'

'You're not suggesting that we disband the society, are you?' I asked in dismay.

'No,' she replied, 'just that we have little choice but to cancel the Christmas party. The story of your little adventure at Foxson has been doing the rounds all week, Isabelle, although fortunately it's only been seen as a lovers' tiff, while Mrs Jellaby's intervention is considered more amusing than anything.'

I found myself blushing at the suggestion that people thought of me being given a public spanking as amusing. But I answered Eliza quickly.

'Surely Dr Treadle's house will be safe?'

'Isadore is concerned that newspaper reporters may get hold of the story and follow you, or Katie,' Eliza told me. 'That may seem over-cautious, but the lower elements of the national press seem particularly keen to paint Oxford as elitist at present, and I dare say a story involving college girls spanking each other would be just the sort of thing they're after. In any event, Isadore has asked that we suspend parties at his house for the time being.'

'I'm sorry,' I said.

'You will be, I assure you,' Sarah replied. 'But Eliza, surely we only need a venue a safe distance from Oxford?'

'Such as?' Eliza queried. 'We can hardly hire a room as if we were having a birthday party.'

'Why not?' Caroline asked. 'Nobody outside Oxford will know who any of us are.'

'Because,' Eliza pointed out, 'there will be staff, who will be sure to wonder about the peculiar noises.'

'All we need are open-minded staff,' Caroline insisted. 'We could have it at the Red Ox, at least if it was held during the week.'

'I am *not* having a Rattaners party at the Red Ox,' Sarah stated emphatically. 'That ghastly man Tierney and his friends would expect to join in.'

'My father would be sure to find out,' Yazzie put in.

'Besides,' Eliza added, 'Cowley is part of Oxford. My suggestion is this. If any of us can find a suitable venue, then we will go ahead. Otherwise we'll have our next meeting in the Hilary Term once everybody has forgotten about Isabelle's little indiscretion. Shall we vote?'

She had raised her own hand, and the others followed suit more or less reluctantly. I voted last of all.

I felt empty, and extremely cross with myself. Thanks to my hot temper and stupidity there would be no Christmas party, and if that meant I would be able to avoid another punishment it was no consolation at all. Besides, I *deserved* another punishment, as the buggering that Duncan had given me didn't make up for one-tenth of my offences.

Somehow I needed to make things right, but obviously the best thing to do was to keep quiet and make sure that I didn't draw attention to myself. I didn't believe for a moment that there were paparazzi scouring the streets of Oxford for the chance of a shot of me with my knickers down – or, rather, with another girl's knickers down – but I could understand Dr Treadle's caution, and Eliza's.

For the next few days I spent most of my time mulling over the situation. But it seemed intractable, and for once I found it impossible to concentrate on my work. I did so badly at Collections that Duncan called me into his room, not for a spanking but to offer me sympathy and advice, which was far worse. The following day I was wandering aimlessly around college when Tierney appeared, popping out from the bottom of a stairwell like a small ugly genie.

'Hello, Isa – been keeping the old fiddlers in trim?' he greeted me, wiggling his fingers at me meaningfully.

It took me a moment to realise that he was referring to the darts match on Saturday and was not asking me if I'd been masturbating regularly. I'd decided to go, under pressure from Yazzie and Caroline, who were stripping that evening, and because I'd been assured that Edna Jellaby was refusing to have anything to do with the darts team after the minibus incident. He spoke again before I could find a suitable answer.

'I hear you've got venue problems?'

'How did you know that!?' I demanded, without even thinking of denying what was the truth.

Tierney merely tapped the side of his nose. Then he went on.

'Osman's the bloke you want. He's well into you, and all. Posh and dirty, he says.'

'Why should he think that?' I asked, although I could guess. 'You told him, didn't you, about what happened in the minibus?'

'No. The Jellabys went into the Boar, didn't they?' he explained. 'When they fetched your bike.'

'Edna?' I asked, as the blood started to rise to my face. 'What did she tell him?'

'Oh, how you were a right little tart and all that,' Tierney said casually. 'You know what she's like.'

I was wondering which was worse: to have Tierney give a no doubt frank account of my behaviour or to have Edna painting me as a slut. It was hard to choose.

'That was very kind of them, anyway,' I said, 'especially in the circumstances.'

'Nah,' Tierney said. 'She'd left her arrows there, that's all.'

'Oh. And was my bike really chained to a different lamp-post?'

'Nah, don't be daft, girl. Jack went out and nicked it while I was making sure you got plenty of whisky inside you.'

'You bastard!'

'It was the only way we could think of to get you out of your knickers,' he replied, as if it was a perfectly reasonable thing to have done.

'You ... you utter *pig*!' I snapped. 'You're unspeakable, Tierney, you really are!'

'Come on, love,' he urged. 'You know you love it, and a little cutie like you, you're bound to get the boys trying it on a bit, ain't you? Anyway, we gave you your bike back, didn't we? You want to get a proper chain, you do, one of those hardened-steel jobs. I know this bloke who ...'

He carried on, but I wasn't listening. I was appalled by his behaviour, although it was exactly what I'd have expected of him. Worse, he'd succeeded, and to add extra humiliation I'd been as willing as they were eager once they'd got me in the minibus. Even more annoying was the fact that while the sudden appearance of my bike at Foxson had led to me spanking Amy Jane and to my current predicament, I couldn't blame Tierney – or at least, not directly. Yet indirectly his actions had led to me being spanked, sodomised and very nearly sent down, while I still had my punishment from the Rattaners to come.

'... But anyhow,' he was saying, 'Osman, he's got a restaurant, he has, fancy Turkish place.'

'Bastard, utter bastard!' I hissed, my mind still obsessed with how he'd used me.

'What's wrong with having a Turkish restaurant?' Tierney asked.

'Not Osman! You!' I spat back.

He merely shrugged, then spoke again.

'So what? Do you want me to have a word with him or not?'

I closed my eyes, struggling to bring my temper under control. The offer of a venue was too good to be dismissed out of hand, whoever it came from, although Osman's place didn't sound particularly suitable.

'Where is it?' I asked. 'In the middle of Bicester?'

'No, outside,' Tierney said. 'Place used to be a barn. Really swish it is, nice and out of the way, plenty of parking. Just the place to get down to some good dirty fun and games. The ladies' loo is like something out of a fucking palace.'

'What would it cost? And how about staff?' I asked, not wanting to know how he knew what the ladies' conveniences were like.

'You'd have to talk to Osman about all that. Me, I just want to be there, that's all I ask.'

If there was one thing I was absolutely determined on, it was that Tierney would not be coming to the Rattaners Christmas party. I wanted him to know about it. I wanted him to know he was excluded. I wanted him to hear every single juicy detail of what happened. But I did *not* want him there.

I decided to approach Osman after the darts match and do my best to charm him into allowing us to have exclusive use of his restaurant at the beginning of Ninth Week, when we'd be able to have the party on a Monday or Tuesday without having to worry about work. As he'd been told what I'd done in the minibus it seemed inevitable that he'd demand sex, although there had to be at least a faint possibility that he was a gentleman. In any event he would have to be there.

There was another matter that needed to be resolved. Somebody was passing Tierney information, but it couldn't possibly be Amy Jane. Only the nine of us knew that we needed a new venue, or ten if Dr Treadle himself was included. Treadle could safely be eliminated from suspicion anyway, and so could Eliza and Katie. Among the others, Sarah's attitude to Tierney was as if he was something nasty that she'd found on the bottom of her shoe, so it was unlikely to be her. But otherwise it was impossible to decide. Jasmine and Caroline knew him well, but they had always been loyal to me. Portia's attitude was much like my own, a mixture of distaste and self-disgusted fascination, and where Portia led, Tiffany followed. Yazzie was an unknown quantity. None of them had anything to gain except to humble and degrade me, which left the finger of suspicion pointed firmly at Portia.

Accusing her would be pointless. I needed proof, and preferably something that I could bring out at the party, which would enable me to have her punished with a vengeance. First, I had to make sure there was a party. On the Saturday I dressed in a manner that I hoped Osman would find alluring: low-cut white jeans with the top of a pair of scarlet thong panties showing at the back, a turquoise-blue skinny top to leave my tummy showing, lipstick-red high heels and no bra. I felt like a slut, and was extremely glad of my long coat and the darkness of the evening as I slipped out of college.

The streets were wet and there was a lot of traffic, making the bike ride up to Cowley extremely unpleasant. By the time I got to the Red Ox even the hot smoky interior seemed welcoming, provoking memories of the night at the Boar and how I'd ended up then. I ordered an orange juice instead of whisky and took a nervous glance around the room, hoping not to find Edna there. She wasn't, and with very few exceptions there were only men present. I remembered it was also striptease night just as Caroline emerged from the tiny back room where the girls got changed. She was in her khaki military gear, her crop top straining across her braless breasts and her shorts so tight over her bottom that the seam had begun to give way. I knew that she and Sarah were supposed

186

to have seen the Owl that afternoon, and I went straight over to her.

'Hello, Caroline. Did you manage to scare Amy Jane away?'

'Er . . . no, not really.'

'What do you mean, "not really"?'

'Newton bumped Keble on the river this afternoon . . .'

'What's that got to do with it?'

'Let me explain. All the rowing crews had come back from the river, and they'd been drinking, and they'd got hold of one of Amy Jane's bras and hung it from a tower with a bowling ball in each cup. She was really upset, and so Sarah went and got the captain of the rowing club. She brought him down from his room holding him by the ear, and she made him apologise to Amy Jane and get it down.'

'Good for Sarah. But I don't see why—'

'Because now Amy Jane thinks that the sun shines out of Sarah's bumhole, that's why. The way she was going on, anybody would think that being a lesbian catering manager should be every woman's ultimate goal. Sarah tried to explain about the Rattaners without giving too much away, but Amy Jane just soaked it all up. She says she wants to come to a party, and that she's open-minded about sex.'

'She'd better be!'

'So in the end Sarah and I decided to leave it open and see what happens next term. After all, Amy Jane may have found herself a boyfriend by then, or more likely a girlfriend after the way she was behaving this afternoon.'

'That's all very well, but if things go to plan I'm hoping there'll be a Christmas party after all. There's a Turkish restaurateur called Osman . . .'

I explained what I was hoping to do, as Caroline alternately nodded and bit her lip. She was the perfect ally and accepted all my suggestions, even promising to help me out if it came down to having to suck cock. I wasn't too happy about the situation with Amy Jane, but it was extremely reassuring to have Caroline with me, so when Mike told me that the darts team's drinks were on the house I decided to have a whisky after all.

A girl I didn't know had come out onto the stage. She was wearing heels, long black and white striped socks, a pair of little black panties and a top hat, nothing more. The music had become so loud that I couldn't hear myself speak, so Caroline and I turned to watch her performance, which involved a lot of posing with a silver-topped cane and her hat. It was a little refined for the Red Ox, who were soon yelling for her knickers to come off. She declined to oblige, leaving the stage with a saucy wiggle of her bottom that left me chuckling with amusement and the men thumping their tables and demanding Caroline.

She went up and gave them her military routine, a piece of sexy slapstick that had them roaring with laughter and encouragement as it grew gradually ruder. By the end she was crawling around the floor with her shorts around her thighs and her top pulled up, with every detail of her body on display. Every man in the room was giving Caroline their full attention, most of them with expressions of stupefied lechery on their faces. But I didn't realise that I'd been staring as hard as any of them until Tierney tapped me on the shoulder.

'If you've finished ogling your mate's arse, Isa, we need to figure out who's playing who in the darts.'

'Er . . . yes, of course,' I replied. Before following him I stole a last glance to where Caroline had begun to spank her own bottom to the delight of the crowd.

The Boar had sent the same team that we'd played in Bicester: Osman himself, the skinny old man, Eddy, the balding woman, Lil, a plumber called John and his wife Maureen. As they saw me there was an immediate exchange of glances and whispers, leaving me blushing to the roots of my hair for what they were almost certainly talking about. Edna, I was sure, had spared no detail and no opportunity to describe my delinquency.

We had changed only a little, with Yazzie in place of Edna, Tierney, Jack, Choker and myself. Yazzie was going to be stripping after the match, and was already in her costume, an abbreviated silk dress that left her panties showing at the back and gave the overall impression of a Japanese *hentai* cartoon. As John the plumber approached he glanced from her to me and back, then spoke to Jack, laughing.

'If you reckon you're going to beat us by dressing up your tarts you've got another think coming.'

I bit down my immediate flush of irritation and forced a smile.

'They always dress like that, those two,' Jack answered. 'If we needed to get one up on you we'd have 'em doing it in the nude. But we don't, do we?'

'We'll see about that,' John answered. 'It was a fluke, last time.'

Jack merely laughed. My skin was burning right down to my chest as they began to discuss the game, and I was earnestly wishing that I'd worn something a little more modest. I was chosen to play against Maureen, as the first pair, but what with one thing and another I played appallingly and lost. Not that it made much difference to the result. Yazzie managed to beat Lil, but both Tierney and Choker lost, leaving the match already decided against us before Osman disposed of Jack with ease.

I wasn't particularly bothered, and Osman was full of himself, which I knew would be to my advantage. The Red Ox was now packed, and a third girl was on the stage, doing an energetic striptease to music that was even louder than before. But I managed to attract Osman's attention by using sign language. He nodded, turned back long enough to watch the girl wiggle her bottom out of a pair of tiny green panties, then began to push his way towards me through the crowd. I'd lost Caroline, but she was only really needed if things threatened to get sticky.

'Can I have a word!' I yelled, gesturing to the door.

Osman gave me a thumbs-up sign and began to plough through the crowd, using the mass of his body to clear a path with me following him. Outside, which had seemed cold and dank before, was now blessedly cool.

'What's up?' he asked.

'I don't know if Stan Tierney has said anything to you,' I told him, 'but I was hoping it might be possible to hire your restaurant on a Monday night in a couple of weeks, or maybe on a Tuesday.'

'Could be,' Osman said, with a knowing grin. 'Some sort of swingers' club, isn't it?'

'Yes,' I answered, not wishing to go into details. 'So we'd need privacy, although I'm assuming you'd want to be there yourself.'

His grin grew broader and dirtier.

'How much is it?' I asked.

'Twelve hundred,' he said, and my heart sank. 'But I'll call it a grand, just for you.'

'I'm sorry,' I told him. 'A lot of us are students, so we couldn't possibly afford that much. Couldn't we come to some kind of arrangement?'

I was effectively offering to prostitute myself, and I knew that I was blushing with shame even as I spoke. Osman didn't seem to realise.

'What if we say eight hundred?' he suggested.

I shrugged, wondering if it was worth bringing the offer to the others. Duncan and Dr Treadle could presumably afford to make a contribution, also Eliza and perhaps Sarah, while Portia and Tiffany presumably had well-to-do parents and so might or might not be able to contribute. The real drawback was that I could guarantee that Sarah would seek to take advantage of the situation by suggesting that those who hadn't put anything in should pay in kind. That would mean myself and Katie.

'Possibly,' I admitted. 'But ... but you like to gamble, so how about a game of darts, and if I can beat you we can use your restaurant for nothing?'

'And if I win?'

'Perhaps a private show from me and Caroline?' I offered. 'Caroline's the girl in the army outfit. She was stripping earlier.'

'The one with the gigantic tits?'

'Yes.'

'Fuck me,' Osman said thoughtfully. 'She in your club, is she? And you two will do ... what? A double strip, or get good and dirty together?'

'Whatever you like,' I offered.

'Jesus,' he breathed. 'Stan said you would be up for a bit, but lezzie stuff ...'

He trailed off, no doubt imagining me and Caroline together and thinking how much better he was at darts than me.

'You've got a deal,' he said. 'What d'you want to play, five-oh-one?'

'I have a better game,' I suggested, quickly running through the details of the game I'd invented for the Rattaners in my head. 'We take turns to call out a number, anything you can get with a single dart, and the other player has three darts and ten seconds to score that number. The catch is, you don't just say five or twenty, you say, for example, ten plus ten, which makes the number twenty. The best out of five is the winner. That's five goes each.'

'Yeah, all right,' he agreed. 'Only to give it a bit of spice, how about every time you don't make it you have to take a piece of clothing off, and every time I don't I have to put a twenty in the kitty, which you get at the end.'

'In the middle of the pub!?' I demanded before I could even think to refuse.

'Why not? Striptease night, innit? Nobody says the girls have to be on the stage.'

I was about to refuse anyway. But I hesitated. To end up naked I'd have to fail every time, and he was right about the stripping. Better still, with Yazzie on stage nobody was going to take any notice of me if I was barefoot, while he obviously hadn't seen the catch. All that mattered was that I'd be better at mental arithmetic than a Turkish restaurateur, just as I knew I was better than Sarah.

'OK,' I agreed and turned back for the pub.

The board was vacant because everybody was watching Yazzie, so we drew only the occasional curious glance as we tossed a coin for who would go first. I won, and stepped up to the line.

'Oh yeah, shoes count as one article,' he said.

'No, two,' I objected.

'No way,' he told me. 'Not when you play strip. Stan'll tell you. Hey . . .'

'No, no, no,' I said hastily as he turned to look for Tierney, who was lost among the crowd of ogling men. 'OK, shoes count as one article.'

I did not want Tierney to know what we were doing, as he would inevitably ask the reason for the game and broadcast it to the entire pub. Having to spend a few minutes barefoot, or even in just my knickers and top, was a risk I was well prepared to take, especially as Yazzie now had every single male pair of eyes in the pub firmly riveted on the way her now-bare bottom stuck out from beneath the hem of her shortened kimono.

'Ten plus nine,' Osman said.

I managed to get the nineteen with my second dart, allowing me to chalk up a victory. Osman took his place and I glanced at my wristwatch.

'The square root of eighty-one.'

He looked blank, then bit his moustache as he struggled to think of the answer, or perhaps even to remember what a square root was. I began to count the seconds down, and had got to four before he spoke.

'Nine, ain't it?'

As he spoke he threw, hitting the twelve twice before successfully sinking a dart into the right bed.

'You sneaky cow,' he told me as he marked up his success.

I was going to have to try harder, but the principle worked.

'Hang on,' Osman said as I took my place. 'OK, got it. Three times thirteen.'

I threw immediately, missed by a whisker, hit the triple four, and the wire. Osman was laughing as I kicked my shoes off. But if he could be awkward, so could I.

'Two hundred and thirty-eight divided by seven,' I told him as we exchanged places,.

'Fuck me . . . um . . . shit . . .'

'Thirty-four, of course,' a small voice said from behind me.

'Thanks, love,' Osman said. I spun round to find the Owl peering up at me from behind her huge round glasses as she sipped at an orange juice.

'What are *you* doing here!?' I demanded.

'Carrie said it would be OK,' she answered.

'Nice shot, Os,' Tierney remarked as Yazzie's striptease music faded. 'What are you two playing?'

I nearly twisted my neck off trying to look three ways at once. Osman had hit the double seventeen with unerring accuracy, and had begun to speak before I could think of any way to stop him.

'This game she made up, clever it is, and if she wins she gets to use the Golden Chalice for her swingers club. But if I win she and little Carrie with the tits have got to give me a lezzie show. Your go, Isa. What's the matter?'

I'd buried my face in my hands. Amy Jane had heard every word that Osman had said, and was staring at me as if I'd just suggested cannibalism. Because the music had stopped at that instant about a dozen other people had also heard, including Big Dave, Jack and Mo, who had at least seemed to have had the decency not to watch Yazzie. Unfortunately, whatever I said could only make the situation yet more embarrassing, even if that was rather hard to imagine.

'Come on, love, up to the oche,' Osman urged, totally unaware of what he'd done.

A good twenty people were now watching us. I stepped up, feeling numb, barely heard his demand for three seventeens, miscalculated and wasted valuable seconds trying to find a way of scoring fifty-three, then missed anyway.

'Bad luck,' Amy Jane said.

I closed my eyes, fighting back the temptation to strangle her, or spank her again. It now seemed likely that I'd lose, and end up having to entertain Osman without getting the restaurant – either that or pay. I also had to remove an article of clothing, either my

194

top or my jeans, and as I had no bra and was wearing only a miniscule pair of thong panties underneath my outer garments it was not an easy choice.

'What's it to be, Isa?' Osman laughed. 'Tits or arse?'

'You playing strip?' Tierney demanded. 'Nice.'

'Do you have to undress, Isabelle?' Amy Jane asked.

'Yes,' I snapped as I decided it was better to go down to my panties than go topless. 'And could you not tell him the answer this time, please?'

'Sorry,' she answered. 'But . . . but are you really going to . . . strip off, and, you know, with Carrie, in front of him?'

'Probably yes, thanks to you,' I told her as I pushed down my jeans.

She didn't answer, but the look of utter horror in her magnified eyes told me all I needed to know. Osman was waiting, and he watched closely as I tugged my jeans off, trying to think of a good sum despite my embarrassment. Somebody had once told me that the triple eleven was the hardest bed to hit on a dartboard. I made a frantic calculation.

'Um . . . the square root of . . . of one thousand and ninety-nine.'

'You what?' Osman demanded.

'The square root of one thousand and ninety-nine,' I insisted. 'And don't you say a word, Amy Jane.'

'I wasn't going to, but . . .'

'Shut up! Right, that's ten seconds gone.'

'But . . .' Amy Jane demanded. 'But how's he supposed to score thirty-three point one . . . five . . . sorry, that's as close as I can get off the top of my head.'

'He's supposed to score thirty-three,' I said. 'Triple eleven.'

195

'That would be the square root of one thousand and *eighty*-nine,' she said.

'Tits out, Isabelle!' Tierney laughed.

'No,' I pointed out. 'That round doesn't count, that's all . . .'

'Yes, it does,' Osman insisted. 'What do you reckon, boys?'

Inevitably they agreed with him, but I insisted on keeping my top on. I was shaking badly as I stepped up once more, and acutely aware that I was showing my panties – although my embarrassment was more because of the Owl than the men.

'Five fives,' Osman said.

It took me maybe a second to remember that twenty-five was the value of the outer bullseye. I forced myself to throw carefully and managed to get the third dart on target, producing a groan of disappointment from the watching men. With two victories I could still win – just.

'This one for the match,' Osman said, stepping forward. 'What's it to be?'

'The cube root of eighty-one,' I demanded.

'I know that one,' he said, 'I had to write it out a hundred times when I was a nipper.'

He'd thrown as he spoke, and not only hit the three but managed to do the same with his remaining darts. With four successes, when I could only hope to manage three in total, he had won. At least I wasn't going to have to strip in front of the Owl.

'Tell you what,' he said. 'Let's go another round, same deal, only . . .'

He leant close as he continued, his moustache tickling my face.

' . . . I get to fuck Carrie's tits while you blow me.'

'No,' I answered immediately.

'All right,' he went on. 'Same deal, but you're

up on your own and you have to win two out of three.'

I made to refuse, but hesitated. The odds were against me, but not by very much.

'No triples or doubles?' I suggested. 'Or the bullseye.'

'OK,' he offered. 'If you take your top off.'

'Good on you, Os,' Tierney said.

'Yeah, get her stripped down,' somebody else added.

I bit my lip, unable to meet Amy Jane's gaze as my fingers went to the hem of my skinny top. All I had to do was tug it up and off to be almost completely sure of winning, and I was trying to tell myself that it was ridiculously stuck-up of me to mind going in just my panties when two of my friends had just stripped naked on stage. I'd done the same myself as well, but never under the gaze of an innocent first-year who was no doubt wondering how I could behave like a complete slut and a whore. My nerve failed me and I shook my head.

'Aw, come on, Isa!' Big Dave urged. 'Tell you what, here's ten just to play.'

Tierney immediately offered up five pounds, and Jack twenty, with other men joining in until there was a pile of money on the table easily sufficient to cover my share of the restaurant hire and Katie's as well. I still had to play to get it, but I had to go with Caroline in front of Osman anyway, and Amy Jane knew. Still I hesitated, glancing at her to find that she looked more like an owl than ever, only a stuffed one.

'Oh, to hell with it!' I swore, and peeled off my top.

The men all started to clap as I retrieved the darts from the board. I'd seldom felt more embarrassed but it was impossible not to react to so much attention, especially when more people were now looking at me than at the strippers.

'Eight and one and one and one,' Osman said, as fast as he could.

I'd launched a dart at the nine before he'd even finished, but missed wildly, sinking it into the eleven and cursing before I even realised I'd actually succeeded.

'Well done,' Amy Jane said.

Her voice was breathless with fear and excitement, but there was none of the disapproval that I'd have expected. I managed a smile for her, realising that her fear was for me. Just one more success and I would not only have won but would come away with well over a hundred pounds. I fetched the darts, determined to succeed. Osman was having a whispered conversation with Mike at the bar, but he started back as I put my toes to the line.

'Cube root of three four three,' he said.

Even as he spoke I felt myself start to panic. I opened my mouth to protest, but the calculation was no harder than those I'd given him and we'd said nothing about getting help. That wasted maybe two seconds before I began to make desperate calculations.

'It's seven, Isabelle!' Amy Jane squeaked.

I threw, far too hard, hitting the wire and sending the dart back at me, so that I was forced to jump aside. Tierney swore and I felt cold lager splash my naked back and bottom, making me jump. I threw again, hit the three, and was just trying to take aim when Osman called out the ten seconds.

'Knickers off, Isabelle!' the men chorused – all except Tierney, who was trying to fish my dart out of his pint.

'Knickers off,' Osman said firmly as I opened my mouth to protest that we hadn't said anything about my strip carrying on.

'Knickers off!' Big Dave echoed. 'Knickers off!'

The other men took up the chant, and despite myself I found my thumbs going to the waistband of my skimpy panties. Amy Jane looked terrified, and I didn't blame her, with twenty or more large rough men baying for me to go naked while she was now the only woman in the pub with all her clothes still on.

'OK, OK,' I said quickly, and pushed down my thong, drawing an immediate cheer from the men as my pussy came on show and my bum was fully bared.

I kicked my panties off and then I was standing stark naked in a half-circle of drunken lecherous men. Yet my nipples were hard and I was shamefully sticky between my thighs; already I could feel my resistance slipping. But I knew that given what looked likely to happen to me it was probably just as well. I knew I could cope as well, if I had to, and so could Caroline, but I was equally sure that Amy Jane couldn't. Osman was grinning at me, quite happy to let me take my time now that I was in the nude, while Big Dave was by the window. I signalled to both of them, speaking in an undertone as they approached.

'You can take me in the back afterwards,' I offered, 'even if I win. But promise me you'll take care of my friend. Nobody's to touch her.'

'You got it,' Dave promised and Osman gave a solemn nod.

As I took up the darts again I was trying to tell myself that I should be cursing the Owl for what I was going to have to put up with for her sake. But it wouldn't wash. I'd sacrificed myself, but willingly, and the only resentment I felt was for my own dirty reaction.

'Ready?' Osman demanded, and I nodded. 'What year was the Turkish Grand National Assembly first formed? Like, just the last two figures.'

I laughed at him.

'I'm reading history,' I said. 'Nineteen-twenty, so . . .'

I took careful aim at the top of the board, showing off by aiming for the triple, and sank the dart dead in the bed's centre. Suddenly being stark naked in a rough townie pub no longer mattered. I'd won, and I gave a crow of triumph, my arms held high.

'Twenty, not sixty,' Osman said.

'We said no doubles or triples,' I pointed out, but with a sudden sick feeling welling up inside me.

'We said I wasn't allowed to give you doubles or triples,' he pointed out. 'Not that they didn't score if you hit one.'

'Yes, but . . .'

I stopped and threw another dart, which scored one, but my third hit the twenty.

'There we are,' I told him, cocking my thumb at the board, only to realise that he was tapping his watch.

'Time's up, babe,' he said.

'Yes, but my first shot . . .'

'Might have counted if you hadn't thrown again, but seeing as you did, well . . . You can't have it both ways, can she, lads?'

The answer was a storm of raucous laughter and shouts of congratulation to Osman. Again I made to speak, but it was not easy in the face of the men's sheer animal lust, while I knew that Osman was right. Naked, sticky with beer and my own juice, beaten, I threw up my hands in despair. Another cheer greeted the gesture and Osman reached out to take me by the hand. I made a frantic signal to Big Dave, who nodded, and allowed myself to be led in among the crowd, too numb with defeat to object to the hands reaching out to squeeze my bottom and breasts.

One of the strippers was still on stage, just finishing a routine, and I was forced to wait, standing naked by the stage with the entire pub aware that Osman was about to take me into the back for sex. The moment she'd given a last teasing flash of her pussy beneath the tiny school skirt that was her only garment I was led up onto the stage to the sound of cheers and catcalls.

'Have a nice wank, boys!' Osman called out. 'Me, I've got the real thing.'

The men responded with yells of abuse and filthy demands so loud and so strong that I found myself scampering across the stage faster than Osman could lead me, which in turn set a lot of them laughing. Caroline was in the storeroom, barefoot but in her army shorts and top. As soon as she saw me naked and with Osman she realised what had happened.

'You lost, didn't you?' she asked.

I shrugged, unable to speak for the huge lump in my throat. The other stripper took one look at Osman and made a hasty exit. Caroline gave a sigh.

'So, what do you want to do first?' she asked.

'You two have got to get dirty, that's the deal,' Osman told her.

'Would you like me to spank her?' I offered, hoping he'd at least allow me to take a dominant role.

'I don't mind a bit of kinky stuff,' he answered, 'as long as there's plenty of T and A on show. But I'd really like to watch you suck each other's tits.'

Caroline's response was to take hold of her tiny khaki top and flip it up, spilling out her great heavy breasts. Osman said something in Turkish and sat down heavily on a beer keg, as if the mere sight of Caroline's chest had been enough to drain him of energy. Her tits were slick with sweat from her dancing and her nipples were stiff, tempting me to suckle on her as she bounced them in her hands. She was smiling, fully aware of the effect her breasts had on men, and on me. I wanted to slap them and leave her pink and aching, then do her bottom and have her go down on her knees to me, sore at back and front. But that could wait until later, I decided. I'd promised Osman a show, and I hadn't given up on the idea of getting the restaurant for free.

'Go on, play with them,' Osman urged. 'I want to see you touch her up.'

I sat down opposite Caroline and took her breasts in my hands, feeling the hot heavy flesh and marvelling at their sheer size. She pushed them out obligingly and I leant forward, first to lick at one salty nipple and then to take it in my mouth, sucking on her. Osman gave a deep groan and changed position, spreading his massive legs to show off the bulge in his crotch. I continued to suckle on Caroline, watching him from the corner of one eye as he massaged his cock through his trousers. He looked big, and was obviously getting hard, making me wonder if I could make him come just by playing with her and spare myself the indignity of a mouthful of spunk.

'Have you ever seen one girl kiss another's bottom?' I asked.

'Not for real,' he answered. 'You do that stuff?'

I smiled and stood up, turning to present Caroline with my bare bottom. She gave me a slap, but put her face close, kissing my cheeks, lapping at my skin, running her tongue slowly up my anal crease, all the while with Osman staring in mingled lust and astonishment. He was completely in thrall to our ability to choose what we did together, making me feel powerful and confident.

'Would you like to see her kiss my bumhole?' I offered.

'Fucking hell!' he breathed, and began to struggle with his flies.

'You're a dirty bitch, Isabelle,' Caroline remarked.

'You're the one who's about to kiss a bumhole,' I reminded her. 'Now come on.'

Osman had freed his cock, a great brown pillar of flesh, long and thick and curving up, immensely virile. Immediately I wanted him inside me, but I was doing my best to keep control. Caroline was still kissing and licking at my cheeks and crease, but was playing with her tits at the same time, a sure sign that she was ready.

'My bottom-hole, Caroline,' I reminded her.

She continued to lick, faster still, and harder, but not where I'd told her to.

'Lick my bottom, Caroline,' I demanded.

She gave a little shake of her head, but I wasn't having it. Reaching back, I took her firmly by the hair and pulled her face in between my cheeks. For a moment she tried to pull away and I nearly let go, only to have her suddenly bury her tongue up my bottom, pushing in, lapping as if to clean me up, then probing once more.

'Good girl,' I said. 'That's where your tongue belongs, up my bottom, isn't it?'

Having given in, Caroline was making the best of it, with her tongue well in and her mouth wide between my bum cheeks. I closed my eyes in bliss, enjoying both the feel of her tongue on my anus and the knowledge of what she was doing. There can be no deeper submission to another woman than to lick her bottom, and I was in my element until Osman spoke again.

'I can't see properly. Stick it right out, Isabelle, and hold your cheeks open so I can watch her tongue touch your hole.'

I hesitated, but we were showing off for him so I did as I was told, spreading myself to let him see my bumhole as Caroline pulled back a little. She'd kept her tongue out, now teasing my anus with its very tip, a sight that had Osman pulling furiously at his cock. I pushed my bottom out a little more, showing everything and hoping that he'd come in his hand.

'You dirty bitches,' he breathed. 'Now swap round.'

'Um . . . that's not really how it works,' I began even as Caroline pulled back.

'Come on, Isabelle,' she urged. 'I licked yours, you have to lick mine.'

'No, I—'

'Come on – it's just for show, remember, and I like my bottom licked.'

Osman gave a groan and Caroline giggled at his reaction. She'd stood up, stroking my cheeks and spanking me gently. Despite myself I wanted to stick it out for more, and to lick her.

'It's true,' she said, deliberately teasing Osman. 'It feels nice to have my bumhole licked, and really, if a girlfriend expects me to lick hers, she should return the favour and lick mine. That's only fair, isn't it, Isabelle? Jasmine licks my bottom.'

Again Osman groaned. His cock looked fit to explode, and I was sure he couldn't last much longer. I stuck my bottom out into Caroline's lap as she ran her hands up my body to cup my breasts, still showing off, but in no sense faking.

'Don't you think that's fair, Osman?' Caroline asked in a voice like honey. 'For good friends to lick each other's pussies and bottoms, and suck each other's titties, and spank each other's bottoms and sit on each other's faces? I think Isabelle should lick my bottom right now, and she should have to put her tongue right in up my hole for being so selfish, right in so she can taste my—'

'Yeah,' he gasped, 'while I fuck your tits. Come here, you little cock-tease, now. And you, Isabelle, get your tongue up her arse.'

Caroline giggled and got down to the floor, holding up her breasts to make a cock slide of her cleavage, while her bottom was stuck out behind. I hesitated for an instant, wanting to do it but not wanting to admit to my need. Yet she was just too tempting, her pretty face flushed with excitement, her huge breasts held out ready for fucking, her tiny waist, her flared hips, the way she filled out her tight khaki shorts.

'I … I'll lick for you,' I promised. 'But only because I have to do as Osman says.'

It was a lie, and we both knew it. I got down anyway, to rub my face against the bulging fabric of Caroline's shorts. She was laughing as Osman took her breasts and folded them around his cock, fucking her in her cleavage as she struggled with the button of her shorts. It came free and I'd pulled them down in an instant, baring her lovely chubby bottom into my face, her cheeks spread to show off her plump pussy lips and her anal star. I stuck my tongue in, tasting her bottom as she had asked, to make her moan and wriggle her big cheeks in my face.

Osman muttered something in Turkish, no doubt calling me a filthy bitch again, and he was right. I was grovelling naked on the floor with my tongue up my friend's bottom-hole, licking her as deeply as I could get, and it was making me want to come. She'd begun to lick at his cock as he fucked her breasts, but was lost to view as I buried my face between her bottom cheeks once more. My hand went back behind me and I was masturbating over being made to lick

Caroline's bottom, only for Osman's voice to break through my rising ecstasy.

'Now suck me, Isabelle,' he demanded. 'You said you would. Suck me while I fuck her titties.'

I forced myself to pay attention, gave Caroline's bumhole a last kiss and knelt up. He had her breasts squashed around his cock, with the fat, purple knob of his glans bobbing up and down between them. I pushed my head in, smothering my face in her soft breast flesh with my mouth wide to make a fuck-hole for his cock. It went in and jammed deep again and again, so fast that I could hardly cope.

'I'm going to spunk,' he grated. 'I'm going to spunk all over you, you dirty sluts. Suck it, Isabelle.'

I was doing my best, but Osman was pumping his cock in and out of my mouth at a furious pace, while I could barely breathe with Caroline's breasts squashed into my face. My own needs were forgotten: everything was focused on getting him off as he thrust harder and faster still. Then he came, full into my mouth. I jerked back, choking, only to get a wad of come shot in my face and all over Caroline's breasts – and that was just the start. Jet after jet of spunk erupted from Osman's cock, most of it going over her, but he was holding my head in place and I got my fair share too, spurting into my open mouth and down my chin, in my hair and in my eyes. He kept pumping too, soiling her cleavage to leave his prick working in a tube of boob flesh that was well slimed with his own mess before pulling my head onto himself once more, filling my mouth with his long slippery cock-shaft and squashing my face against the soft sticky pillows of Caroline's breasts.

'Suck me clean,' he grunted.

Most men lose interest when they've come, at least for a while. Not Osman. He held me down against

Caroline's breasts with his cock jammed deep in my mouth until he was satisfied that I'd cleaned him up properly and only then did he let me go. I came up panting, my face smeared with come, one eye blurry and stinging, my mouth full of jism, but now eager to take my own pleasure.

'Lick it up,' Osman puffed. 'And you can both swallow it.'

We didn't need telling. Caroline's tits were a mess, and we both began to lick up the spunk. A thick white streamer was hanging from one of her nipples and I stuck my tongue out to catch it and lap it up, deliberately showing off as I reached out to cup her pussy. She immediately returned the favour and then we were masturbating each other as we kissed and licked at her filthy boobs and each other's faces. Almost immediately I could feel myself starting to come, and I rubbed harder as our mouths met in a long sticky kiss, with bubbles of white froth escaping around our lips and dribbling down our chins as we shared our dirty mouthfuls.

I was vaguely aware that the door was open and that people were watching us. But I didn't care. All that mattered was that I was coming under the motions of Caroline's fingers as we shared our mouthful of Osman's spunk. He'd made me strip naked in front of dozens of men, had made me show my bumhole for Caroline to lick and, best of all, had made me lick hers and had then spunked all over us. As the first peak hit me I swallowed what was in my mouth, deliberately taking his come down into my belly as I'd been ordered to, a thought I held just as I held Caroline in my arms until at last the shudders began to die down and my dirty, delicious experience was complete. Or almost.

'Was that nice?' I asked as I sat down on the hard concrete floor.

Osman was beyond words. His face was puce in colour, his mouth slack, but he managed to nod. He'd continued to pull on his cock after we'd broken away, and there was still come dribbling from the tip, making his orgasm the longest I'd ever seen for a man. Quite a bit of what he'd done was still plastered across my face, and I took a moment to wipe my eyes before speaking again.

'There might be more,' I suggested.

'But only if you let us use your restaurant,' Caroline added. Once again Osman nodded.

I was exhausted, and also filthy. But Big Dave was peering in at the door and spoke as I looked up.

'It's all right, Mike's looking after your mate behind the bar. How about mine, then?'

All I could do was shrug. I was not really up for more but was grateful that he'd taken care of the Owl and I was aware of my promise. He waddled forward, flopped out his cock and sat down on a case of wine. I took him in my mouth, telling myself that it was only fair and that it wouldn't take long, only to hear Jack's voice from the door.

'Here, you lot. They've put Carrie and Isa in the back for blow jobs.'

'Oh, come on – not all of you!' I protested, pulling back.

'Just the lads,' Jack assured me, sounding hurt. 'Me and Stan, Mike, Mo and that's your lot!'

'Five men?' I queried.

'I'll help,' Caroline offered with a sigh. 'Come on, then. Get your cocks out, boys. We'd better do them all at once, Isa, or we'll never get finished.'

I nodded and went back to sucking Big Dave's cock. The others pushed in, Jack inserting himself in Caroline's mouth and Mo unzipping to place my hand on his cock. There wasn't really enough room for Tierney, who stood in the doorway, masturbating as he watched the others get their cocks sucked. Only when Osman left did he get in, feeding his prick to Caroline as she began to toss Jack off. I followed his example, alternating between Mo and Dave in my mouth, and soon all four men had stiff wet erections for us to play with. Dave had obviously been touching himself while he watched Osman use Caroline and me, because he was soon ready.

'I'm going to do it in your face,' he grunted, and immediately suited his action to his words. Come exploded from the tip of his cock into my mouth and flooded down my neck, then more spurted over my nose and cheek.

Mo laughed to see what had been done to me and pressed closer as Dave moved back. He began to masturbate into my mouth and I was expecting the same treatment again at any moment when Mike appeared, tugging down his zip as he entered the room.

'Os and that little piece with the big tits are doing the bar,' he said, 'so this has got to be quick. Give over, Mo.'

I let Mo slip from my mouth and took Mike in, the fourth cock I'd sucked in the space of a few minutes. Naked, plastered in spunk and still with two men to suck off, I couldn't help but start to get excited again. Letting my spare hand sneak between my thighs made it much easier to accept what I was doing. I decided to finish Mike off quickly and then come with Mo in my mouth, although if they'd chosen to fuck me I'd have spread my thighs or stuck my bum high on the instant.

Neither of them did. Mike jammed himself deep to spunk down my throat and force me to swallow what he'd done and Mo popped himself back in my mouth before I'd caught my breath properly. I began to rub harder, knowing that he wouldn't be long, and watched Caroline as she dealt with her two men. Both were about to come, and my pussy gave a delicious twitch as she was given a double faceful, which she immediately began to rub into her tits and cunt. That made me want to go to her again, and I began to push my lips onto the head of Mo's cock, hoping he'd come so that Caroline and I could share another orgasm with our mouths full of spunk. It was going to happen at any moment, but as my thighs began to squeeze together the door slammed open. Mo jerked back at the exact instant he came, ejaculating full in my face even as he swore in shock and a coarse female voice roared out.

'Get here, you filthy little whore!'

I screamed as a finger and thumb like a pair of pliers closed on my ear, and again as I was hauled to my feet. Mo had spunked in my eyes and I could barely see, but I recognised the massive backside and tree-trunk legs of Edna Jellaby as I was pulled staggering from the room.

'Hey, no!' I managed. 'No, not . . . why are you . . .? Hey! No, not on the stage! No, Edna!'

It was too late. I'd been dragged out onto the stage, naked and filthy in front of several hundred people.

'I'll teach you to go with my hubby, you dirty whore!' Edna screamed, snatching a chair up from the floor.

'No!' I wailed as I was jerked down across her lap, my naked bottom presented the audience. 'No, Edna, please, not a spanking . . . not in front of everybody, no!'

My words were choked off by a squeal of pain as Edna's hand smacked down across my bottom. Her palm was so big that it covered almost the entire area of my cheeks, and the blow was delivered so hard that

I was jammed forward, leaving me head down over her lap with my legs waving in the air and my cunt spread to the stares of maybe a hundred gaping men, and to Amy Jane Moffat.

I could see her through the legs of the chair I was bent over, her hand to her mouth as she stared in horror. Osman was next to her, but he was laughing, as were most of the other men in the place, their voices raised in a chorus of derision and delight at what I was getting – and what I was showing. I burst into tears, beating my fists on the wooden floor of the stage in an agony of shame as Edna's huge hand slapped down on my bottom again and again.

'I didn't know he was your husband!' I screamed. 'I didn't! I didn't!'

She only spanked harder, tightening the grip she'd taken around my waist to leave me with my legs flailing in every direction and my bottom bucking frantically up and down as I fought to escape the pain and hide my swollen juicy cunt from the stares of my audience. They were getting a full show of my bumhole, too. It was still wet with Caroline's spit, but for once that wasn't the worst thing to be showing, because for all my pain and the blubbering, screaming tantrum I was gripped in, I was about to come.

I just couldn't help it. Edna was spanking me right over my cunt, furiously hard, and it just happened. My orgasm kicked in with unstoppable power and my screams of pain and humiliation turned to shrieks of ecstasy. The observers realised what had happened, men calling out in astonishment as my body jerked and shook in the throes of orgasm, and all the while Edna still spanked my blazing bottom, until she too realised that something was wrong.

'Why, you filthy, dirty little . . .' she gasped, and let go of me.

My bottom hit the stage first as I tumbled off her lap, leaving me spread-legged in front of the audience, gasping for breath, tears and snot and spunk dribbling down my face and over my tits, my wet cunt still on show. I was still in the middle of my climax and I lay back, lifted my legs high and opened them wide to make sure the men got a good eyeful, stuck one finger up my slippery bottom, a thumb in my gaping cunt, and finished myself off with my fingers. Every single member of my audience watched me in stunned silence, but none was more stunned than the Owl.

Nine

There was no chance whatsoever of hiding what had happened. I'd come because I'd had my bottom smacked, and not a playful erotic spanking but a hard punishment spanking given to me in the nude and in front of an audience, which was about as humiliating as it can possibly get. Everybody had seen and everybody knew, including Amy Jane.

I spent most of what remained of the term trying to avoid her and the consequences of my behaviour. The perpetual look of astonishment in her huge brown eyes was more than I could bear, and while she might want to talk about it I very definitely did not. Even to think about it was too much, filling me with shame and arousal all at once, so that I didn't know whether to cry my eyes out or stick a hand down my panties. At night, once I'd finished reading and could no longer stop my mind from wandering, it was generally both. I'd lie there with the tears trickling gently down my face and my thighs spread open to the dark as I ran over the same awful memory again and again. Sometimes I'd come over how powerless I'd been to prevent my spanking, sometimes over the way my orgasm had welled up inside me and I'd been unable to stop it, sometimes over how I'd masturbated on stage. But I always came.

For all my woes I had at least succeeded in securing the Golden Chalice restaurant as the venue for the Rattaners Christmas party, and without Tierney. What I'd failed to do was establish any link between Portia and Tierney, but that was just going to have to wait. He knew about it but wasn't coming, which was good enough for the moment. My revenge on Portia would come in due course, preferably when I was able to spring it on her as a horrid surprise.

The gossip about my behaviour at Foxson had begun to die down, and there had been no evidence of reporters or photographers. But we had decided not to meet up in Oxford again until the following term and so we simply passed messages from one to the other as convenient. My suggestion that we should use the Golden Chalice was immediately accepted, and we also agreed that the female full members should arrive half an hour earlier than the men to go through society business.

I was still due to be punished, at least in theory, but I was fairly sure I had a way of avoiding that. In any case, Eliza hadn't mentioned anything and didn't send any instructions for me to dress in a particular way. I was still feeling extremely delicate, so I decided to present as dominant an image as I could, choosing leather jeans and jacket, which I'd bought on one of the rare occasions I'd had any money, heeled boots, and a black top. With my hair back I looked aggressively feminine, but with a boyish touch that I rather liked and which I hoped would deflect Osman's interest onto one of the other girls.

As usual I'd changed at Jasmine and Caroline's, along with Katie, and this time with Amy Jane too. She had been taken in hand by Caroline, and it was already obvious that if she was going to fit in with the Rattaners it would be as a submissive. Whatever was suggested to her she accepted it, although the colour of her face gave away her rising embarrassment as she was put in a red satin corset with French knickers and stockings to go with it, all of them Caroline's. Out of her normal baggy clothes, and with her figure enhanced by the corset, Amy Jane looked intensely feminine – and also exceptionally vulnerable. Her breasts were very nearly as big as Caroline's, and rather firmer, while her inability to keep them in her corset properly caused her constant embarrassment. She also had a well-formed bottom, round and firm, but even in all her finery I found it hard to see her as sexual. In an effort to make Amy Jane feel comfortable Caroline had dressed the same way, only in a blue corset rather than a red one. Standing together they might almost have been sisters, one a slut, one an innocent dressed up by her wicked sister.

Katie was also in lingerie: a bedtime crop top, panties with 'Spank Me' printed across the seat, long white socks and sandals – a curious mixture but very appealing when on her. Jasmine seemed more determined than ever to exert her dominance, and had dressed in an elegant black silk sheath along with stockings, high heels, a hat and veil, which gave her a very pretty 1950s look. She was also showing off, and I promised myself that by the end of the evening she'd be in the nude with a red bottom to show for her trouble.

With the five of us together the car was going to be full, so Sarah had agreed to collect Yazzie, who also had to change at Jasmine and Caroline's to avoid raising the suspicions of Mo and her appalling stepmother. Yazzie was in her usual simple dress and was carrying several hanks of rope. Sarah had decided to be a schoolmistress, complete with gown and mortarboard, and she had both Portia and

Tiffany in identical school uniform: smart bottle-green skirts and blazers, white blouses and socks, sensible black shoes and green ties with the same crest.

'You two look very authentic,' I commented. 'Did you go to a real school outfitters?'

'These are our real uniforms,' Portia told me. 'All Saints Ladies College.'

'We were at school together, silly,' Tiffany laughed. 'Saints girls always go to Erasmus Darwin – or try to, anyway. Didn't you know that?'

'No,' I admitted. 'But you look nice anyway, and perfectly spankable.'

'I'm a prefect,' Portia pointed out, instantly sulky, but there was honey in Tiffany's voice as she addressed me.

'You look as if you've just got off a motorbike.'

'If you three have finished flirting,' Sarah remarked, 'it's time to go.'

We climbed into the cars and drove north, a journey that seemed to take for ever, with my excitement gradually building along with my concern for what might happen. They all knew about the Red Ox, but I was determined to exert myself, and I resolved that if any of them teased me I would take it out on their bottoms.

To do Tierney and Osman justice, the Golden Chalice was everything they had claimed and rather more. Located in open farmland nearly a mile off the main A34, there were no neighbours to worry about at all, while by closing the gate at the beginning of the old farm track we could cut ourselves off from the world. The main restaurant was more or less as I'd expected, with a bar in one corner and the rest of the floor area given over to seating, which we could rearrange as we pleased. A door opened to the kitchen, which was in a separate building, and another to the loos, which were housed in a large lean-to at one side. If there was a problem it was that the restaurant area was about three times larger than we could possibly have needed. But it was easy to make a cosy space at one end, while the high black-painted beams had definite potential.

We were the first to arrive, aside from Osman, and we had the tables arranged before Eliza arrived, with three pushed together for our meeting and five arranged around an open space. Eliza was in her usual immaculate tweeds, but with a heavy tawse clipped to her skirt, immediately making me worry that it might be my bottom that it was intended for. I took my place at one end of the table and she chose the other. Osman busied himself setting up Christmas decorations.

'The gentlemen will be with us presently,' Eliza told us, 'although I'm afraid Isadore is unable to come. We have several matters to attend to, so let us proceed.'

'Isabelle's punishment for a start,' Portia demanded.

'All in good time,' Eliza told her. 'Isabelle?'

'Thank you,' I replied after a brief glare at Portia. 'First, I'd like to welcome Amy Jane to our society. I have shown her the rules and explained how we work, including using "red" as a stop word, which she was very grateful to discover. Please be gentle with her, because she's a little unsure of her sexuality. But she does like the idea of looking up to a stronger woman.'

'Thanks to Sarah,' Portia remarked.

'Secondly,' I went on, ignoring her, 'we've had a difficult term, which was at least in part my fault—'

'*Entirely* your fault, Isabelle,' Jasmine pointed out.

'Getting horny in front of my stepmum was a bad idea,' Yazzie agreed, 'and as for what you did with my Dad . . .'

'I didn't know that she was your stepmum!' I protested. 'I didn't know what she was like, either. Anyway, please hear me out. I know that I've caused us some problems, and created some tensions within the society, which I think it would be best to sort out now. My own feeling is that what I went through to get us this venue – for free, I might add – along with my very public spanking from Yazzie's stepmum should count as my punishment. If the majority of you think I should be given further punishment then I accept that. Let's vote.'

'Firstly,' Eliza said, 'does anybody feel that this has gone too far to be resolved in the traditional fashion?'

Nobody spoke.

'I'm glad to hear it,' Eliza went on. 'Who accepts Isabelle's proposal, that she has already suffered sufficient punishment?'

'Not from us!' Portia pointed out. 'I want her across my knee – and I'd like to borrow your tawse, please.'

'Just raise your hand, Portia,' Eliza ordered.

I gave a worried glance around the table as hands were raised, fast or slowly. Portia's was up, and inevitably Tiffany's, also Sarah's and Yazzie's, but that was not enough.

'Caroline?' Portia demanded. 'After what she made you do? And how about you, Amy Jane? She spanked you, without your consent and in front of half of Foxson College!'

Caroline merely shrugged.

'I didn't mind,' Amy Jane said in a tiny voice.

'You're such a mouse!' Portia retorted.

'She's not a mouse, she's an owl,' Tiffany put in. 'A fat owl, as if she was Billy Bunter's sister.'

Portia laughed and Amy Jane went pink. I quickly raised my hands.

'That's decided, then. Thank you. And Tiffany, I think you should say sorry to Amy Jane.'

'*You* always call her the Owl,' Tiffany pointed out, and I found myself blushing as well, and stammering apologies.

'It's all right,' Amy Jane said quietly. 'Everybody calls me that.'

'I'm sorry, anyway,' I assured her. 'OK, if that's all shall we decide what game to play? Have you got your cards, Sarah?'

'There is one other thing,' Eliza said. 'Something rather important, in fact. The fact is, Isabelle, that when I said your training was complete last term I only meant insofar as your skills and understanding of what it takes to make a dominant woman were concerned. However, even when I gave you what should have been your last-ever caning I couldn't help but notice how much it excited you. That is why I asked Sarah to devise some form of test to see where your true desires lay. She in turn consulted Jasmine, and Portia, who administered the test with some help from Tiffany.'

'What test?' I asked. But even as I spoke an awful suspicion had begun to grow in my mind. 'You two told Tierney about our meetings, didn't you, Portia?'

'Yes,' she admitted. 'But don't get on your high horse. We had it all under control, and he promised not to interfere.'

'In return for giving me rough spankings,' Tiffany added with relish. 'The man is such a pig!'

'And the rest of you knew about this?' I demanded.

'I didn't,' Katie said quickly.

'I did,' Sarah said, 'and it think it was an excellent test. No truly dominant woman would go within a mile of Tierney if she could help it, never mind fellate him in the back of a minibus.'

'I was not aware of the details,' Eliza added. 'But I have to agree with Sarah that the test was both fair and effective, if a little cruel. You did what you did, Isabelle, and apparently enjoyed it.'

'No, I didn't!' I lied.

'Yes, you did,' Yazzie put in. 'I got the full description from my stepmum, remember.'

'Not to mention being spanked bare by her in the Red Ox!' Tiffany giggled. 'And you came while you were over her knee. I've never met such a slut!'

'We also have to consider your reaction during your punishment at the last party,' Eliza pointed out, 'and afterwards with Sarah and Tiffany.'

'That was between you and me, Tiffany!' I said. 'And you, Sarah, you said . . .'

Sarah's mouth turned up into a condescending little smile and I shut up.

'It was part of the test, Isabelle,' Tiffany told me, 'but still very nice.'

I was blushing hot and felt close to tears as the full reality of the situation sank in.

'I've failed, haven't I?' I asked.

'You shouldn't look at it as having failed,' Eliza said gently, 'more as having come to accept your true sexuality, which is not dominant, but switch, just as you are not a lesbian, but bisexual. There's nothing to be ashamed of.'

I made a face, unable to find a reply as a huge bubble of consternation began to swell in my throat.

'Or do you think that being dominant makes you superior?' Tiffany demanded. 'Do you think you're better than me, or Caroline, or Yazzie?'

'No, of course not,' I managed. 'It's just that . . .'

'It's just that you're too proud to accept who you really are,' Eliza interrupted. 'But what you have to understand, Isabelle, is that there is far more to be proud of in being able to accept your true self than there is in continuing to attempt to deny it, both to others and to yourself.'

I gave a single weak nod.

'I'm just the same,' Jasmine admitted.

'And you're both young,' Eliza went on. 'Most women have far less understanding of their sexuality at your age.'

I drew a heavy sigh. They were right, and my behaviour over the course of the term made it pointless to argue.

'Fair enough,' I admitted. 'Maybe I did need to be tested, but I don't think it was right to effectively give me to Tierney. Sarah could easily have tested me herself.'

'We needed to give you a hard choice,' Sarah pointed out, 'hence the situation in which you would know that by offering sexual favours to Tierney you could avoid problems for the Rattaners. It was really very noble of you to fellate him.'

'Not to mention the other two,' Portia giggled.

'I want all three of you punished!' I snapped. 'You know what Tierney's like, and the risk you were taking. He might easily have brought half a dozen of his friends around to Dr Treadle's . . .'

'He didn't know the parties were at Dr Treadle's,' Sarah pointed out.

'He could have worked it out, Sarah – he's not as stupid as he looks. At the very least I want all three of you spanked, now.'

'Why?' Portia demanded. 'We only set the situation up. If you had the slightest scrap of dignity or any real dominance you'd have told Tierney to mind his own business.'

'Instead of offering to suck his penis,' Sarah added in disgust.

'Ladies, please,' Eliza interjected. 'There is some truth in what Isabelle says, so I think we had best put the matter to a vote, and Isabelle is only suggesting a brief over-the-knee spanking. Aren't you, Isabelle?'

The tone of her voice brooked no argument and I nodded.

'An open vote, then,' Eliza said. 'All those in favour of Sarah, Portia and Tiffany having to accept spankings before the party?'

I raised my hand, as did Jasmine and Caroline, Yazzie and Katie. Eliza kept her hand down, leaving the decision in the hands of the Owl.

'Amy Jane?' I asked.

She glanced at Sarah.

'Perhaps just Portia and Tiffany?' she suggested.

'All three of them,' I insisted, 'or none.'

This time her gaze went to Tiffany, and there was a flicker of resentment in her big mild eyes. I was smiling even before she'd raised her hand, making the vote six to four in favour of the spankings. Sarah threw an angry glance around the table and Portia had begun to pout. Tiffany merely shrugged.

'Oh, very well,' Sarah said testily. 'But not from Isabelle. You'll have to do me, Eliza.'

'Isabelle has the right under the rules,' Eliza pointed out.

'I think I should at least choose,' I suggested. 'But I don't insist on doing it.'

Sarah gave me a doubtful look. I could see she was far from happy about having to be spanked, but I knew she'd follow the rules and accept the vote, if only because the time was sure to come when the situation would be reversed.

'If you insist,' she said.

'Thank you,' I told her, trying not to let the sadistic glee welling up inside me show too obviously. Then I

222

decided that I might as well make the best of it while I had her at my mercy.

'Knickers down and bare bottom, of course. In fact, pop them down now and you can sit bare while I choose.'

Tiffany immediately lifted herself from her chair to flip up her school skirt and push the big bottle-green knickers beneath it down to her thighs. Portia followed suit more reluctantly, but Sarah stayed as she was.

'Come along, Sarah,' I teased. 'Bare bottie on the chair, please.'

She threw me a glare of utter fury but quickly adjusted herself, lifting her long dark schoolmistress's skirt and tucking it up before pushing down the black French knickers underneath to sit her bottom, now naked, back on the chair. I could no longer keep the grin off my face as I admired the three of them.

'Very pretty,' I said. 'Now, who first? Yes, Portia. I bet it was your idea to get Tierney involved. Let me see, who would you really hate to get it from ... Eliza spanks hard, but you wouldn't have any difficulty accepting discipline from her ... I know: Jasmine, would you like to spank Portia's bottom for her?'

'Very much, thank you,' Jasmine replied promptly as Portia's mouth came open in dismay. 'Over my knee, Portia. Now!'

I was laughing openly as Portia stood up, her face working with resentment and shame. She'd tucked her school skirt up into its own waistband, and had taken her knickers down just far enough to leave her bottom ready for spanking while showing as little as possible, an image that brought out the worst in me, and in Jasmine, who knew just how to handle her.

'Panties down properly, Portia,' she said, adjusting

the bottle-green knickers as Portia got into position across her lap, 'so all the girls can see your pussy.'

I certainly could, Portia's smooth, full sex lips pouted out from between her thighs in that thoroughly rude way that brings so much shame and so much excitement. She was already wet.

'Naughty girl,' Jasmine said, and began to spank, not all that hard but thoroughly enjoying the feel of her slaps on Portia's bottom. 'Take some photos, Carrie, please?'

'Hey, no!' Portia squealed. But Caroline already had her camera out, and Portia only succeeded in ensuring that her face was in the photo as she tried to twist around.

Jasmine laughed and continued to spank, showing off to Caroline's camera as more photos were taken, but still really only patting Portia's full, smooth cheeks.

'It *is* supposed to be a punishment,' I pointed out.

'I think being over my knee is the best punishment for her!' Jasmine laughed. But then she began to spank harder anyway.

Portia had tried to speak, possibly to agree with Jasmine, but all that came out was a squeak as the slaps got abruptly harder. Her bottom was starting to bounce and she was having trouble keeping her thighs together, which gave me an even better show of her pussy and the occasional glimpse of the little fleshy wrinkle of her anus. Jasmine was grinning and, encouraged by Portia's reaction, she began to spank harder still, setting her victim's thighs kicking in the bottle-green panties.

'That's enough, I think,' Jasmine finally announced as she gave Portia's bottom a last hard smack. 'Almost, anyway.'

She pulled Portia's now pink cheeks apart to show off her bottom-hole, holding them wide.

'One for the album, I think,' she said, smiling up at Caroline.

'No! You bitch!' Portia spat, but too late. 'You just wait, both of you – and you, Isabelle!'

I just laughed, thoroughly enjoying her embarrassment.

'Now for Tiffany,' I said. 'Let me see . . .'

Tiffany stood up, her mouth set in an insolent smile and her hands on her hips, completely unashamed of being bare behind or having her school knickers around her thighs.

'I wish there was a man around to do you,' I told her. 'Although after Tierney I don't suppose even that would get to you. So let me see . . . yes, why not? Amy Jane, would you like to spank Tiffany?'

Tiffany's sassy, confident expression vanished.

'The Owl!?' she demanded. 'The Owl can't spank me!'

'I'm not really sure . . .' Amy Jane began. But I cut her off.

'If you're going to be a member of this society you're going to need to smack other girls' bottoms occasionally, and who better to start with than this brat?'

'But I . . .'

'She said you look like Billy Bunter's sister, Amy Jane,' Caroline pointed out. 'Spank her.'

'It's easy,' I added. 'Just put her over your knee, make sure her bottom's fully bare and slap her cheeks until they're both nice and pink. Come on, Tiffany – over you go.'

'You are such a bitch, Isabelle,' Tiffany said. But she went, genuinely embarrassed as she draped herself across Amy Jane's lap with her bottom lifted.

She'd pushed her knickers down a lot further than Portia had and her pussy was already showing, but

Amy Jane adjusted them anyway and also tucked the little school skirt up higher to make sure that Tiffany was left with no modesty whatsoever. As she did it she repeatedly glanced at me, and at the others, as if seeking reassurance.

'That's good,' I told her. 'You got her nicely in position, and we can see everything, can't we, Caroline?'

The camera flashed and Tiffany gave a little angry jerk as she realised that she too had been photographed in spanking position. Her long red hair was shading her face, but I could easily imagine her expression, and her feelings.

'*Almost* everything,' I corrected myself. 'It might be a good idea to open her blouse.'

'Her blouse?' Amy Jane asked.

'So her tits show, to humiliate her,' Jasmine explained.

Amy Jane gave a doubtful nod. But her hand was already under Tiffany's chest, fiddling with the buttons of her school blouse.

'Pull it up,' I instructed, 'or Caroline can't get a decent shot of her breasts.'

'Not that's she's got much,' Caroline said as Tiffany's tits came on show. 'Now *you*, Amy Jane, would look good in that position.'

Amy Jane's face immediately coloured up, but she was smiling too. Tiffany's blouse was now right up, and she hadn't bothered with a bra, leaving her little round breasts dangling bare under her chest. Caroline took several photos, with Amy Jane waiting patiently and Tiffany growing increasingly fed up until her nerve finally broke.

'Just spank me, if you're going to, you fat Owl!' she snapped.

'Don't be nasty,' Amy Jane said, and smacked her hand down on Tiffany's bottom.

226

'Do it hard,' Caroline urged. 'She deserves it.'

'Yes, she does,' Amy Jane agreed, applying a second smack. And then, suddenly, it was as if she'd gone berserk.

I could imagine how she felt, with all the years of snubs and put-downs from girls like Tiffany coming to the surface at once when she finally had a chance for her revenge. She spanked furiously hard, holding Tiffany tight around the waist and applying smack after smack after smack to the wriggling little bottom. Tiffany kicked and screamed and swore, her legs waving wildly in the air and her hair tossing in every direction, so lost in her pain that she was indifferent to the thoroughly rude show that she was making of her gingery pussy and furry bottom-crease, or to the fact that Caroline was still taking pictures. Soon she was in tears, but Amy Jane continued to spank until finally Tiffany's insults and curses gave way to broken pleading and apologies babbled through a haze of pain.

'. . . I'm sorry,' she was saying. 'I really am . . . you're not fat and you don't look like an owl . . . but I'm a nasty little brat and I deserved that, but no more, please, Amy Jane, no more!'

'Do you really mean it?' Amy Jane asked, raising her hand above Tiffany's bottom, which was a great deal redder than Portia's had been.

'Yes!' Tiffany wailed. 'I do mean it, really. I'll do anything . . .'

'Make her lick your bum,' Caroline suggested, laughing.

'Be fair, she's had enough,' Portia put in, and Amy Jane let her victim go.

Tiffany picked herself up, her legs shaking as she wiped her tears and put one rueful hand to her smacked bottom. I knew Amy Jane wouldn't take her up on her offer, which was a pity, but it might also have meant that we'd forget something more important: Sarah's spanking.

'Which leaves us with Sarah,' I stated, smiling at her.

Sarah gave a nervous glance at her watch, but I was determined to take my time. Tiffany had gone to Portia and the two of them compared bottoms and exchanged kisses.

'Later, you two, if you wouldn't mind,' I told them. 'Hmm, perhaps the pair of you should spank Sarah? That's a thought.'

'I'd rather be done by Eliza, if I have to be done at all,' Sarah replied.

'I think not,' I told her. 'It's your pride I want to hurt, Sarah, not your bottom. As you clearly realise, the men will be here any minute. In fact, I'm sure I heard a car, didn't you?'

'You can be such a bitch, Isabelle . . .'

Sarah went silent as the door opened to admit Duncan, Walter Jessop – and Stan Tierney.

'What's *he* doing here!?' I gasped, my triumph forgotten on the instant. 'I didn't invite him.'

'No,' Eliza answered me. 'I did, on Sarah's recommendation.'

'Why would you . . .' I began, and stopped.

It was obvious why she'd invited Tierney. It was so that the punishment she'd expected me to have to take could involve him.

'We had to,' Sarah said desperately. 'He knew the venue and—'

'And was quite happy as long as he had Tiffany's bottom to smack,' I finished for her. 'And the occasional suck, I expect, knowing him. OK, since you want him here, Sarah, *he* can spank you.'

'What's all this?' Tierney demanded as he reached us.

228

'We want you to spank Sarah,' I explained.

She had gone white and was staring at him in dumb horror. But he merely gave her a lewd grin and carried on talking to me.

'Give us a chance, Isa, I ain't even had a drink yet.'

'Take your time,' I told him. 'Osman's around somewhere, but we're allowed to help ourselves from the bar as long as we keep a tab. You might fetch me a glass of whisky while you're at it. The Glenfiddich will have to do, I think. One for Sarah, too – she looks like she needs it.'

'Red,' Sarah said firmly as Tierney made for the bar. 'I can't, Isabelle, not from him. Anybody else, but not him.'

'You brought him up here to help punish me, didn't you?' I demanded, genuinely cross. 'I don't know what you were planning, but I'd have been going over his knee, wouldn't I? And probably a lot worse, too. I wouldn't have used the stop word, and you know that. I'd have taken my punishment.'

'Yes, but you're . . .'

'Bisexual? A slut? You shouldn't dish out what you can't take, Sarah – you told me that yourself.'

'Oh, all right!' she snapped. 'He can spank me. But you wait, Isabelle, that's all!'

'Thank you,' I said, and I meant it.

Tierney was coming back towards us, a bottle of beer in one hand and two whiskies in the other, his finger and thumb pushed well down in the glasses. Duncan had been talking to Eliza and Walter to Jasmine and Caroline, but both now took seats.

'Did I hear you say there was about to be a spanking, Isabelle?' Duncan enquired.

'Tierney's going to spank Sarah,' I told him.

'That will be a rare treat,' he remarked, settling back in his chair.

'I'm ready now,' Tierney announced. 'How d'you like it, love, over my knee like a naughty little girl, or rolled up so I can pat your cunt, or what?'

'We agreed over the knee,' I said before Sarah could find her voice. 'And don't forget that she has to be bare-bottom.'

'This ain't the first time, love,' Tierney laughed. 'I know how to do it.'

He'd pulled a chair out into the centre of the space that I'd cleared and now he sat down on it, still holding his beer. As Sarah approached him he took a swig, then put it down on the floor. Osman had come back in and was watching with interest from the door of the kitchen as Sarah draped herself with utmost reluctance across Tierney's lap. Her skirt had fallen, covering her, and it was hard to contain my satisfaction as it was raised once more, revealing her stockings, the French knickers tangled at thigh level and her full, womanly bottom.

'Knickers down ready, huh?' Tierney joked. 'Shame, really – I like to pull 'em down myself, I do. Yeah, can't miss that bit.'

'Do you *have* to play with my underwear?' Sarah demanded as he hauled her knickers back up over her bottom.

'Yes,' he said as he placed a hand on the curve of her bottom, smoothing out the silk across her cheeks. 'Nice arse, by the way. I like 'em meaty.'

'Get on with it!' Sarah demanded.

'Temper, temper!' Tierney chuckled. 'Right, then – down come the knickers.'

He'd stuck his thumbs into the waistband as he spoke, and now he began to push, his face set in a grotesquely coarse leer as Sarah's bottom came slowly bare once more.

'I love doing that,' he declared as he tucked them down around her thighs. 'One more time.'

230

'Mr Tierney!' Sarah protested. But her knickers had already been pulled up again.

Tierney stripped her bottom a second time, and a third before he grew tired of the game. But on the last occasion he pulled them right off and pressed them to his face.

'Ahh, cunt!' he said happily, and tucked the knickers into his top pocket. 'Right, ladies, how many does she get?'

'As many as you care to give her,' Eliza instructed. 'But you are only to spank her . . .'

'Yeah yeah, I know the deal,' Tierney interrupted her. 'I'll keep my fingers dry, don't worry. You'll want to see her cunt and arsehole though, yeah?'

'You bastard!' Sarah squeaked as her bottom cheeks were hauled apart. But Tierney merely laughed, spent a moment inspecting her anus and her sex, and then began to spank her.

She tried to keep her legs together, but he spanked hard, and with her knickers off there was nothing to stop them spreading wide. Soon we were being treated to a fine view of dark well-furred pussy and, better still, her bottom-hole, while her cheeks were getting distinctly red. She'd begun to whimper, too, and was obviously and painfully aware that Caroline was taking photos of her humiliation.

Tierney was having fun, and was in no hurry at all, grinning as he spanked Sarah and taking care to vary the power of his slaps and occasionally hit her thighs so that she'd kick and show herself off behind. I was enjoying the view as much as he was, my only regret that she wasn't going to be put on her knees and made to suck his cock once he'd finished with her. Yet it was still immensely satisfying to see her spanked and humiliated for what she'd done to me. At last he stopped, only to begin to stroke her

231

bottom, a liberty that drew no more than a little choking sound from her throat.

'That's enough,' I said. 'And you do have a beautiful bottom, Sarah, although that doesn't really matter to me just now. What matters is that it's bare, and rather pink.'

'Very pink,' Tierney remarked, still fondling her as he picked up his beer. 'Hot, too. I reckon you need cooling off, love.'

As he finished speaking he tipped the bottle of beer and poured out a pale golden stream over Sarah's naked bottom. She gasped in surprise as the cold liquid splashed on her hot skin and she jumped up immediately, clutching at her wet red bottom. Tierney laughed at her, and for a moment I thought she was going to slap his face. But she contented herself with calling him a bastard once more, then hurried for the Ladies, still with her skirt held up around her waist.

'Nice wiggle, too,' Tierney laughed, cocking a thumb at Sarah's retreating bottom cheeks. 'So what's up?'

'Once Sarah has recovered her poise,' Eliza said, 'and assuming that you can behave yourself, Mr Tierney, we are going to play a game of something called joker.'

'I love dirty games,' Tierney answered. 'And don't you worry about me, love. I'll be a good boy, you know that.'

I shook my head in despair, knowing exactly what he meant by being a good boy. But at least I wasn't going to be on the receiving end for once.

'What's joker?' Amy Jane asked nervously.

'The rules are simple,' Eliza said, and began to explain.

I took a look around. Portia looked sulky, Jasmine smug, the others more or less expectant. Tiffany seemed to have got over her spanking, but she still had her knickers down and her school skirt tucked up behind. As long as Sarah could pull herself together it looked like being an excellent evening, and one during which I would be able to firmly establish my dominance, for all my failure to make it absolute. After all, if Sarah still got spanked, and in theory even Eliza, then it wasn't really a problem if I had to take it occasionally. This evening I had escaped.

'. . . So the first thing is for the submissive girls to choose the punishments,' Eliza was saying. 'Which we can do without Sarah. Portia, would you like to go first, so that Amy Jane knows what sort of thing to choose?'

'I think I should take Isabelle's place,' Portia said.

'Why you?' Jasmine asked her. 'It should be me, if anybody.'

'You took her place last time,' Portia pointed out.

'Exactly,' Jasmine retorted. 'Just like I should have, and you've already had your bum smacked, so you're ready—'

'Girls, please,' Eliza interrupted. 'We have voted against a punishment for Isabelle, so I think it only fair that she should retain her usual place.'

Portia opened her mouth to speak but quickly shut it again, looking sulkier than ever.

'Your punishment?' Eliza asked.

'It's all right, I'll start,' Amy Jane put in, with a tremor in her voice. 'To be held down, with my, er . . . whatever it is, er . . . you know, with her arm twisted behind her back, and spanked, hard.'

It was almost exactly what I'd done to her, making me wonder what went on in her head, especially when she was alone at night.

'That's a good punishment,' Eliza said, writing it down. 'Yazzie?'

'To be suspended from the beams,' Yazzie said, 'naked. I have enough rope.'

'I'm sure you do,' Eliza replied. 'Tiffany?'

'A dozen with your tawse,' Tiffany said, 'while held in place.'

'Katie?'

'To be maid all evening, and subject to my Mistress's orders, or my Master's, I suppose – but no penetration.'

'That's fair. Caroline?'

'Waxed boobs and the candle stub up the pussy.'

'Amy Jane is still a virgin,' I pointed out.

'Up her bum, then, if she gets it.'

'Carrie! Isabelle!' Amy Jane exclaimed, colouring up.

'You do have your stop word,' Eliza reminded her. 'Jasmine?'

'I think a bit of bum-licking would do some people around here good. Yes, oral sex, including anal, and I mean right out in the middle of the floor.'

Jasmine gave Portia a smug grin as she finished. Eliza nodded thoughtfully but wrote the punishment down before she spoke again.

'Portia?'

Portia nodded and threw a cautious glance around the group, clearly unsure what to do. I could appreciate her difficulty, because while she would have loved to land Jasmine or any of the girls who'd voted for her spanking in trouble, the rules of the game meant that if she chose a severe punishment she might end up having to take it herself. Just watching the indecision in her face made me feel deliciously cruel. When she finally spoke there was a tremor in her voice and she was looking directly at Jasmine.

'Tied up, properly, fully clothed, until she wets herself, then an enema. Have you got the equipment, Eliza?'

'Yes, in my bag,' Eliza told her. 'But that's very strong.'

'I'll risk it,' Portia replied. 'I won't blame Amy Jane if she gets it and chickens out, but anyone else should go through with it.'

She gave a shrug, so dismissive, so full of contempt that I knew I wouldn't have dared to refuse the punishment, not that I was going to be getting it anyway. Sarah had just emerged from the door to the loos, looking none too pleased, and had heard what Jasmine had said. Personally, I was wondering if she had any panties on under her dress and found it hard to keep the smile off my face as she took her cards from her bag and placed them on a table.

'Ladies, gentlemen,' Eliza said. 'If you'd care to cut?'

I cut the pack, no longer able to contain my smile as I saw the ace of diamonds, the third-best card in the deck. Sarah followed and got an eight, Eliza a jack. Osman could only manage a four, and to my delight Tierney cut a two. Duncan got the ace of spades, slightly to my annoyance, and Walter a three.

'Excellent,' Duncan declared. 'First choice, although not an easy one at all. Hmm . . . I confess that I am smitten with your girlfriend, Isabelle. Katie.'

She smiled and went straight to him, sitting down on his lap and kissing him, making me feel jealous but also relieved. I still wanted to protect Amy Jane, but she was just going to have to take her chances, because I badly wanted to put Jasmine in her place.

'I'll have Jasmine,' I stated, and gave her a pointed look. 'She is, after all, supposed to be my slave girl.'

'In which case I shall have Caroline,' Eliza said.

It was a sadistic choice, leaving Portia making pleading eyes at Sarah. If she wasn't chosen she would go to a man.

'Portia,' Sarah said. 'I can't leave you, darling, not after Tierney's behaviour.'

'Thank you,' Portia breathed, kissing Sarah hard on the mouth.

'I'm next, am I?' Osman said. 'Only one choice for me – no offence girls, but I like tits. Sorry, what's your name, love?'

'Amy Jane,' the Owl squeaked.

Osman licked his lips. Amy Jane looked terrified, but she'd been chosen before both Tiffany and Yazzie, and there was a little smile playing at one corner of her mouth.

'Yazzie,' Walter said, clearly pleased with his voice.

'Fuck me, that's a relief,' Tierney said. 'I could never have looked Mo in the face again, and I get the most gorgeous of all.'

He gave Tiffany a dirty leer, to which she responded with a nervous smile.

'And if the girls would like to cut?' Eliza said. 'Most junior first, as always.'

I saw Amy Jane swallow hard as she cut the cards, and was relieved to see the king of spades come up. She glanced at Osman, and I could see her thinking how hard a man of his size was likely to spank.

'I . . . I think I'd like to be your maid, please?' she said.

'One of us might get an ace, you know,' Portia said. 'Go on, Tiffy.'

Tiffany only managed a six, and was biting her lip as she went back to Portia. Yazzie got the ace of clubs, giving her an almost certain first choice, but as she glanced upwards I already knew what it would be. Katie cut a queen, but was still left looking nervous, even after Caroline had cut the two of hearts.

'Oh shit, looks like a tube up my bum,' she said,

giving Eliza a weak smile. 'And these are really expensive panties!'

I found myself smiling at her consternation and Portia stepped up to cut the pack. She got a jack, and let out a long sigh of relief, no doubt quite happy to lick Sarah's bottom and everything else.

'Let it be a two,' she said as Jasmine put her fingers to the pack.

'You wait, Portia,' Jasmine said, and cut the pack, revealing a joker.

She looked puzzled, then smiled and turned to Sarah.

'Doesn't that mean I get to swap?'

'It does,' Sarah said, and I had never seen such a delighted expression on a human face as she turned to me. 'With Isabelle.'

'But . . . but you take out the jokers!' I managed to splutter.

I was going to,' Sarah said sweetly. 'But when you started playing I was cleaning up my bottom in the Ladies after Mr Tierney had poured beer all over me. Ironic, isn't it?'

'But which punishment do I give her?' Jasmine asked.

'Whichever is left over, I suppose,' Sarah stated.

'But jokers are usually wild,' I said desperately. 'She should have first choice.'

'OK,' Jasmine said. 'I'll choose Portia's.'

'No, Jasmine!' I gasped, realising what I'd done an instant too late. 'You can't do that to me!'

'You'd do it to me,' she pointed out. 'Osman, could you bring Isabelle a bottle of wine, please? The house white should do, and a pint of lemonade – no, better make that two.'

'Jasmine, please,' I begged. 'Choose something else, anything—'

'No,' she interrupted me. 'You'll take it, and like it. Now shut up and drink your wine.'

I went quiet, too numb even to listen properly as the girls chose their punishments. Amy Jane was already being used as maid, and had brought my drinks on a tray. Yazzie wanted to be suspended, and was trying to explain to a doubtful Walter what he could do to her once she was helpless, until Jasmine tapped her on the shoulder.

'I need your help first, Yazzie. Drink up, Isabelle, and you can take off your jacket.'

My stomach already felt bloated from the pint of lemonade I'd swallowed, along with a large glass of wine. I poured another, hoping my ordeal would be more bearable if I was a bit drunk. Katie had opted to be spanked, and was kneeling on a chair with her bottom stuck out and her Spank Me panties taut across her bum cheeks, but even that failed to get to me as I gulped down the second glass of wine, and then a third.

Jasmine waited patiently, watching me drink until I'd finished both pints of lemonade and nearly all the wine. My tummy felt hard and round, and I shook my head in the hope that she'd let me off the rest of the bottle, but she poured it out and held it up to my mouth. I took it, forcing myself to swallow it down, although it left me feeling dizzy and a little sick.

'Good girl,' she said. 'Now, come with me. You too, Yazzie.'

Jasmine took me by the hand and led me to the Ladies, a large space with three cubicles and a row of basins with a huge mirror above them. The floor was tiled in white, so clean and shiny that I could see a vague reflection of myself. Like the main area, the roof was supported by black-painted beams, but only a foot or so above my head.

'Tie her up,' Jasmine ordered, 'so that's she's helpless. But I'll need to get her bare later.'

'Yes, Jasmine *Kyou*,' Yazzie replied. 'Kneel on the floor, please, Isabelle.'

I obeyed, feeling as if I was kneeling for execution as I got down on the cold hard tiles.

'Place your arms behind your back, please,' Yazzie said.

My arms went back to allow her to bind them together, tight, using an elaborate criss-cross of ropes that left me pretty well helpless.

'Feet together, Isabelle,' she ordered.

Again I obeyed, this time for my ankles to be lashed together as tightly as my arms, so that I could barely move at all but was forced to set my knees apart in order to keep my balance. This in turn meant that my sex felt open and vulnerable. Even then Yazzie hadn't finished. She led another rope from my bound wrists up to a beam, tying it off to leave me in an upright kneeling position, and virtually immobilised.

'Thank you, Yazzie,' Jasmine said from where she was standing by the basins. 'Open your mouth, Isabelle.'

I twisted my head around to see her unwrapping a large bar of soap. It was obvious where she intended to put it.

'Jasmine, please,' I begged. 'That wasn't part of the punishment!'

'How many times have you made *me* wash my mouth out with soap?' she asked.

'Not many. Three? Four?'

'Six,' she told me. 'And I'm only going to do it to you once, so stop whining and open up!'

Grimacing ruefully, I did as I was told, allowing Jasmine to wedge the cake of soap into my mouth. It tasted foul, and my face screwed up in disgust.

239

'It would be unwise to spit it out,' Jasmine told me, something I'd already guessed. 'Now, I want to watch Katie's spanking, so I'll leave you to think about all the cruel things you've ever done to me. Have fun.'

She gave a little wave, fluttering her fingers, and walked away, closing the door of the Ladies behind her. I hung my head, keeping still, because even with nobody to see me I felt that making faces and wriggling would delight my tormentors. That was assuming they were even thinking about me, because I could hear the sound of smacks, squeals and laughter from the main room. Katie was being spanked, a thought that sent a stab of jealousy through me and brought me one step closer to tears.

My fate was inevitable, and I knew that I'd soon be kneeling in wet jeans and soggy panties. But I stayed as I was, moving only to ease my aching muscles. It was utterly humiliating, when I should have been taking my turn with the girls, perhaps even enjoying putting Jasmine through the same wicked ordeal, not kneeling bound and helpless on the hard tiles with my mouth full of soap.

Yazzie had tied me too well to permit escape, and even if I got free I knew they'd simply put me back in place, no doubt with some new cruelty to add to my woes. All I could do was try and keep my suffering to a minimum, which meant behaving myself, a thought that brought me fresh humiliation. I also wondered if I shouldn't just wet myself and get it over with, but even as I felt the first hint of pressure in my bladder I'd begun consciously to hold back. I knew it would happen, but I was too proud to just let it come.

Minute after slow minute passed, with the noises outside changing – fresh smacks and cries of pain as Tiffany was given the tawse, mingled with laughter from her persecutors. Now I just felt sorry for her, because I was grimacing at the rising ache in my tummy and at the disgusting taste of the soap, which had begun to go soggy as it dissolved in my mouth. I could have spat it out and called out to beg them to take pity on me, even to cry out my safe word and bring it all to a stop. Again, I had too much pride, even with the strain in my bladder starting to become painful and my whole mouth clogged with slimy bitter muck. For a second time I told myself I ought to just let go, and for a second time I held back, even though I was in danger of losing control of both my body and my will.

I clenched my teeth, struggling to keep control, but it was my will that snapped – the whole overwhelming humiliation of the situation became just too much for me. Given what Jasmine was going to do to me, what did it matter if I pissed my panties? I was going to do it anyway, and I was just being arrogant and stubborn by holding out. With that thought I let go, my mouth opening wide in a shame-filled sob as the pee exploded into my knickers. The soap bar fell out to land on the floor with a squashy noise, but I barely noticed. My panties were filling up, the urine gushing out to wet my pussy and up between my bum cheeks, soaking in over my bottom and into my expensive leather trousers.

I was shaking and gasping as I felt the warm, damp sensation spread out across my bottom cheeks, my piss soaking into the leather of my jeans. Outside I heard the click of Jasmine's heels and I looked up as she came into the Ladies. She was no longer wearing her dress: now she was naked except for her high heels, her knickers and a pair of rubber gloves.

'Say hello to nurse!' she teased, and held up her hands to show off her gloves.

My pee was still coming, bulging out the seat of my trousers and seeping through the seams, trickling out also from around my ankles. Jasmine smiled as she saw that I was doing it, a cruel smirk that broke the last of my resistance. Now I was punished, well and truly, brought so low that had my arms not been tied behind my back I'd had have my clothes down in a minute and would have shown her what she'd done to me by masturbating in front of her.

As it was I could only kneel there and let my bladder drain into my soiled knickers and filthy jeans. I'd done rather a lot, and most of it had now leaked out, so that I was kneeling in a big yellow puddle on the white-tiled floor, making it doubly obvious that I'd wet myself. Jasmine watched, enjoying the view, and I'd barely squeezed the last dribble of piss into my now-sodden panties when I heard somebody else coming. It was Caroline, grinning as she looked down on me. Like Jasmine she had a pair of rubber gloves on, but she was otherwise stark naked, with her breasts spotted with wax and the stubby end of a large red Christmas candle protruding from the hole between her legs. In her hand she held a smart black bag, one with which I was painfully familiar – Eliza's enema kit.

'Carrie asked if she could help give you your enema,' Jasmine told me, 'and I thought it was only fair after what you made her do at the Red Ox.'

'And one or two other things,' Caroline added. 'Now, let's get you bare, shall we?'

I hung my head, helpless to stop her. She gave a soft chuckle at the condition I was in as she squatted down beside me, first to retrieve the soap and jam it back into my mouth, then to slip a hand under my belly, pop the button of my jeans and tug down my zip. I was going to be stripped bare, have a tube stuck up my bottom, perhaps be masturbated as my rectum filled, and I was already sobbing in reaction.

'Dirty little baby,' Caroline taunted as she tugged my jeans down. 'Imagine wetting your knickers, at your age!'

She had exposed my sodden panties, which in turn were peeled down over my bum. Yazzie had tied me well to make sure that I would have to keep my bottom cheeks open, and that my pussy would show once I was stripped, with my anus available for the insertion of the enema tube.

'Dirty, *dirty* little baby,' Jasmine echoed Caroline as she took a sponge from the bag and moistened it at a basin. 'Wetting your panties. Honestly, whatever is to be done with you?'

Caroline took the sponge and dabbed it between my thighs. The water was cold, first making me wince as she began to wipe my bottom down, then gasp as the sponge was pressed firmly to my pussy, squeezing chilly water up my cunt-hole and over my mound. Jasmine tutted and retrieved the bar of soap, which had fallen out again. It was now nothing but a soggy, shapeless mass, which allowed her to jam it well in, completely filling my mouth and leaving me panting through my nose in order to breathe.

'Actually,' she went on. 'I know exactly what is to be done with you. First, a wet-bottom spanking. Excuse me, Carrie.'

Caroline was still wiping my pussy but quickly pushed the sponge up my hole, leaving me well plugged and gaping. I could well imagine how I looked behind, with my open vagina bulging with wet purple sponge and my glistening bottom stuck out at them. Jasmine knelt down and began to spank me, slapping my wet bottom as she chided me for wetting myself and pausing occasionally to spread my cheeks.

Caroline soon joined in. They took a cheek each and giggled together as they spanked me. The smacks stung, but they weren't hard enough to stop me thinking about the state I was in, or about what was coming.

'. . . And hopefully that will teach you to control your bladder,' Jasmine said as the spanking stopped. 'Now, don't wriggle.'

I couldn't have done so even if I'd wanted to, but I still twisted around to see what she was doing. She'd pulled open the bag and I saw the fat red shape of a rubber enema bottle, already full for my bottom, which almost certainly meant that there was something other than water inside. Panic welled up inside me and I began to squirm in my bonds, but Jasmine merely smiled as she hung the bottle from the door of one of the cubicles. A long tube dangled from it, ending in a bulbous nozzle designed to go up my bottom hole and stay there while my rectum filled.

'Naughty baby – I said not to wriggle,' Jasmine chided. But that didn't stop me.

She took a tube from the bag, ordinary toothpaste, but I knew she planned to use it to lubricate my bottom hole, and that it would sting. Jasmine also knew, and she was grinning as she showed it to me before turning to give the tap on the bag a twist. A squirt of pinkish-white liquid emerged from the nozzle, quickly cut off as Jasmine adjusted the tap. They saw the look on my face, and laughed.

'Milk,' Caroline explained, 'with some of Osman's extra-strong Turkish chilli sauce and a measure of Stan Tierney's spunk stirred in. Me and Tiffy tossed him off into the jug. It must be very nutritious.'

The thought of drinking the revolting mixture made my stomach lurch. But it was going up my bottom, not down my throat, and it was going to

sting as badly as the toothpaste. Jasmine had removed her gloves and she now took Caroline's
camera from the bag, adding a whole new dimension
to my degradation as she began to take photographs.
Even that didn't stop me wriggling as Caroline got
down behind me, and I continued to do so despite
several firm slaps to my already smarting cheeks and
a great deal of telling-off. It made no difference
anyway. She simply took me firmly around the waist,
used two fingers to spread my anus, squeezed out a
worm of toothpaste, and stuck one rubber-clad finger
up my bottom.

'There, is that anything to make a fuss about?' she
said gently.

My answer was a queer gulping noise as my eyes
popped and a froth of soap bubbles plopped from my
mouth. The toothpaste burned like fire, but it had
certainly done its job, making my bumhole loose and
slippery after just a few pushes of Caroline's finger. I
was still wriggling in her grip, indifferent to the show
I was making of myself, but she held me firmly in
place, enjoying my reaction and the feel of my
bumhole too.

'You're lovely and tight,' she said, 'almost as if you
were a virgin . . . only in your bum, of course. Your
pussy hole's huge, but then I suppose it *is* full of
sponge.'

She pulled her finger out as she finished, and began
to whistle happily as she retrieved the enema hose. I
felt the bulb press against my burning anus, and then
I was writhing in her grip as my soft slippery ring
spread from the pressure.

'Hold still for nursey,' Jasmine warned, 'or it will
be spanky times again.'

I didn't care, squirming desperately in Caroline's
grip as the bulb was pushed deep up my rectum,

attaching me to the enema bag. She held it in and nodded to Jasmine, who gave me a wicked grin and turned the tap on. I jerked as I saw her action but there was nothing to feel at first. Then a mild, cool sensation around my bottom-hole and pussy lips. The liquid was leaking.

'Hmm, maybe not so tight after all,' Jasmine remarked. 'Maybe we should have used a bigger nozzle?'

'I think I used too much toothpaste,' Caroline suggested. 'Or maybe I shouldn't have fingered her for so long. She's gone all sloppy.'

She let go of me, unexpectedly. I fell over into my pee puddle, unable to keep my balance because of the sensations of my body, and was left lying on my side with my arms held up by the rope that attached me to the beam. My muscles ached dreadfully, my mouth and lips stung, my bumhole was burning and the chilli sauce in the enema had begun to take effect, warming my wet cunt lips and the sensitive skin between my bum cheeks. The liquid was still running up my bum, and now I could now feel the pressure as my rectum began to swell, inducing fresh panic for what I would undoubtedly do all over the floor if I wasn't untied.

Jasmine made a small adjustment to the camera to make sure that I was fully in view and then took another photograph before she ducked down. Her fingers went to the knot binding my arms and I began to babble incoherent thanks through my mouthful of soapy mush. A single tug and I felt my arms loosen a little, a sensation that brought out in me a flood of deeply pathetic gratitude to her, and to Yazzie for the skill with which she'd tied me. Once more Jasmine stood up, quickly peeling off her panties before straddling me.

'You can undo yourself now,' she told me. 'But the question is, can you hold your enema long enough to get free? They're taking bets, and most people think you'll mess yourself. Whether you do or not, you're to frig yourself off once you're free, and your punishment will be over when you've come. Take some pictures, Carrie.'

Caroline nodded, quickly peeled off her gloves and took the camera from Jasmine. I thought Jasmine was going to sit on my face, but she put her hands on her hips, stuck her belly out, and just let go. Pee erupted from her sex, catching me completely unawares. A lot of it went into my mouth, mingling with the soap to create the most revolting taste imaginable. She began to laugh at the expressions I was making, and continued to piss on my head even when I'd twisted my face away. Then she urinated all over my top, plastering the material to my breasts, and lastly she peed on my bottom and over my already badly soiled jeans where they were tangled with my panties at thigh level.

'That was fun!' Jasmine said with a laugh as she squatted to shake the last few drops of pee from her pussy and onto my skin. 'Now you can try and get free. And get on with it – Carrie's got a tenner on you making the loo.'

I'd forgotten all about untying myself while Jasmine had urinated on me, but the pressure in my rectum was beginning to get uncomfortable and I'd begun to try even as she stepped away from me. First I spat out the wad of soap in my mouth, although it made little difference. I could reach the knot that she'd loosened – just – and tug on one end of the rope. If the knot was a bow I'd be free, but if it wasn't I'd have secured myself again, which I was sure they'd think was absolutely hilarious. Both of them were watching me as I squirmed in my puddle, their arms around each other, their faces full of cruelty and excitement. I pulled the rope, which came loose.

'Clever girl,' Jasmine remarked. 'Maybe you'll make it.'

She cuddled up to Caroline, sharing a kiss to taunt me as I struggled to free myself from the elaborate criss-cross of ropes binding my arms. Everything hurt, but the enema was still pouring into me and I was already having to clench my cheeks and squeeze with my bumhole to stop myself leaking. I tried to be calm but I was too far gone, with little waves of panic welling up every time the rope wouldn't give way.

Finally the rope came fully loose and with it the leash holding me to the beam. I wrenched my arms free, grimacing as I squeezed the pins and needles from my flesh, an act more urgent even than extracting the enema hose from my bumhole. I pulled that out next, but immediately regretted it. Without the plug in my anus it was far harder to hold on, and it would be nearly impossible to get onto the loo with my ankles lashed together, at least without letting go.

My teeth were gritted with the strain as I fumbled for the knots binding my legs. There were two, one at my ankles, the other behind my knees. I grabbed the nearest and pulled hard, only to discover that it wasn't a slip knot. Jasmine laughed. Caroline gave a delighted little squeal despite being about to lose her bet. I was sobbing with frustration as I began to pull desperately at the knot, now much tighter than before. It wouldn't come loose and I could feel the muscles of my belly and bottom and thighs starting to contract in reaction to the weight of liquid in my straining rectum. It was going to happen at any second, and still the knot wouldn't come free. I burst into tears, sobbing and swearing as I tore at the knot – which gave way at the same instant as my bumhole.

A great gush of dirty milk exploded from my gut, to arch high in the air above my bottom, which by ill luck had been stuck high at the instant my anal ring gave way. It went all over the floor, and I found myself laughing hysterically for the view I was giving them, with spurt after spurt of the mixture of milk and chilli sauce and Stan Tierney's spunk erupting into the air from my gaping bumhole. All the while Caroline was taking photographs, but I was too far gone to care. I rolled onto my back, the ropes still around my ankles, liquid still bubbling from my anus. All that mattered was getting free, and I was full of a weird exhilaration as I tore off the rope. My trousers followed, my boots and socks, all pushed down and off as one soggy mass. I jerked my top up, showing off my naked tits, glistening wet with Jasmine's pee. My thighs came up and open, spreading my cunt to the camera lens, the hole still plugged with the fat purple sponge.

I began to rub at myself, wriggling on the filthy floor, snatching at my sex and squirming my bottom around in the piddle, my mouth wide open to show off the slimy, soapy mess inside, my spare hand clutching at my tits and jerking my nipples as if I was trying to milk myself at the same time as I masturbated. They wanted me to come. I was going to, to show them what they'd done to me, how they'd broken me down to a grovelling filthy little slut, which was exactly what I wanted to be. Then I came with such power that my vision went black and I was driven to the edge of consciousness before my climax finally broke. As my ecstasy faded I was giggling, happy in a way that I'd never been before, as if nothing in the entire world mattered except my state of pained, exhausted bliss.

'Mop your mess up,' Jasmine instructed. 'And then you can do us both.'

Caroline was already playing with the candle in her pussy, and it obviously wasn't going to take long. I hurried to obey, trying to ignore my aching muscles. Jasmine had the key to a cupboard full of cleaning things, and they watched as I mopped the floor, both of them teasing themselves. My clothes were filthy but I stayed nude anyway, because I wanted to be. When I was finished my two tormentors took turns to sit on one of the loos while I licked them to orgasm. Then I was finally taken by the hand and led back into the main area.

Most of the others were sitting around a pair of tables, drinks in their hands. Katie was on Duncan's lap and gave me a knowing smile. Tiffany was sitting splay-legged on Stan Tierney's knee, his hand down the front of her bottle-green school panties. Portia and Sarah were cuddled together, kissing lazily and toying with each other's breasts. Yazzie was suspended from one of the beams, stark naked, her pussy open and obviously newly fucked. Osman was behind the bar, looking thoroughly pleased with himself. Amy Jane was carrying a tray of drinks to the table, still in her pretty red corset but with no knickers. I'd never seen her look so happy.

'Ah, there you are, Isabelle,' Eliza said. 'I hope you enjoyed your enema?'

'Yes, thank you, Mistress,' I said, the words slipping from my mouth without conscious thought.

'That's what I like to hear,' she said. 'We've been having a little talk, and everybody agrees that you should say sorry to Amy Jane for spanking her without her consent, and for being rude to her.'

'Gladly,' I said. 'Sorry, Amy Jane.'

'Properly,' Eliza stated firmly. 'You are to give her a nice kiss.'

'Yes, of course,' I said. I stepped forward, only to be brought up short by a cough from Eliza.

'I think you know what I mean, Isabelle,' she said patiently. 'Get on your knees.'

I got down, still feeling far too submissive to even think of disobedience but a little shocked for what I was expected to do.

'Do you really want me to do this?' I asked as Amy Jane stepped close.

'From the day I met you,' she told me. 'Something, anyway, not this ... I never imagined that any woman could want to do anything as rude as this, except me. Now I know better.'

I managed a weak smile. For all her looks and all her shy manner, the Owl's fantasies had been as dark as mine all along.

'I'm sorry,' I told her, 'genuinely sorry, and I'll show you. Make me do it from behind.'

A murmur of appreciation ran around the room. Amy Jane hesitated, but then she turned, presenting me with the full cheeky globes of her bottom, fat and nude, her bum cheeks parted to show a deep, tightly puckered bumhole and a sweetly pouting virgin cunt. I moved forward, closing my eyes in blissful submission and very real apology as I began to lick, tasting her pussy and anus as the others started to clap. Amy Jane gave a soft moan and reached back to take me gently by the hair, pulling me against herself to smother me in ripe meaty girlflesh. I stuck my tongue up her bottom in response, probing deep in her anus to let my mouth fill with the taste as my hand slipped between my own thighs. She started to gasp, her big cheeks already squeezing against my face, and I put my mouth to her pussy instead, licking eagerly even as my own ecstasy rose up. I had Amy Jane's bum in my face, the Owl's big round bottom, the perfect humiliation to make me come, especially when I so thoroughly deserved it. I was rubbing myself hard as she came full in my face, bringing myself to climax seconds later.

'Good,' Eliza said as our mutual shivers died down. 'Very good, in fact. Keep her there, please, Amy Jane, but not too tight.'

The grip in my hair grew looser and I moved back a little, held with my face just inches from the cheeky peach of Amy Jane's bottom as Eliza carried on. It was an awful position, kneeling with my face held to a girl's bottom, and not just any girl. But Eliza had ordered it and that was enough for me.

'We have also decided that it is important to allow each member of the Rattaners to fully express her sexuality, and that we need to give greater consideration to those men who know about the society, which we hope will also avoid some of the difficulties we've experienced this term. This also has to be formal, and fair. You evidently need regular spankings, Isabelle, so you will be dealt with once a week . . .'

'Once a week?' I asked.

'Once a week,' Eliza said firmly. 'Or more frequently if necessary, and by either Duncan, myself or Sarah . . .'

'Sarah?'

'Yes, Sarah. Why not? And please will you let me finish.'

'Sorry, but . . .'

'In addition to which,' she went on, 'we have agreed to establish a rota among the eight of you . . .'

'Eight?'

'Yes, eight. Not Sarah or myself, obviously, but you, Portia, Jasmine, Caroline, Katie, Tiffany, Yazzie and Amy Jane, who are to make themselves available for oral sex . . .'

'Oral sex! With who?'

'Duncan, Isadore, Walter, Stanley, Osman and perhaps one or two others. And please don't try and pretend you won't enjoy it every bit as much as the others, Isabelle.'

'Yes, but that's not fair! At least—'

'Do make her shut up, please, Amy Jane,' Eliza said.

My protests were reduced to a muffled gulping noise as my face was pulled firmly back between the Owl's bottom cheeks. But it wasn't really necessary. I would be doing as I'd been told, because only that way would I be true to myself.

nexus

The leading publisher of fetish and adult fiction

TELL US WHAT YOU THINK!

Readers' ideas and opinions matter to us so please take a few minutes to fill in the questionnaire below.

1. Sex: Are you male ☐ female ☐ a couple ☐?

2. Age: Under 21 ☐ 21–30 ☐ 31–40 ☐ 41–50 ☐ 51–60 ☐ over 60 ☐

3. Where do you buy your Nexus books from?

☐ A chain book shop. If so, which one(s)?

_____

☐ An independent book shop. If so, which one(s)?

_____

☐ A used book shop/charity shop
☐ Online book store. If so, which one(s)?

_____

4. How did you find out about Nexus books?

☐ Browsing in a book shop
☐ A review in a magazine
☐ Online
☐ Recommendation
☐ Other _____

5. In terms of settings, which do you prefer? (Tick as many as you like.)

☐ Down to earth and as realistic as possible
☐ Historical settings. If so, which period do you prefer?

_____

☐ Fantasy settings – barbarian worlds
☐ Completely escapist/surreal fantasy
☐ Institutional or secret academy

- ☐ Futuristic/sci fi
- ☐ Escapist but still believable
- ☐ Any settings you dislike?

_____

- ☐ Where would you like to see an adult novel set?

_____

6. In terms of storylines, would you prefer:
- ☐ Simple stories that concentrate on adult interests?
- ☐ More plot and character-driven stories with less explicit adult activity?
- ☐ We value your ideas, so give us your opinion of this book:

_____

_____

_____

7. In terms of your adult interests, what do you like to read about? (Tick as many as you like.)
- ☐ Traditional corporal punishment (CP)
- ☐ Modern corporal punishment
- ☐ Spanking
- ☐ Restraint/bondage
- ☐ Rope bondage
- ☐ Latex/rubber
- ☐ Leather
- ☐ Female domination and male submission
- ☐ Female domination and female submission
- ☐ Male domination and female submission
- ☐ Willing captivity
- ☐ Uniforms
- ☐ Lingerie/underwear/hosiery/footwear (boots and high heels)
- ☐ Sex rituals
- ☐ Vanilla sex
- ☐ Swinging
- ☐ Cross-dressing/TV
- ☐ Enforced feminisation

☐ Others – tell us what you don't see enough of in adult fiction:

_____

_____

_____

8. Would you prefer books with a more specialised approach to your interests, i.e. a novel specifically about uniforms? If so, which subject(s) would you like to read a Nexus novel about?

_____

_____

_____

9. Would you like to read true stories in Nexus books? For instance, the true story of a submissive woman, or a male slave? Tell us which true revelations you would most like to read about:

_____

_____

_____

10. What do you like best about Nexus books?

_____

_____

11. What do you like least about Nexus books?

_____

_____

12. Which are your favourite titles?

_____

_____

13. Who are your favourite authors?

_____

_____

14. Which covers do you prefer? Those featuring:
(Tick as many as you like.)

- ☐ Fetish outfits
- ☐ More nudity
- ☐ Two models
- ☐ Unusual models or settings
- ☐ Classic erotic photography
- ☐ More contemporary images and poses
- ☐ A blank/non-erotic cover
- ☐ What would your ideal cover look like?

_____

15. **Describe your ideal Nexus novel in the space provided:**

_____

_____

_____

_____

16. **Which celebrity would feature in one of your Nexus-style fantasies? We'll post the best suggestions on our website – anonymously!**

_____

THANKS FOR YOUR TIME

Now simply write the title of this book in the space below and cut out the questionnaire pages. Post to: Nexus, Marketing Dept., Thames Wharf Studios, Rainville Rd, London W6 9HA

Book title: _____

NEXUS NEW BOOKS

To be published in October 2008

THE PERSIAN GIRL
Felix Baron

Sir Richard Francis Burton was a soldier, spy, explorer, linguist, diplomat, master of disguise and the greatest swordsman of his time. He was also a notorious rake, and during the period of his life recounted in *The Persian Girl*, he carouses and womanises his way around the world. From the depraved 'governess' Abigail and her debauched young wards, to the Ethiopian Amazon who takes him prisoner, Burton's journey leads him to his greatest challenge of all – schooling a dozen lusty young wenches in the more arcane arts of the bed chamber.

£7.99   ISBN 978 0 352 34501 1

NEXUS CONFESSIONS: VOLUME 5
Various

Swinging, dogging, group sex, cross-dressing, spanking, female domination, corporal punishment, and extreme fetishes . . . *Nexus Confessions* explores the length and breadth of erotic obsession, real experience and sexual fantasy. This is an encyclopaedic collection of the bizarre, the extreme, the utterly inappropriate, the daring and the shocking experiences of ordinary men and women driven by their extraordinary desires. Collected by the world's leading publisher of fetish fiction, these are true stories and shameful confessions, never before told or published.

£7.99   ISBN 978 0 352 34144 0

To be published in November 2008

BARE, WHITE AND ROSY
Penny Birch

Natasha Linnet has a weakness for older men, preferably those with sufficient confidence to take her across their knee. The directors of old-fashioned wine merchants Hambling and Borse seem ideal for the task, and they invite her to work for them. It's an offer too good to refuse, but Natasha quickly finds that she is expected to give a great deal more to her employers and their customers than she had bargained for. Will the temptations being dangled in front of her persuade her put up with what is going on behind?

£7.99   ISBN 978 0 352 34505 9

If you would like more information about Nexus titles, please visit our website at www.nexus-books.co.uk, or send a large stamped addressed envelope to:
  Nexus, Thames Wharf Studios,
  Rainville Road, London W6 9HA

NEXUS BOOKLIST

Information is correct at time of printing. To avoid disappointment, check availability before ordering. Go to www.nexus-books.co.uk.

All books are priced at £6.99 unless another price is given.

NEXUS

☐ ABANDONED ALICE	Adriana Arden	ISBN 978 0 352 33969 0
☐ ALICE IN CHAINS	Adriana Arden	ISBN 978 0 352 33908 9
☐ AMERICAN BLUE	Penny Birch	ISBN 978 0 352 34169 3
☐ AQUA DOMINATION	William Doughty	ISBN 978 0 352 34020 7
☐ THE ART OF CORRECTION	Tara Black	ISBN 978 0 352 33895 2
☐ THE ART OF SURRENDER	Madeline Bastinado	ISBN 978 0 352 34013 9
☐ BEASTLY BEHAVIOUR	Aishling Morgan	ISBN 978 0 352 34095 5
☐ BEING A GIRL	Chloë Thurlow	ISBN 978 0 352 34139 6
☐ BELINDA BARES UP	Yolanda Celbridge	ISBN 978 0 352 33926 3
☐ BIDDING TO SIN	Rosita Varón	ISBN 978 0 352 34063 4
☐ BLUSHING AT BOTH ENDS	Philip Kemp	ISBN 978 0 352 34107 5
☐ THE BOOK OF PUNISHMENT	Cat Scarlett	ISBN 978 0 352 33975 1
☐ BRUSH STROKES	Penny Birch	ISBN 978 0 352 34072 6
☐ CALLED TO THE WILD	Angel Blake	ISBN 978 0 352 34067 2
☐ CAPTIVES OF CHEYNER CLOSE	Adriana Arden	ISBN 978 0 352 34028 3
☐ CARNAL POSSESSION	Yvonne Strickland	ISBN 978 0 352 34062 7
☐ CITY MAID	Amelia Evangeline	ISBN 978 0 352 34096 2
☐ COLLEGE GIRLS	Cat Scarlett	ISBN 978 0 352 33942 3
☐ COMPANY OF SLAVES	Christina Shelly	ISBN 978 0 352 33887 7
☐ CONCEIT AND CONSEQUENCE	Aishling Morgan	ISBN 978 0 352 33965 2
☐ CORRECTIVE THERAPY	Jacqueline Masterson	ISBN 978 0 352 33917 1
☐ CORRUPTION	Virginia Crowley	ISBN 978 0 352 34073 3

☐ WHAT SUKI WANTS	Cat Scarlett	ISBN 978 0 352 34027 6
☐ WHEN SHE WAS BAD	Penny Birch	ISBN 978 0 352 33859 4
☐ WHIP HAND	G.C. Scott	ISBN 978 0 352 33694 1
☐ WHIPPING GIRL	Aishling Morgan	ISBN 978 0 352 33789 4
☐ WHIPPING TRIANGLE	G.C. Scott	ISBN 978 0 352 34086 3
☐ THE WICKED SEX	Lance Porter	ISBN 978 0 352 34161 7
☐ ZELLIE'S WEAKNESS	Jean Aveline	ISBN 978 0 352 34160 0

NEXUS CLASSIC

☐ AMAZON SLAVE	Lisette Ashton	ISBN 978 0 352 33916 4
☐ ANGEL	Lindsay Gordon	ISBN 978 0 352 34009 2
☐ THE BLACK GARTER	Lisette Ashton	ISBN 978 0 352 33919 5
☐ THE BLACK MASQUE	Lisette Ashton	ISBN 978 0 352 33977 5
☐ THE BLACK ROOM	Lisette Ashton	ISBN 978 0 352 33914 0
☐ THE BLACK WIDOW	Lisette Ashton	ISBN 978 0 352 33973 7
☐ THE BOND	Lindsay Gordon	ISBN 978 0 352 33996 6
☐ THE DOMINO ENIGMA	Cyrian Amberlake	ISBN 978 0 352 34064 1
☐ THE DOMINO QUEEN	Cyrian Amberlake	ISBN 978 0 352 34074 0
☐ THE DOMINO TATTOO	Cyrian Amberlake	ISBN 978 0 352 34037 5
☐ EMMA ENSLAVED	Hilary James	ISBN 978 0 352 33883 9
☐ EMMA'S HUMILIATION	Hilary James	ISBN 978 0 352 33910 2
☐ EMMA'S SUBMISSION	Hilary James	ISBN 978 0 352 33906 5
☐ FAIRGROUND ATTRACTION	Lisette Ashton	ISBN 978 0 352 33927 0
☐ THE INSTITUTE	Maria Del Rey	ISBN 978 0 352 33352 0
☐ PLAYTHING	Penny Birch	ISBN 978 0 352 33967 6
☐ PLEASING THEM	William Doughty	ISBN 978 0 352 34015 3
☐ RITES OF OBEDIENCE	Lindsay Gordon	ISBN 978 0 352 34005 4
☐ SERVING TIME	Sarah Veitch	ISBN 978 0 352 33509 8
☐ THE SUBMISSION GALLERY	Lindsay Gordon	ISBN 978 0 352 34026 9
☐ TIE AND TEASE	Penny Birch	ISBN 978 0 352 33987 4
☐ TIGHT WHITE COTTON	Penny Birch	ISBN 978 0 352 33970 6

NEXUS CONFESSIONS

| ☐ NEXUS CONFESSIONS: VOLUME ONE | Various | ISBN 978 0 352 34093 1 |

------- ✂ ---------------------------

Please send me the books I have ticked above.

Name   ....

Address   ....

....

....

.... Post code ....

Send to: **Virgin Books Cash Sales, Thames Wharf Studios, Rainville Road, London W6 9HA**

US customers: for prices and details of how to order books for delivery by mail, call 888-330-8477.

Please enclose a cheque or postal order, made payable to **Nexus Books Ltd**, to the value of the books you have ordered plus postage and packing costs as follows:
   UK and BFPO – £1.00 for the first book, 50p for each subsequent book.
   Overseas (including Republic of Ireland) – £2.00 for the first book, £1.00 for each subsequent book.

If you would prefer to pay by VISA, ACCESS/MASTERCARD, AMEX, DINERS CLUB or SWITCH, please write your card number and expiry date here:

....

Please allow up to 28 days for delivery.

Signature ....

Our privacy policy

We will not disclose information you supply us to any other parties. We will not disclose any information which identifies you personally to any person without your express consent.

From time to time we may send out information about Nexus books and special offers. Please tick here if you do *not* wish to receive Nexus information.   □

------- ✂ ---------------------------